MEAL TICKET$

A Novel by

-Avery Goode-

13 Digit: 978-1-953230-04-1

Meal Tickets:
*People or things that
serve as the ultimate
source of another's income.*

Dedication

To all the mothers and fathers who strive to take care of their children with or without the help of the non-custodial parent.

ACKNOWLEDGMENTS

Once again, I am grateful to my family and close friends who were right here supporting me when I came up with another idea. You all never tell me how crazy I really am. Instead, you all give me that side-eye that lets me know I am on to something Goode. Thank you all for your honest opinions and the hard work you do daily that helps me make writing look easy. You all keep me on my toes, and I am truly thankful.

For this book, I am not going to list people individually because I always forget someone and hear about it later. Instead, I want to say thank you to every person in my life personally and professionally who have helped me, supported me, and assisted me with making Goode books. You all rock!

To my readers and all the amazing book clubs I have had the honor of reaching, thank you all for your prayers, feedback, and continual support. Each and everyone of you are DOPE!

Remember, you only have one life to live so make it a Goode one. Be blessed, be Goode, or be Goode at it!

Avery

CHAPTER 1

First Round Draft Picks

EVERYTHING THAT MALIK JEFFRIES worked so hard for all of his life was about to be culminated in one big event. The NFL Draft. It wasn't confirmed, but the rumor mill was abuzz with talk that he would be among the NFL's first picks. To him, it didn't matter which round he was picked in, he just wanted to play. The young man fell in love with the game when he was only four years old and had first started playing little league football at his community recreation center, Ben Hill in Atlanta. Even then, his coaches saw that he had great talent and potential. They weren't wrong. Now here he was, just a couple of months after college graduation and a few hours away from the first round of draft picks. This was the best Thursday of his life.

"How're you feeling, Son?" Jackson Jeffries asked, patting his son on the shoulder.

"I'm excited and nervous. So many things, Pops. I can't believe this night is finally here."

"I understand. This is a big night for you. For all of us really. I'm very proud of you, Malik. You've proven that hard work and dedication really does pay off."

"Thanks, Pops. I couldn't have done it without you and Mom's love and support."

MEAL TICKET$

The two men embraced one another in a tight hug at the same moment, Eloise Jeffries, Malik 's mother, walked into the room.

"Now this is what I like to see. Two of my favorite men showing one another some love. Can I get a little of that?"

Malik turned and hugged his mother, kissing her on the cheek before saying, "you know there's always plenty of love for you over this way."

What did he say that for?

"I can't tell lately. It seems all your love has been for that girl who lives on the other end."

"Ma, her name is Aisha, and she is my girlfriend. Has been since ninth grade. You need to start respecting that and respecting her."

"Humph. Here you go. I just don't understand why you had to go by the food stamp office to find a girlfriend. Those people who live on the other end of Cascade road are...are..."

"Are what, Ma? Hardworking? Honest? Loving? What are you trying to say?"

"They're not on our social level, Malik. Most of them are unemployed and uneducated. Just like your gold-digging trollop is."

"Dad, get your wife." Malik's nostrils flared and he clenched his jaw. "Aisha is not a gold-digging trollop, and she is just as smart, if not smarter than I am."

"I beg to differ. She's not the one about to graduate from The University of Georgia, you are. If she was so smart, then why did she drop out of college?"

"Eloise, that's enough!" Her husband barked. "Aisha didn't drop out of college and you know that. She attends the community college part-time. You know that her mother got sick, and they needed the money to cover the rising cost of her medical expenses. Now your son has asked you nicely to respect his girlfriend, but I'm not asking. I'm telling you. This is his big night, and he wants everyone here with him who he loves, who loves him back. That includes her. Don't make me bring this up again."

Just then, the doorbell rang.

"Well look what the wind blew in," his mother said sarcastically under her breath when Aisha walked into the room.

"Good evening Mister and Misses Jeffries. How are you?"

"We're well, Aisha. How about yourself?"

"I'm doing pretty well, Sir. Thanks for asking."

Eloise Jeffries rolled her eyes and sucked her teeth, annoyed.

"How're your parents?" Mister Jeffries inquired.

"They're well. My mom is doing better. The hospital said she may be able to come home soon. I know that will make my dad happy. Between work and going to sit with her, he's hardly ever home. I think he went five days without even sleeping in his own bed and-"

"How awful, dear," Eloise interrupted. "Malik and Omari, please hurry along. We don't want to be late."

Aisha looked at Eloise but said nothing. She was aware that Malik's mother didn't like her. All because she wasn't born with a silver spoon in her mouth, and they lived within the perimeter of Interstate two-eighty-five. She'd overheard Misses Jeffries referring to her as 'the girl from the other end' on several occasions but always blew it off.

Eloise Jeffries was as stuck up as they came. Aisha knew from Malik that Misses Jeffries came from a well-to-do family in South Carolina whose ancestors had passed for white. Beautiful and intelligent, Eloise met Jackson Jeffries at Howard University where he was studying business and she was studying accounting. The two of them had an instant love connection and married shortly after graduation. That old saying that opposites attract was the truth because Jackson was a down-to-earth, humble man and his wife was a pretentious snob.

Malik and his family lived in a gated community called Cascade Palms where the median income was $350,000 and the cheapest house was about a million dollars. Mister Jeffries owned his own security company and Misses Jeffries was a high-powered accountant at one of Atlanta's most prestigious accounting firms.

On the other hand, Aisha's mother used to be a cook with the Atlanta Public School System before her diabetes worsened; causing her to take a medical leave of absence and Aisha's father is a mechanic for the same school system.

While they didn't live like the Jeffries, they weren't paupers either. Aisha and her family lived in a four-bedroom home in a good neighborhood. She and her siblings, Clifford, and Rhonda were fortunate enough to come from strong, hard-working parents who loved them all very much.

The young lady stood in silence and thought about her boyfriend. They were in love and his mother would have to get over it. The hateful woman had been giving her the blues since day one and although it bothered her, she endured it for Malik's sake. She was determined not to allow anyone or anything to come between them. It was obvious that her boyfriend's mother thought her to be a gold-digger, but she was nothing of the sort. It didn't matter to her how much money he had as long as he was good to her, which he was.

Deep in thought, Aisha didn't hear Malik walk up on her. He threw his arms around her neck from behind and gave her a bear hug.

"Hey Eesh. How's my favorite girl doing?" He kissed her on the top of her head.

"Hey babe. I'm great. Are you nervous?"

"Man, am I ever. I'm so ready to get this over with its crazy."

"You are going to get drafted. Mark my words. The league needs players like you. Just think, NFL draft pick in April, college graduate in May."

Yeah, that's something, huh? I'm glad that I am graduating. A friend of mine declared for the draft and he's only a junior. If he isn't selected, he can return to college but can't play ball. That part sucks." He fidgeted with the tie around his neck. "This thing is killing me."

Rawr. A soft rumble noise came from his stomach.

"My bad. I haven't been able to eat or sleep much these past few days."

"I can only imagine. But you must take care of yourself or else you won't be any good for anyone, especially one of those teams. Come on, lemme make you a sandwich."

His mother, who was listening to every piece of their conversation stepped closer to them.

"I've already made reservations for us to have dinner. There's no need to dirty up my kitchen." The contempt in Eloise Jeffries voice was evident.

"Let the girl fix the boy a sandwich, El. We're not eating until after the draft anyway and Lord knows how long that'll be. Just clean your mess up, Son."

"Gotcha, Pops."

Eloise spun around on her heals and headed toward the stairs. She was going to stay as far away from her son's girlfriend as much as she could.

"This little heifer is overstepping her bounds. Who does she think she is, volunteering to cook in my kitchen? She's got some nerve," Eloise huffed, once she was out of earshot.

In the kitchen, Aisha fixed all three men a sandwich and they chatted away.

"Are we going to be late?" Aisha asked.

"Nah, we're still waiting on some of my family to arrive."

"But your mom called you and Omari and told you to hurry up."

"Girl you've been coming around here long enough to know how our mom is," Omari replied. "The woman is a micromanager."

"He's right," Malik added. "It's only six. We have to be there at eight and we're only 15 minutes away."

They talked and ate until the other family members arrived at the Jeffries' home an hour later. Like a convoy, the large group headed to the Georgia World Congress Center. The main event was still being held at Madison Square Garden. But because of the large number of Georgia and Alabama players entered the draft, hosting a remote ceremony for the players and their families made sense. Everyone who was anyone in the state of Georgia would be in attendance, not to mention those from the surrounding states.

It was smooth sailing once they left the house and got on the road. They even managed to catch every green light until they got near the venue. When they hit Northside Drive, near the new Mercedes Benz Stadium, traffic was at a complete stand still.

"See, I knew this was going to happen. If your little nappy headed girlfriend hadn't wasted so much time, we wouldn't be in this mess."

"Eloise, that was mean and uncalled for. Aisha is no more responsible for this traffic than you are. Apologize at once," he demanded.

"I will do no such thing."

"Oh yes, you will. Or else-,"

"It's okay, Mister Jeffries. She can keep her apology. Even if she said it, you and I both know she would not have meant it." The softness of the young girl's voice revealed a deep pain. Tears pooled in the corners of her eyes, but she turned her head and blinked them away before they could fall. She felt Malik's hand tighten around her own. The more his mother spoke, the tighter it got.

Malik was the best thing that had happened to her. He was not only her lover; he was her best friend. Maybe one day, he would be her husband. But with the way his mother was, Aisha wasn't sure how long the relationship would even last.

"Mom, you know I love you. But for real, for real, you're pushing it. Dad…"

His father turned his head and stared at his wife before saying, "El, this is my final warning."

Eloise did not respond. Instead, she held her head still and focused on a spot on the windshield until they pulled into a spot in the parking garage. She got out of the car and held her purse close to her body like she was afraid of being mugged. Her husband grabbed her free hand and the two of them led the way to the elevators.

Inside, the large group walked to their assigned area. The room was crowded with draft hopefuls, their families, their agents, and the media. Not long after they were seated, did the ceremony get underway. Malik's knee shook vigorously under the table and even banged it once. To calm him, Aisha placed her hand over it and gently caressed it until he settled down. Even though this wasn't about her directly, she was a bit nervous as well. This draft was going to change their relationship in a major way.

She had seen different shows about baller's wives and saw how relentless some women could be in their pursuit of a man of means whether he was married or not. Once Malik was selected to a team, he would become even hotter than she already believed him to be and that may pose a problem for her down the line.

Stop it, she thought to herself, shaking her head to rid it of the negative thoughts. *He loves you and you guys are in this together.* As if he sensed her inner battle, Malik slid his arm around her shoulder and pulled her close to him. The move was one of reassurance for her and it quieted her noisy thoughts. She looked up at him and smiled and he leaned toward her to kiss her. Just before their lips touched, Eloise pulled him by the shoulder.

"Look who's decided to join us, dear. Selena, you remember my sons, Malik and Omari, don't you?" Eloise stood to hug the young lady.

"Why, of course. Nice to see you all again. Mister Jeffries, you're looking dapper. Armani?" She said of his tailored suit.

"Indeed, it is. It's so nice to see you as well. Are your parent's here? I'd love to see them."

"Dad is in Germany on business and Mom is in Kentucky working with the Derby League."

"Oh, okay. So, who are you here with?" Mister Jeffries asked.

"She's my guest," Eloise answered, then turned to look at Aisha. "Scoot over a seat and let my dear, Lena Pooh take a seat."

Aisha did not want to move but she did not want to cause a scene either, so she grabbed her small clutch bag and was about to move.

"What are you doing?" Malik snapped.

"Um, moving down like your mom asked."

"Yes, dear. She needs to move," his mother said.

"No, the fuck she doesn't. If you want your friend to sit down at this table, then you need to move. My woman is staying where she has been since the day, I met her, by my side."

Eloise placed her perfectly manicured hand over her chest and stood with her mouth open.

"Malik Kasim Jeffries, I've never heard you use such foul language. You will not disrespect me. I am your mother."

"And I'm your son who deserves the same respect."

Selena shifted her weight from her left foot to the right. Her slight movement, reminded everyone that she was there, witnessing the exchange between mother and son.

"Damn, I'm sorry you had to see this. You are more than welcomed to sit here at the table with us, over there." He pointed to the empty seat between his brother and dad.

"No problem. Thank you. I'm not trying to intrude. I just want to celebrate your being a first round draft pick. I'm a big fan of yours." She reached out and touched his arm softly before walking to her seat.

Aisha noticed how her man blushed at the woman's compliment and how long the woman's hand lingered on his arm before she moved it. Malik turned around to see his woman staring at him. Her eyes burned a hole in his arm, the same spot that Selena had touched.

"Uh, thanks. But we don't know what round I'm going to go in, if I get picked at all."

"Oh, I have it on good authority that you are most definitely being picked."

"I hope so," he said.

The lights in the auditorium dimmed slightly and the commissioner of the NFL stood at the podium. After welcoming everyone and giving a few words of encouragement to the draft hopefuls, he said the words that every player who loved the game of football, longed to hear.

"With the first pick in the 2017 NFL draft, the Arizona Eagles select, Murray Tyler, quarterback, Oklahoma."

Loud cheers rang out and Malik watched on the big screen as the young man was hugged and congratulated by his family, while making his way to the podium. Malik's agent had told him that he thought he should have flown to New York to attend the draft in person, but had he done that, all his friends and family who were with him right now, would not have been able to make it. No, he was happy with this village surrounding him.

"Babe, did you know that Atlanta has the next pick?" Aisha asked him.

It was still so loud in the room; he could hardly hear her.

"Huh?" He said, leaning closer to her.

Instead of repeating what she said, she simply kissed him on the cheek and placed her hand over his, giving it a gentle squeeze.

Overhead, they showed a few highlights of the Heisman winner to remind people why he was the number one pick in the league. Then the commissioner cleared his throat to continue.

"The second pick in the 2017 NFL draft, the Atlanta Kings select, Malik Jeffries, Georgia."

The table shook as his family jumped to their feet in excitement but for Malik, it took a moment to register, and he just sat there.

"Ahh," Aisha screamed, hugging him tightly around his neck.

Slowly, realization set in and Malik jumped to his feet, taking Aisha with him, lifting her in the air.

"Nah, we did it, babe," he said swinging her around in the air. Before placing her on the ground, he caught her bottom lip between his teeth, gently. Their tongues danced slowly, causing heat to form of both of their private parts.

"Get a room," his brother said, patting him on the back. "Congrats, Bro. You deserve this."

Both his parents hugged him tightly and told him that they were very proud of him. Lastly, Selena walked up to offer her congratulations.

"See, what did I tell you?" She beamed.

"You were right," he agreed.

"Congratulations, Leek."

Leek? Aisha mouthed. When did this chick start calling him that? Malik noticed the use of the pet's name as well.

"Nah, just Malik."

"Hmm, well, I like it. It suits you. Nevertheless, you deserve this." She stood on her tiptoes, wrapped her arms around his neck and kissed him full on the mouth. His mother clapped at the exchange.

He pushed her back so fast, she stumbled into his father, who gave her a hard glare.

"Damn, it's starting already. Broads are about to be tripping over their feet to get to you now, bruh," his brother said.

Malik looked at Aisha and saw a hint of anger in her eyes, but it was quickly replaced with hurt. He lifted her chin with his index finger and kissed her tenderly.

"I don't care about no thirsty, clout chasing chicks. My only concern is this woman right here. You, are my number one draft pick."

Eloise Jeffries smiled as she took her seat and whispered to herself, "not if I can help it."

CHAPTER 2

Three on Three

THE BEST WAY TO celebrate a win is by getting some pussy and Kyle Hudson, Jr, was celebrating in a very big way. He had not one, but two beautiful women about to join him in his bed, to service him like he was the Prince of Zamunda. One was his on-again-off-again girlfriend, Tika and the other was an associate of hers. At present they were on. Tonight, was special in a few ways. First, his team, the Georgia Heat made it to the playoffs. That was due largely in part because of a great team effort. Although he was one of the three franchise players the organization had, along with his ex-brother-in-law, Justin Wade and Griffin Blakely, all the players rocked it. The bench even put up almost fifty-eight points themselves.

Another reason the night was special was because his little cousin, Malik was drafted to the NFL, so his family was winning all the way around. But lastly, and most importantly, his girlfriend told him that if he made it to the playoffs, she would do a threesome with him like he wanted. And tonight, she was keeping her promise. For the past few weeks, he had been asking her about it, but she kept denying him. For some reason, she was trying to play the demure, conservative roll. That was so far from who she really was. Hell, when he first met her three years ago, she was a stripper at Black Diamonds, one of Atlanta's hottest clubs. Not to say that all strippers got down like that, but he had heard his fair share of rumors concerning her. Truth be told, one of the main reasons he approached her was to see if any of them were true.

"What's taking y'all so long in there?" He yelled from the bed. His dick was rock hard in anticipation.

"Just a moment, Babe," Tika said, peaking her head out the door. "We're both a little nervous so we're giving one another a pep talk."

"Ain't no reason to be nervous. You've rode the stallion before and know how good it is. Tell your friend she's in for a treat."

"Mmmm, yes. And so are you, baby."

Tika shut the door softly, locking it behind her.

"You sure you wanna do this?" Her friend asked.

"Hell, yeah. Have you seen Larissa's new place? Bitch, I'm trying to live like that, too."

The friend hunched her shoulders. "Okay, but you already have one baby. Why do you need two?"

"Insurance," Tika answered.

"Well, I have everything that you need. So how are we going to do this after we're done?"

"Let me handle that. You just suck the shit out of his dick so when he cums, we have a lot to work with."

"Got it."

Tika picked up the tissue box that sat on the counter in the hotel's bathroom and removed all the tissues out of it. Then she placed a small, black pouch inside the box, before replacing the tissues.

"Let's go get this money."

Before she opened the door, she scrolled through the applications on her phone and found her music library. She had created a playlist especially for tonight. Once she found the song she was looking for, she hit play and she and her friend, sauntered out the bathroom, toward a ready and impatiently waiting, Kyle.

Chris Brown's sexy hit, "Back to Sleep" played on Tika's phone as she and her friend, twisted and gyrated to the beat.

"That's my jam," Kyle said. He was leaning back on the pillows, propped up, watching the two former strippers, put on a show.

"This is for you, baby," Tika said. She leaned in and kissed her friend hard on the mouth for a few seconds. "Mmmm, your tongue tastes like mint."

The other woman used her tongue to trace the outline of Tika's lips, before sucking her bottom lip like a pacifier. She used her small hands to caress the firm mounds that pressed against her naked flesh. Slowly, one hand traced a line from Tika's left nipple, down her stomach to her clean-shaven pussy. Two short fingers penetrated the hot, wet box, in and out, until they were coated with cream.

"Fuck," Kyle said through gritted teeth. He wanted to stroke his dick, but he promised his girl that he would not touch himself. Only the women could touch him. Beads of sweat formed on his brow due to the mounting pressure that formed in his loins.

"Come kiss me, KJ," the friend said.

He looked at his girlfriend for approval, smiling when he saw her nodding her head.

"I've been waiting for this for a long time," he admitted.

"Shhh," the friend said softly. She stood on her tip toes and kissed him passionately on the lips. Her soft touch caused his member to jump reflexively, and she looked down at it, licking her lips. "Mmm, you're next."

When she dropped to her knees, Kyle leaned over and kissed his woman.

14

"Thank you," he whispered into her mouth. In response, she placed her hands on his cheeks and pulled his head down to meet her lips. As she kissed him, her friend took his hard penis into her hot mouth, getting it nice and wet.

Kyle threw his head back. "Hssss." He sounded like a snake about to attack its prey.

The friend concentrated on the head of his member when she realized that was where he was most sensitive. She swirled her tongue around the small opening and looked up into his eyes. That was his undoing. He bucked his hips back and forth, pushing himself further down her throat with each stroke. His member was on fire as he reveled about how much the thin layer of skin inside her mouth, felt the same as a deep, soaking pussy.

Another intense feeling began to overtake Kyle. One that he could not hold much longer.

"Uh, I know this could not be happening at the worst time, but I have got to pee. Either you let me go now, or you can get a golden shower."

The friend removed her mouth from his engorged shaft and leaned back on her heels.

"Handle your business," she said.

He trotted to the bathroom and closed the door. Inside, he turned on both the hot and cold faucets at full blast then tip-toed slowly to the door and locked it.

Earlier, he had spoken with his big sister, Kayla and had filled her in on his plans to have a threesome with Tika. She was against it.

"Are you crazy. You're already going through a child support battle for one child. Do you want to make it two?" She had said.

"Don't worry. I got it covered, Sis. I'm using two condoms. Ain't nothing getting through either of them."

Kayla slapped her forehead with the palm of her hand. "Dude, don't you understand that a woman looking to trap you does not care about a damned condom. Don't you know about the turkey basting bitches?"

"The who?"

"The chicks who use turkey basters to remove the semen from use condoms and then inseminate themselves with it. Those chicks."

He sat down, deflated. "Hell no. I've never heard of them. Damn, and I really wanted this to go down. This is every man's fantasy, you know?"

She nodded her head. "Yeah, so I've heard. All may not be lost though. You just need to be wise and take extra precautions."

Kyle rubbed his hands together in anticipation. "Cool, cool. What do I need to do?"

"First of all, check every damned thing. Look in your towels, soap dishes, toilet tanks, all that for paraphernalia. Tika is smarter than a basic turkey basting broad. She will probably have a disposable syringe and an at home insemination kit for intracervical insemination."

"A what?"

She exhaled, frustrated. "A high-tech turkey basting kit."

"Oh, well why didn't you just say that?"
"I did, stupid. Anyway, just do as I say, and you should be fine. Do not leave anything to chance."

And he did not plan on it. While the water ran, he lifted the toilet tank and took out a small, metal lock box that fit in his hands. A key was in the lock. He removed it, set the box on the countertop, and began quickly searching his bathroom. He looked between the towels and found nothing. Next, he checked beneath his cabinets. Still nothing.

"Mm-ch," he smacked. "Kayla and her damned conspiracy theories got me in here tripping."

"Hurry up, baby. We need you," Tika yelled from the other room.

"I'm on my way. Washing up now," he said.

Kyle pressed the soap dispenser and lathered his hands. The hot water felt good as he rinsed the suds off. His mother and sister had come over and decorated this bathroom for him and had hung some nice hand towels for him to use, but he thought they were too nice to get wet. Instead, he reached for one tissue to dry his hands. When he pulled one, they all came out the box.

"What the fuck?" He said as he tried to stuff them back inside.

It was then that he saw the black pouch. With the water still running, he hurriedly unzipped it to see what was inside. Sure enough, there was a syringe and a tube that he had never seen before. There were also step-by-step insemination instructions for the woman looking to impregnate herself at home. He unfolded the paper and a small pill fell on the counter.

"Oh, so she was going to slip me a mickey and knock me out while she and her friend played O-B-G-Y-N. These bitches got me fucked up. If it's a game they want, then a game I will give them."

He put the contents back into the bag, locked it in the small box, dropped the pill in the toilet and flushed it. His Murray's hair pomade sat next to the tissue box.

"Perfect," he said when an idea popped into his head.

Before he exited the bathroom, he made sure that the box was safely tucked away in the tank. Whether they found the box or not, neither of the women would be able to get inside because he had pressed the key to the bottom of his hair grease container and smoothed it over. Everything in the bathroom looked exactly the way it was when he walked in.

"What were you doing in there all this time?" The friend asked nervously.

"Just when I was about to come out, my stomach," he lied, rubbing it, "had other plans. But no worries, I'm good to go now and made sure that everything was spic and span back there because, Tika, I need you to toss my salad."

Grinning from ear to ear, Kyle crossed his arms and stood with his feet spread and planted near his bed.

"While she's licking my ass, I need you back on this dick. It needs hella attention."

Reluctantly, the two women did as they were told. While neither of them was aware of what exactly went down in the bathroom, it was obvious that something had changed while he was gone. Before he went to pee, Kyle was pliable and willing to do whatever they suggested. They were in control. Now he was.

The friend sucked his dick so long, her jaws began to tire, and they became numb. Kyle intentionally withheld his ejaculation as punishment until he could no longer control it.

"Here it comes," he said through clenched teeth.

"Wait, babe. Let me get a rubber," Tika said, jumping into action.

"No! She needs to swallow this, and you need to finish your job," he barked, holding the woman's head in place.

"Fuck," Tika mouthed behind his back. This was not going the way she had planned it at all.

He had Tika and her friend bent over in so many angles one would think they were playing twister. The beauty of being in control was that he was able to make the two women pleasure each other and he did very little work. It was no holds barred with him. Every position that he wanted to try, he did.

When he and Tika had talked about doing a threesome, she only had two rules that he had to abide by. One was that he could not touch himself for pleasure. That had to be left up to the women. And the most important one was that she would choose the girl and he could not know anything about her, including her name. The rules that she proposed were not outlandish, so he went along with them.

Shit, he didn't care if he knew the broad's name or not. It's not like he was ever going to call her. All that mattered to him was that he would be able to do exactly what he was doing right now, ramming his stiff dick in one woman's ass while she ate the other woman out.

"Ah, ah, ah," she screamed as he handled her none too gently.

Smack. He slapped her right cheek. Pop. He slapped the left cheek.

"Damn. This. Is. So. Tight."

His halted speech was filled with tension as the beginnings of, yet another orgasm began to form in his toes.

A sense of euphoria began to overtake him as tiny pulses of electricity ran through his body.

"Ooh, Kyle. Yes. Fuck this ass, baby. Play with my clit. Make this wet ass pussy soak the sheets," she said between slurps.

Tika lay in front of her with her legs spread wide. Her friend nibbled and bit on her hard nub, driving her wild. The model loved getting head no matter whose tongue it was. But she wasn't feeling this as much as she should have been. Her hands held onto her friend's ears, who happily ate at the 'Y', but Tika's eyes were squinted and her nostrils slightly flared.

"Uhn," she moaned involuntarily as pleasure began to come crashing down on her like waves on a beach. "Eat it, bitch."

Her friend glanced up for a moment, slightly startled at the force behind Tika's words. The young woman smiled because it was becoming clear that her friend was getting jealous. Kyle had spent very little time dicking Tika down and most of the time with her. That was her plan all along. She had been wanting to fuck Kyle ever since Tika was pregnant, but her friend was not having it. Also, she was not trying to get pregnant like her friend was. Nah, she got paid by dudes without the baby. Her tongue made sure of that.

"I'm coming," the friend announced.

Tika forced the woman's face into her pussy, almost cutting off her air supply. Through squinted eyes, she saw Kyle kiss the woman's back as his hips bucked, in and out. He had moved his dick from her ass to her pussy and the squishy noises were driving Tika crazy. Her friend was getting the best dick ever. This was partly the reason she did not want to do a threesome to begin with. Women did not share good dick and she was territorial when it came to Kyle. If any of her friends had the chance to experience his good loving, then they would surely want him for themselves.

"Come on, baby. Daddy is about to come with you," Kyle said.

The friend twirled her tongue around Tika's clit and began sucking it like a pacifier. This was a move that would send her friend over the edge.

"Ahh, I'm coming too."

The trio orgasmed until each was spent.

Kyle did not know if it was anger, excitement or a combination that increased his virility. but for almost three hours he had fucked, sucked, and worn the chicks out. Now, he laid on his back, legs crossed at the ankles and his hands behind his head. A smile stretched from East to West and it reached his eyes. This was a moment of sheer pleasure for him. On either side of him, Tika and her friend lay, breathing hard.

"Babe, we need to get that DNA test done," he mentioned.

"Mmm, hmm," she said noncommittally. "Um, I need to take a shower," his scandalous girlfriend said.

Kyle giggled. Her plan did not work out and she wanted to get into the bathroom and remove any traces of deception before it was found. Not that she was worried about Kyle finding it. He never paid any attention to anything and never used those tissues anyway. No, it was his housekeeper who she was concerned about. If the nosey lady found it, she would tell Kyle about it and he would stop messing with her for good.

"That's a great idea. We can all go." Thanks to his sister putting him up on game, Kyle was thinking with his big head now. He figured she would want to get into the bathroom to get rid of the evidence. He was not going to make it easy for her.

Tika gave him a half smile and grudgingly went along. After the shower, Kyle did not leave either of the ladies alone for even a second. There was no way to retrieve the little bag and finally, they had to leave his place, empty-handed.

"So, what are you going to do now since you didn't get any sperm?"

"I'll get some more pills and the next time he and I are alone, I will slip a few into his drinks. Looks like I'm going to have to do this the old-fashioned way. Get on top and ride that thang like a mechanical bull."

The friend laughed. "And what about the DNA test? Are you finally going to give it to him?"

"Oh no," she said, shaking her head.

"You know proof of paternity is required in order for you to get an increase in child support."

Tika shrugged her shoulders. "Yep, but I don't care right now. I mean, I know I've been saying he does not take care of Malia, but he does. The ten grand he gives me is cool for now.

MEAL TICKET$

Keeping up with the lie that he's a deadbeat is profitable. These gossip shows and blogs pay to interview me. Shit, bitch, I'm living my best life."

"I see. You haven't fucked up with your baby daddy enough for him to stop fucking with you. Why don't you just give him the DNA test like he asks?"

"Because I don't who Malia's daddy is and if the test says he's not, then my well will dry up."

CHAPTER 3

Life's a Breeze

BABY MAMA DRAMA. The headline, along with Breeze Coleman's face was plastered over the screen of his boss' laptop. Up until that day, his music career and image were untarnished. But now, thanks to his ex-girlfriend and former backup singer, Larissa MacIntosh, all that has changed.

"Keyon, I'm sorry. I didn't mean to bring all this drama to Man of Steele. I mean, your record company, this label," he looked around the office, "you have an image to uphold."

"Don't worry about that. Man of Steele has seen its share of drama. That's the nature of the music industry beast. Besides, your situation isn't that bad. Social media has a way of making things appear a lot worse than they really are."

"Nah, bruh's situation is pretty fucked up."

Keyon wadded a up a piece of paper and threw it at his brother.

"Shut up. This was you not too long ago. Your ass was blessed when the DNA results proved you were not the father."

Shymon leaned back in his chair and rubbed his chin. "Yep, I'm blessed like that. I learned my lesson though. I strap up with two rubbers now. That's what we get for fucking with ratchet back-up singers."

Breeze exhaled. "Yeah, you're right. You beat your situation but what am I going to do? This girl won't stop talking to the blogs and these entertainment news people."

"She's just trying to capitalize off her fifteen minutes of fame."

"You're right, Shymon. When both of you signed to Man of Steele, I told you the same thing. Fame and fortune attract the fake. Leave these Mattel-made chicks alone. A real woman will not care about what you do, or what you have. All she will want is you," Keyon said.

"I know that. Now. This shit is for the birds," Breeze shook his head. "All I want to do is see my daughter. She is everything to me."

"I know how you feel. My kids and my wife are my world," Keyon said.

Before he spoke, Breeze looked at Shymon and then back to Keyon. "Um, you have three kids right, Key?"

"Yep, a set of twins and a six-month old son, Keyon, Jr."

"I know these blogs are full of shit, but is any of the stuff they wrote about you true? Like, were you really engaged to Mon's sister?"

"Yep," Shymon said. "Sadly, most of that stuff is true. My sister kinda went off the deep end. A lesbian who obsessed over her, created this intricate plot to get her and Keyon to break up and when they did, the stud went in for the kill."

"Damn, I read about that. How did that make you feel, Key? No disrespect."

"None taken. Shit I was fucked up about it but things between us had been bad for quite a while. Donnie, the chick she left me for, used my wife to get to me. Even though I was drugged, I was coherent enough to know that even though she was complicit in me and Symone's breakup, she was a different kind of woman. One worth getting to know. It took a minute for me to find her, but once I did, I never wanted to let her go."

"Man, what you went through almost makes my stuff seem so elementary."

"Shit, I told you that your situation was not that bad."

"Breeze man, I keep telling my big bro, that he could write a book about his life. The truth is way better than fiction."

"I see. I'm interested in hearing it all."

"Hmph, I bet you are," Keyon said. "But that's a story for another time. I need you to concentrate on your baby, your music and your new relationship."

"My new relationship? You know about that?" Heat formed around Breeze's collar.

"I make it my business to know about everything you all do. And you can hardly sneak around with A & R manager without Judy telling me. She's my eyes and ears around here."

"I'll remember that."

A buzz from the desk phone interrupted their conversation.

"Speaking of the devil." Keyon pressed the button to answer. "Hey, Judy what's up?"

"You have a call on line one. It's G-Steele."

"Thank you. Hello?"

"What's up, my nig? Do you know what today is?"

"No, what day is it?"

"It's Four-twenty day. Come put something in the air with me."

"You know I don't smoke weed. Hold on. Listen, you guys have been on the road for a week. Get home and get some rest. The rest of the band have already left."

"Yeah. Hey, Granny," Shymon said loudly.

"That's his grandmother he's talking to?"

"Yeah. She is something else. A whole mood."

All Breeze could do was shake his head. "You all are quite colorful. Let's chat tonight so we can coordinate a rehearsal time for the King's half-time show this Sunday."

"Bet. I'll hit you up after I wake up. My ass is beat."

They gave one another some dap, bumped shoulders, and parted ways. In his car, Breeze held onto the steering wheel for a moment before turning the ignition. He gripped it so tightly, his knuckles paled.

"Relax, dude. God is in control," he said to encourage himself. He exhaled, started the car, and made his way home. There were two pretty girls that he loved that he wanted to see. His woman and his daughter.

He didn't think he could love anything more than music until God blessed him with his daughter, Brely. He sat on his bed staring at a picture of the Cherub-faced little girl, who had managed to capture his entire soul and had the performer wrapped around her fingers. At two-years old, she was smarter than most children twice her age and could hold a conversation better than some adults. And he loved every moment spent with her.

Although the dancing, singing, rapping sensation loved being on tour, he did not like being away from his baby girl. The road was no place for a child, but he seriously considered hiring a nanny so she could be with him all the time. He had asked his ex-girlfriend, if the baby could come with him before he left last week. Unfortunately, she would not allow that.

"Breeze, you know Bre gets sick too much for that. Hell, she just got out the hospital for the severe rash. So, what you gon' do? Hire an entire medical team to accompany you on the road?"

She took his brief silence as an answer.

"I didn't think so," she finished, smacking her lips.

"If I have to, I will. But she never has any of those episodes when she's with me. Maybe it's something in the environment of your house."

"It ain't shit wrong with my house. Do you know how much money I pay for a house note?"

"A note implies that you are buying. You're simply renting and yes I do, consider I'm the one actually paying it," he said, poking his chest.

"It's always about money with you, ain't it? I already told you, I don't want the damned child support. All I want is for us to be together again." Her voice softened and she caressed his cheek. "Don't you miss us, baby?

He jerked his head away from her touch. "Miss what? The cheating? The sex tapes I found with you and other dudes? Or you wilding out on me after getting pissy drunk?"

"I quit drinking when I found out I was pregnant, and you know it so stop holding that against me and the sex tape? Well, I didn't know he was filming us."

"You were my woman, Larissa. You shouldn't have been fucking him in the first place. Fuck! All these other entertainers are out here screwing this one and the next one, but I was faithful to your ass. Nah, I don't miss none of that. All me and you can ever be are co-parents. If it weren't for my baby, you would never see me again. That's on my, mama."

He shook his head and put his phone away. When Breeze wasn't on the road, he kept his daughter with him as much as he could. The two had developed an unbreakable bond and for the child to be as young as she was, he sensed that she understood what was going on around her.

Once he was home, he went straight to his room and sat on his California king-sized bed. As much as he loved the comfort of hotel beds, they were no substitution for his own.

A pair of soft hands slid up his back, over his shoulders and gently kneaded them.

"Are you alright, honey?" She said, kissing his neck.

"Yeah, I'm good. Just thinking about Bre. I can't stand not having her with me all the time. It seems like every time she is at Larissa's house she is vomiting or dizzy."

Caresse giggled. "I'm not laughing at you being separated from her, but wouldn't it be something if she were allergic to her mother? I mean, when she is here with us, she is bright-eyed and bushy-tailed."

"You're right about that. She's totally different when she is here."

"Have you given any thought to what we talked about?"

"Going to court for full-custody? Hell yeah. I already put my lawyer on it but told him don't file anything until the tour ends though. I need to be able to show the court that I am able to be a full-time parent."

"You're a great man and an excellent father. They will see that. You have nothing to worry about."

"I'm not worried. With you by my side, I can conquer the world."

There were knots in his shoulders, so his girlfriend massaged them to ease the tension.

"Damn, babe that feels so good. You're so gentle and tender."

She leaned over slightly and nibbled his ear lobe. "Well, that's what Caresse means in French. A woman with a tender touch."

"Hmm, and this whole time I thought you were named after a bar of soap."

Playfully, she slapped him against his head. "Whatever, nut."

"Oh, it's like that? You want to hit somebody? It's on now."

He pulled her into his lap and tickled her until she could not breathe. Breeze sobered and his piercing brown eyes questioned Caresse from under his furrowed brow.

"Does it bother you that Larissa doesn't know about you or that our relationship isn't public?"

"Nope. I value my privacy and I know where I stand with you. Not only do you tell me that I am the only woman who matters you show me."

"Damn, skippy. You never have to worry about that cheating shit from me. My dad would kill me if I did you like that. He acts like he loves you more than he does me and I'm his flesh and blood."

"Don't hate the relationship he and I have. Mister Coleman is my main man."

He smacked his lips. "That's right."

"Plus, the people who need to know about me, do."

The sunshine broke through the crack in the curtain. Caresse got up and opened them, allowing the light to fill the room.

"I know you planned to rest today but look how pretty it is outside today. Why don't you call Larissa and ask her if you can pick Brely up and take her to the park?" She handed him his cellphone.

"Good idea," he nodded, dialing his exes' number.

Larissa answered the phone, smacking bubble gum. "What up, baby daddy?"

He exhaled slowly. Breeze hated when she called him that. "Nothing much. I'm back in Atlanta and would like to take Bre to the park. Can you have her ready?"

"Don't you think you should axe me if she can go?"

"I am *asking* you, Larissa. Can you please have her ready?"

"You got five racks?"

29

Caresse covered her mouth to prevent the sound from escaping.

"Are you actually charging me five-thousand dollars just to be able to take my daughter to the park?"

"You damned straight, nigga. The fuck you think this is? Ain't shit free this way."

"I already pay child support. You're not extorting more money from me."

"Well then I guess you don't wanna see Bre that bad." Click.

"Gold-digging ass," he said. Shaking his head. He rapidly typed in a text and hit send.

On the other side of town, Larissa doubled over in laughter. Her baby daddy had her fucked up. If he really wanted to see their child then he would have cash apped her the money like he had in times past, but a little over a month ago, things changed. When she asked him for extra money, he would tell her no. So, since he would not give her what she asked for, she denied him what he wanted...visitation with their baby.

"Fuck him," she said and returned to putting lotion on her legs.

The sun was out and that meant that titties and asses would be too. No one could have asked for a more beautiful day in the A. Seventy-five degrees, no humidity and not one cloud in site. Shit, Larissa was about to be in the streets, turning the fuck up.

She stood in the mirror, fanning her eye so the eyelash glue she had just applied, could become tacky.

"Get it, Bitch. Where you going?"

Oh, hey, Mama. I'm on my way to get a mani-pedi. My feet all jacked up like I've been kicking rocks."

Her mother lifted her own hands and inspected them. "Damn, mine too. Lemme put my wig on."

"Cool. After I finish my lashes, I'll be ready."

Five minutes later, Larissa and her mother, Laquanda, were ready to walk out the door.

Larissa snapped her fingers. "I forgot to tell you that Breeze's bitch ass called me, asking if he could come swoop, Bre."

"Oh yeah? What you tell him?"

"Shit, the only thing I could tell him. Run me some money. He said no, so I did too then hung up in his face. He ain't seen his daughter in a month 'cause he wanna be stingy with the gwap. Fuck him and feed him beans."

Laquanda gave her daughter a high-five.

"That's what the fuck you supposed to do, baby girl."

"His ass doesn't understand how much it costs to look this good on a daily basis."

"Damned straight. Beauty like this comes at a very high price," her mother said.

Larissa grabbed her Birkin bag from the arm of the sofa, reached in and pulled her car keys out. "Jarell!" She yelled at the top of her lungs.

"What?"

"Watch, Brely. Me and Mama are going to the nail shop and to run some errands and shit."

"But I have soccer practice," the little boy said, walking into the living room.

"Boy what have I told you about that white ass game," his mother screamed. "Your punk ass needs to get into football like I told you. Then you would be worth something. Shit, I need one of y'all bastard asses to buy me a house. I'm tired of struggling."

"I ain't no bastard," Larissa said. "Hell, I'm the one who takes care of all the bills around this place."

"No, Breeze does that," the little boy said. "All you did was open your legs for the right one and managed to get pregnant. I'm still astonished that Brely is actually his. Will wonders never cease."

"You need to watch your fucking mouth and stop biting the hand that feeds you."

"Both of y'all stop the dumb shit. Rissa you do a good job around here, but Jarell, your ass need to start pulling your weight. I know Tank will give you dope sack or some shit to slang for him. Your ass is almost grown."

"I'm eleven years-old, Mother. Hardly anywhere near being grown."

"When I was your age, I was pregnant with your big brother, Hitta. Now that's who you need to be more like."

"You want me to sell drugs and end up in prison like him? Thanks, but no thanks. I have greater dreams and aspirations than that."

She rolled her eyes. "My motherfucking son is a hustler and knows how to handle business. But you know what? Your sister is right. Your ass do got a smart mouth. I was gonna leave you some money to get y'all something to eat but since you wanna talk like a grown-up then you feed yourself like one." Laquanda stormed out the house.

"But what about Brely?" Jarell question, Larissa. "She needs food."

"It's some Top Ramen in the cabinet. Cook those," she said as she walked out the door, slamming it behind her.

The little girl peeked her head around the corner. She was so astute; she was checking to see if the coast was clear.

"Mommy gone?"

"They both are, Niecy Pooh. It's just the two of us."

"Yayyy," she squealed. "You call, Daddy? I've been a big girl. I keep the secret."

"Not yet, but I am about to. And yes, you are a very big girl. We can never tell anyone about this, okay? Your daddy loves us and takes care of us. If our moms found out, they would stop it. Don't forget, it's our secret. Shhh."

"Shhh." The little girl sucked her thumb and nodded as Jarell sent a text message.

Breeze, who was still holding his phone, opened the message immediately.

"The pigeons have flown the coop," he read out loud to Caresse.

She smiled. "I think it's great that you and Jarell have this system. If it weren't for him, you would probably never get to see your baby."

"Yeah. It's a damned shame. Larissa and her mother are two peas in a pod. Neither of them takes care of their kids."

"But you keep that little boy dressed so well. Where does his mother think the clothes and shoes come from?"

"Jarell told her that he has been stealing them."

"What? And she hasn't said anything to him about it?"

"On the contrary. Jarell told me that she was happy about it. Said that she told him that school was for suckers and hustling was the most important thing."

"Un-fucking-believable." Caresse shook her head in disbelief.

"My sentiments exactly. Let's go. We can go to the park after we get something to eat. If I'm hungry, I'm sure the kids are, too."

Breeze and Caresse walked to the garage and got into a Burgundy, 2010 Chevy Malibu. He pressed the garage door opener, reversed and they were on their way.

"I love this car," she said. "It's so normal. No flash."

"That's why I bought it. It's so low-key, no one knows it's me in here and when I pick up Jarell, none of Larissa's neighbors can say he was picked up in a fancy car."

"I get it. It takes the heat off both of you. Clever babe."

"Thank you. I was thinking that I'm going to send Larissa a couple of thousand via cash app and then tell her I'm going to take Brely for the weekend so I can keep my baby."

"What about, Jarell?"

"I'm keeping him, too. Monday morning, I'm taking your advice."

"Oh yeah? What's that?"

"I'm going to call my attorney and have him prepare the custody papers. Something has got to change."

CHAPTER 4

Zone Blocking

FOOTBALL SEASON WAS IN full-effect and the Atlanta King's season opener was the hottest ticket in town. The team had had a stellar pre-season, giving their fans a taste of what they could expect for the remainder of the year. For Malik this was his chance to show his team that although he was a rookie, he earned his spot. The veterans rode him hard during practice, making him a stronger player, mentally and physically. This would be the first game the coach allowed him to start, since the starting wide receiver was out for a few games due to injury. Now, he was ready to show his team and the world what he could really do. More importantly, he wanted to show his woman what he could do.

For Aisha, she was just happy to be there, supporting the man who she loved. The man she knew loved her in return. Thinking of him made her smile. She was in la-la. That is, until his mother brought her back to reality.

"This is an important for Malik, young lady. Please do not do anything to embarrass him or us."

"Embarrass you? How could I do that?"

"You know, all that screaming and yelling that you people do when you are," she snapped her fingers, trying to help her memory recall the word she sought, "turned up. Try to act with some decorum and class if you can."

It took every ounce of restraint for Aisha not to respond to her man's evil mother. Instead, she offered a fake, half smile and moved away from the nasty woman. The stadium was packed. Fans milled around the concessions area, laughing, and talking.

"Kick-off is in fifteen minutes. Does anyone want anything from the concession stand before we head to our seats?"

Eloise was about to say no, when she spotted, Selena walking their way. Immediately, she gave her husband a laundry list of things to grab for her and he and their son strolled off.

"Selena, so good to see you dear. I'm glad that you made it." The woman leaned over and kissed the late arrival on both cheeks.

"I almost did not make it. Traffic was horrible. And, unfortunately, I was not able to get a ticket in the same row as you guys. Mine is a few seats behind you."

She showed Eloise the ticket in her hand.

"Oh, that's okay. You can use her ticket," Eloise said, pointing at Aisha. "You don't mind do, you?"

Without waiting for a response, she snatched the ticket from Aisha's hand and throws the other ticket to her. It fell on the floor. As Aisha bent down to pick it up, she was pushed by a fan, rushing to his seat and she stumbled to the ground. By the time she got up, The Jeffries had vanished, and she was alone, surrounded by a group of strangers.

"What the fuck? A few seats behind my ass." Aisha began breathing heavily and she tapped her foot, frustrated. Selena's ticket was in section three-fifty, row twenty-five, seat nine.

"Hell naw. She got me fucked up if she thinks I'm sitting way up there."

Aisha walked to the club level where she knew the Jeffries would be seated.

"Ticket please," the gate greeter said.

"I don't have a ticket for this section anymore. I'm looking for someone who does."

"I'm sorry, honey. Without a ticket, I cannot let you pass."

"Oh, um, I have a ticket," she said. "It's just not, well. My boyfriend's mom took my ticket and gave me this one. She said it was only two rows behind her seats but it's not."

"She exchanged her ticket with yours?" The lady asked.

"Not exactly. This ticket belonged to someone else. It's a long story."

The gatekeeper looked at Aisha's ticket and shook her head.

"Unfortunately, that ticket is for another area. I'm going to have to ask you to step aside so that I can get all these people to their seats."

Aisha nodded and moved aside. She called Misses Jeffries several times, but the lady forwarded her calls to voice mail each time. Omari, Malik's brother, nor his father answered their phones either. She was ass out of luck. At that point, she had two choices. Stand around, pout, and miss her man's game altogether, or take the lousy seat and watch him on the Jumbo-Tron. She opted for the latter. The seat was in the last section in the Benz Stadium, and it was God-awful. There was a church group there that had brought their teens to the game. Not that she had anything against the church or teens, but they were talking loudly, listening to music on their phones, and disturbing those who tried to watch the game.

There were some animated fans in the section that made cheering fun. Sitting alone, Aisha was able to be herself and cheer wholeheartedly for her man. That's something she would have not been able to do had she sat with the family. Turns out, the church teens were not that bad, especially when it came time for the half-time show. Her favorite group SKY-Hi and Breeze Coleman were the acts.

"A-T-L," the DJ announced overhead. "Are you ready?"

The crowd went wild.

"Well get up on your feet and make some noise for Atlanta's own, SKY-Hi and Breeze."

The cheers were so loud, Aisha was sure folks in Buckhead could hear the fans.

Fweet. Fweet. Fweet. A whistle sounded and then two drum majors came bursting from the tunnel, followed by a marching band. Behind them, a large Man of Steele float carrying their award-winning artists rolled out. Bass filled the stadium and fans young and old were on their feet when the beat dropped. Even Aisha twerked to a song or two.

 Their performances were worthy of a Super Bowl show, but because they were from Atlanta, they always put on for their city. It was the best twelve-minute show she had ever witnessed. She, along with everyone else in the stadium, danced and sang along with a medley of both performers' hits. Despite her elevated seats, she was having a very good time.

"Breeze, we love you!" The teens screamed.

Aisha smiled.

"That was a great show, wasn't it young lady?" An older gentleman asked.

"Yes, it really was. I haven't danced that much in ages."

"I'm headed to the concession stand to grab a bite to eat and drink. May I bring you something back?" He offered. Her pride, nor her stomach would allow her to turn him down.

"I really appreciate it. Thank you."

She assumed that many people had the same idea as he did because it took a minute for him to get back. The game had begun again shortly after he left his seat. He got back just in time to see the best play of the game.

The Saints defense was aggressive. But the King's offensive line formed a wall of protection around the quarterback, giving him just enough time to find an open receiver and to pass the ball. A few of the players took some hard hits from the defensive line. The offensive line held them at bay. The quarterback threw a deep pass, just as he was tackled. On the other end of the field, Malik bobbed and weaved, and with the grace of a ballet dancer, he leaped in the air, caught the ball and set off toward the end zone.

"The Crown Prince, Malik Jeffries has caught the ball. Look at him go," the commentator yelled overhead.

Aisha jumped to her feet. "Go baby! Go baby! Go!" She yelled so loudly, those on the fifty- yard line probably heard her. The Kings protected Malik as he ran for a seventy-two-yard touchdown. When he crossed into the endzone, the camera man filmed him doing The Dougie. She watched on the jumbo-tron as her man danced proudly.

"Young lady, you sure love football."

"Yeah, and I really love him," she mumbled out of ear shot.

The Kings won the game forty-two to seven. Many Kings players killed it on the field, but her man scored fourteen points. She could not have been happier for him.

"That was a great game, huh, young lady?"

"It sure was, Sir. Thank you so much for the refreshments. Watching the game with you was fun."

"Well, if you're not busy, I'll be here next week." He winked at her and she laughed.

"Thank you. You have a great day."

Getting down to the club level proved to be difficult. Fans were not in a hurry to leave as they were to arrive.

"Excuse me. Pardon me. Sorry."

No one wanted to move out her way. She bobbed and weaved trying to be careful but ended up stepping on a woman's foot.

"Oh my gosh, I am so sorry," she gushed.

The woman looked up from her shoe. "Aisha? How are you?"

"Kayla. I did not realize that was you. I'm sorry about your foot."

"No worries. With all these people milling around, it was unavoidable. What are you doing on this side of the stadium?"

Aisha told her about the ticket switch.

"Eloise needs her ass slapped. I swear she and my sister, Kalia, are like twins. Both are stuck up and out of touch with reality. Snobby bitches."

"I couldn't agree more. It is so irritating to hear her refer to me as "the girl from the other end." Like, I only two miles away from them."

"Yeah, in the wrong direction. My dad said that the entire family was surprised when he married Eloise." Kayla shrugged. "I guess opposites really do attract."

"Perhaps. I've never done anything to give her a reason to dislike me so much."

"Eloise does not like people who do not have money or status. Don't worry about it. Just continue to be the best girlfriend and future wife of my little cousin."

That made Aisha blush. "I hope so."

"Trust me. That boy is sprung. It was so good to see you again. I got to go meet my parents for dinner. If you need anything, you have my number. Please use it."

"Thank you."

She and Kayla hugged, and the ladies parted ways.

By the time she made it to the level where the Jeffries had been seated, they were nowhere to be found. She tried calling and texting Misses Jeffries again, but the older woman still did not answer. None of them did. Because Malik had played so well, she figured that he was probably being interviewed by the press, but she called him anyway, just in case. Like she thought, he did not answer either. It was an hour after the game was over. The stadium was still packed. And she was still alone. Just as she was about to exit the stadium and walk to the bus stop, her phone rang.

"Where are you?" Malik asked.

"Walking around looking for your family. Where are you?"

"I'm with them, by the tunnel entrance. How did you get separated from them?"

She could hear the agitation in his voice.

"Long story. Stay where you are, I'm on my way."

Aisha hightailed it to her man. This was not the way she envisioned this day going. At all.

"Damn, I'm out of shape," she said, huffing and puffing, running toward the elevator to take her down the three levels to her man. The ride allowed her the chance to catch her breath and compose herself. She took a towelette out her purse and wiped the beads of sweat from her forehead and brow.

"Oh, Alicia. How nice of you to join us," Selena said, sarcastically, when she joined the group.

"You know my name. It's Aisha."

Malik stepped between the two women.

"Where were you?"

She rolled her eyes in the top of her head and pointed upward. "In the nosebleed section."

"What! How in the hell did you end up there? You were supposed to sit with us," Mister Jeffries said.

"I thought so, too. But Misses Jeffries gave my seat to her," she said pointing to Selena, "and gave me her ticket. It was in three-fifty."

"The fuck! That's the worst section in the building. Mom, why would you do some shit like that?"

"Watch your mouth, Son. Selena forgot her glasses and I wanted her to be able to see the game. Plus, it is not good to have someone of her stature sitting with a group of paupers," she finished haughtily.

"So, what you're saying is, is that it's okay for Aisha, who's your son's woman, to sit up there, but not the daughter of one of your friends? Fuck outta here with that."

Misses Jeffries rolled her eyes. "Well, it's not like she's not used to bargain basement discounts. Afterall, she does shop at Ross. The ten-dollar seats were perfect for her."

Aisha gasped.

"Damn, shots fired," Omari, said.

"She belongs with me." Malik pointed to his chest. "Babe, I'm sorry. This will never happen again. And don't worry about where she used to shop because she can shop wherever she wants to from now on. On me!"

"Of course, she can. That's what girls like her live for."

"Excuse me?" Aisha said.

Selena giggled.

Omari covered his face with both hands.

With his fists clenched down to his side, Malik breathed deeply and slowly.

His father cleared his throat.

Malik put his hand up to stop his father, who had just opened his mouth to speak.

"Before you say anything to me, Pops, you need to check your wife. Time and time again, she steps out of line. And girls like her deserves dudes like me who will treat them like the queens they are. Come on, Eesh. Let's go."

"And where do you think you're going? We have reservations at Claude's," his mother said.

"You go. I'm going to celebrate with my woman." He threw up two fingers, grabbed Aisha's hand and strutted away.

"Eloise, I will not continue to allow you to disrespect that young lady any further. I have had it up to here." Jackson motioned with his hand above his head. "One day you are going to go too far and when you do, you will be sorry."

"Let's go, Omari."

"Jackson, we have dinner plans."

"Since you're so fond of Selena, take her. Me and my son are heading to The Beautiful Restaurant for some good ol' soul food. Selena, you don't mind going to dinner with Misses Jeffries now do you?"

"I, uh" Selena fumbled over her words.

"I thought not. Peace." Like his oldest son, he chucked up the deuces and walked off, his other son in tow.

Not in a million years did Eloise think she would be subjected to this level of disrespect. Especially not from her husband or sons.

"Shall we go?" The older woman said.

Selena nodded and they headed to her car.

Misses Jeffries strapped on her seatbelt and faced her young friend.

"My son is clearly enamored by that low-income trollop because of sex. But mark my words, he will come around and I will pair the two of you. He needs a woman of your caliber who can help him leverage these wonderful opportunities that are coming his way. Someone who can help him socially."

"Thank you, Mother Eloise. I believe you and I'm patient. I know Malik will be mine."

MEAL TICKET$

On the way to the restaurant, they made small talk and kept the conversation light.

Eloise was seething, but her anger was frighteningly under control. Hate was a strong word, but it was the only one that accurately illustrated how Eloise Jeffries felt about Aisha Graves. She did not know how, she did not know when, but one day, she was going to get rid of that girl once and for all.

CHAPTER 5

Un-reality Show

BALLER BABES WAS A new reality show that chronicled the lives of the baby's mothers of entertainers, athletes, and their kids. And this show was a new thorn in Kyle's side because, Tika, had just been cast to appear.

"It's bad enough that everyone in Atlanta knows my business. Now that she is on this show, the entire world is going to know what's going on."

Kyle dropped his head in his hands and exhaled deeply.

This was not the space he ever imagined being in. Before he made it to the NBA, he thought that he would meet and marry a sweet, beautiful woman who had her own dreams, yet supported his as well. Kind of like his mother. But that's not what happened. He did not take into consideration how his money and status would attract a different type of woman. Specifically, gold diggers. Nor did he realize that having his pick of women would increase his already voracious sexual appetite.

"Ma, I don't know why I am so surprised about the women who chased me. Hell, look at my little sister. All she wanted was a man with money to take care of her and she did not care how she went about getting what she wanted, either."

Kyle looked around his parents' house. "Where is she, anyway?"

"She is in her room. You know she does not come out much," his mother answered.

"Her vanity will not allow her to be seen by anyone. Not even us," his father added.

"That's a damned shame," Kyle said.

No one said anything for a minute. As angry as he was with his little sister and the choices she had made, he could not really pass judgement. Although they went about it differently, both used their positions to get what they wanted. And for both, it didn't end well.

He was not just Kyle Hudson, Jr., star basketball player, he was a baby's dad. Repeat, baby's daddy. Not husband. Not fiancé. Just baby's daddy. He did not like that at all.

"What were you thinking, Son?" His father, Kyle Hudson, Sr, asked him.

"That's the problem, Dad. I wasn't."

"You were thinking, but not with the right head."

"Ma!" Kyle's eyes widened and he turned quickly to look at his mother.

"Oh boy, don't look at me like that. How do you think all of you got here?"

"Trust me, that is not something that I think about. Eww, thanks the for the visual." He shook his head trying to rid it of the thought.

"Whatever. When will you find out if the baby is yours?" His mother asked.

"I want to do a paternity test, but she keeps avoiding it. Kayla said we were probably going to need a court order to force the issue."

"Probably," his mother began, nodding her head.

Kyle stood up and walked across his living room. "Until then, what do I do?"

"You make sure whomever you are out here messing with that you use protection. Every interaction. Every time. No exceptions. And take care of that little girl like you know she is yours until you find out definitively that she is not."

"I hear you, Dad. I really screwed up big time."

"Don't beat yourself up. We all make mistakes."

Both his parents stood to hug him. KJ could always count on the support of his family.

"I know I told you that I was leery of developing an attachment to her if she was not yours, but I think I am ready to meet her," his mother said.

His father nodded in agreement.

"I will get with Tika and see if she will let me come get her soon. I have practice back-to-back and games too."

"We know your schedule is busy. Take care of that first. Malia is little, she will not remember when she met us, but I want her to know all of her family if she is a Hudson."

His mother put emphasis on the 'if'.

"Yeah. The problem is, is that it's a big 'if' right now. The crazy part is that even though we have not had the DNA test yet, she is taking me to court for an increase in child support. That's not fair. Malia is a baby. I know kids are expensive, but does it really cost ten grand a month to take care of a six-month old?"

"Absolutely not. Me and Gayle Halpern are working on something that may help non-custodial parents when it comes to child support."

"Oh yeah, Dad?"

His father jots some notes on a pad quickly.

"You know Gayle's son is a real estate mogul. Apparently, he got into a relationship with a young woman a few years back and she had a baby. Gayle's son was paying out the ass for a couple of years. The child got sick or hurt and needed some blood. That's when they found out that the child was not his. Gayle was devastated. The woman was not even using the money to support the child but to fund her lavish lifestyle. That's just not right."

"At all," Kyle, Jr. agreed. "Well, whatever you all come up with, I pray that it helps us all."

"It will. Trust me. This is why I ran for office. If there are changes that need to be made, it must begin with us."

Kyle hugged his father and kissed his mother on the cheek.

"I'm going to head out. Kayla is expecting me in her office in an hour and you all know how she is about being on time."

"Indeed. Have a great day, Son."

Across town, Tika swung her thirty-inch weave and blew a kiss into the camera when the basketball she shot went through the hoop.

"And go," the director said.

"When I shoot my shot, I always score," she said.

"Cut. Perfect. Okay everybody, let's break for the day. We will resume filming tomorrow at eight sharp, in the morning not at night. If you're late, don't bother begging to stay because you're off the show. Got it?"

Tika and the other cast members nodded. When the director walked off, they slapped high fives and headed toward the dressing and makeup area.

"Heyyy, get it bitch," a girl said as Tika twerked in the mirror.

"Oww," Tika squealed, with her tongue hanging out. "Y'all know this show is about to make us rich and famous right? We are going to be better than any housewife or hip-hop show on the air."

"You got that right. We finsta blow up." Larissa said. "Shit, if I would have known that having a baby by Breeze was going to keep me paid like this, I never would have had those two abortions. I could have been a millionaire by now."

"Hoe, if you're going to be on television then you need to start talking like you got some fucking class. The word is finna, not finsta. Damn."

The other cast members side-eyed both Larissa and Tika before laughing at them.

The make-up artist who was touching up someone's makeup spoke up. "Actually, you're both wrong. The phrase is fixing to. But if you really want to sound like you have class, perhaps you could say "getting ready to," that way, once this show airs, viewers won't compare you all to the other ratchet reality broads that already grace their television screens."

Larissa turned her nose up to the woman and rolled her eyes.

Tika waved the comment off then looked at herself in the mirror and touched her eyelid. "Oh, uhn, uhn." She turned to face the young lady doing makeup. "Can you touch up my eyeshadow? I need it to really pop because a bitch like me look to good to be sitting in somebody's house tonight. I'm hitting the club."

"Who watching your baby?" Larissa asked.

"Fuck. That's a good question. I forgot tonight is Mama's bingo night and you know she ain't missing that for shit."

Larissa picked her teeth in the mirror.

"Well, you can always bring her over my house. Jarell will watch her 'cause the little nigga certainly watching my baby."

"Must be nice to have a built-in babysitter. Kyle needs to step his motherfucking game up off the court, fo' he finds himself in court. Hell, I'm tired of raising this baby by myself."

"Hmph, he still tripping?"

Tika nodded. "Yeah, for now. But I gotta plan. I'ma put this good pussy on him again and make him see what he's been missing. Once he's all up in these guts again, he will be back under my spell."

"If he ain't then you need to take his punk ass to court just like I did Breeze. Shit a bitch like me, sitting pretty. Look," Larissa turned her backside to Tika. "How you think my ass turned out? Dr. Shapes hooked it up."

Tika rubbed her friend's booty. "Damnn, hoe. I forgot you had this done. No wonder you been shaking it everywhere we go. If mine looked like that, I would too. Shit a bitch like me is low-key jealous but I'm happy for you."

"Thanks, boo. You'll get everything you want, watch. After that judge smash that gavel on Kyle's ass, you'll be just like NeNe Leakes, rich bitch!"

"Fa show. But you know I ain't really trying to see no judge. My ass stays with warrants plus, you know I'm still uncertain about you know what."

"Right, right. I got something for that though. I know people and we take care of ours. Trust."

The makeup artist shook her head at the pathetic conversation she was hearing. One of the cast members, who was engaged to a pitcher for the Atlanta Tomahawks baseball team, laughed out loud as she walked past them on her way out of the room.

"I think my I.Q. just dropped fifty points listening to this rubbish. This show is sure to become popular because people will tune in merely to see what shenanigans you two are getting into," the makeup artist said.

Neither Larissa nor Tika caught the shade that was thrown their way.

"You think we gon' help make this show good? Seriously? Ooh that's good then. The more camera time we get the bigger our checks will be."

"Word up, Tika," Larissa said. "Now we got another reason to celebrate tonight. For real though. Tonight, I'm gonna shake that ass, so niggas gimme they cash. I'm gonna shake that ass, so niggas gimme they cash," she chanted as she twerked on her friend to the beat.

"I'm done," the makeup artist said.

She packed her tools quickly and rolled her suitcase out the room as fast as she could. Although all she did was apply a fresh coat of shadow to Tika's lids and replaced a jewel that had fallen, time seemed to stand still. The faster she tried to work, the slower it felt like she got. Listening to them was torture.

"Have a great day, ladies," she said, closing the door behind her.

Tika gave herself another once over in the mirror and then nodded her head in approval.

"That hoe know what she's doing with this makeup thing. Once my money starts really rolling in, I'm going to have her at my beck and call."

"Word up. Let's go. If we hurry, we can hit the mall and get us something to wear for tonight."

After grabbing her new Celine bag, she and Larissa trotted out the studio, jumped into her leased, Maserati and jetted to Phipps Plaza. Tika stepped into the Bottega Veneta store with her sights set on a new handbag and matching wallet. She spent money like it was nothing because to her, it wasn't. Even though she and Kyle did were not together, he made sure she had money above and beyond what he paid in child support. That is one of the reasons why she had to get him back.

A loud buzz sounded from Tika's purse. She pulled it out and got excited when she saw who was calling her. Quickly, she pressed the talk button and rushed to Larissa's side, showing her the caller I.D. on the phone.

"Oh, shit," Larissa mouthed.

"Hello? Oh, hey Rhona. How are you? Nothing really. Me and Larissa were going to go the club tonight. For real? Oh my gosh, that would be great. Okay, I'll let her know. Thanks. Yeah, we'll be on time. Bye."

Larissa tugged at her arm. "Was that Rhona Stewart-Older, the show's creator? What she want?"

"Bitch, she said that she wants to send cameras to the club with us tonight, to get footage for the show. So, we really need to look our best. But she also said, if we go out, we still need to show up on time in the morning. You know that means that we can't drink too much. We don't want to get fired before we are officially hired."

"Word. Let's hurry up. Grab that bag hoe and let's get to the Fendi store. It's some shit in there with my name on it."

Excited was not the word that Tika would use to describe the way she was feeling. All that she wanted was beginning to fall into place. The last piece of the puzzle was Kyle. Once she had him, her life would be perfect.

The camera man followed Tika from her house to Larissa's. When she got there, she took her baby girl upstairs and came down with a drink in her hand.

"She has a bar upstairs?" The man asked incredulously.

"My girl got drinks everywhere. Why? You want one?"

"I'm good. Thanks, though. I'm going to get a little footage here before we leave, okay?"

"Yeah, that's cool."

Just before he turned the camera on to begin filming, Kyle called. Tika looked at the phone before letting out an exasperated sigh.

"Is that KJ?" He asked.

"Yeah, but I ain't answering it."

The phone stopped ringing.

"How do you think Kenya or any of the other Housewives are holding a peach in the opening credits of the show? They create drama to keep their storylines hot to make viewers want to watch them. You need to call him back. Trust me, when Rhona sees this footage, she is going to give you all the camera time you want."

"You think so?"

"I know so."

Taking his advice, Tika pressed his number and waited for him to answer. She put the phone on speaker so that the cameraman could film the entire conversation.

"Hey, KJ. You called?"

"Uh, yeah. How are you?"

"I'm good. What's up?"

There was a brief pause before he spoke. "We need to talk about Malia Janae."

"Hmph, so you finally want to stop being a dead-beat baby daddy?"

"That's bullshit and you know it. I pay child support religiously on a child that...," he stopped mid-sentence.

"A child that what, Kyle? Gon' head and finish what you were about to say."

"Fine. A child that may not even be mine."

"What the fuck? She looks just like you. Here you go with this crap again."

"Man whatever. We're on the road for the next couple of games but when I get back, we're having that talk. A very long one."

"Okay then, boo. You know I love it when you get all forceful and shit."

"Bye, man."

The phone call disconnected and the light from the camera went out.

"Perfect," the cameraman said, giving her the 'okay' signal.

"Boop. Thank you. Damn, Larissa. Let's go."

There was a knock at the door.

"Five minutes hoe, damn. Get the door for me."

Tika rolled her eyes and walked over to the door. She heard loud voices on the other side and instantly knew what time it was.

"Larissa, I know you didn't call these ratchet ass hoes to go out with us."

Larissa walked down the steps.

"Chill, bestie. We're going to have a good time and give this fine ass white boy right here something to do."

She blew the cameraman a kiss, pushed Tika out the way, and opened the door.

"What took you so long to open the door. A bitch gotta piss."

"Have some class, Shante'." She leaned in and whispered in her friend's ear. "Be cool, bitch. We filming tonight. If you act right, I'll get you on the show."

Shante nodded quickly. Slowly the corners of her mouth turned up and she flashed a smile so big you could see all her teeth.

"Got it.'

The camera man shook his head. He was used to chicks like her. What she was doing was nothing new. Making empty promises that she had no way in hell of fulfilling. He snickered. His boss had done a little digging on her and she was a bit skeptical of keeping her in the lineup. While she was busy trying to secure spots for her friends, she barely had a spot of her own.

"She'll find out soon enough," he whispered as he grabbed his equipment and headed for the club.

The club was jumping, and the music was blasting. To get the best footage, Rhona had taken the liberty to call the club and have a VIP section reserved for her reality stars.

"I can get used to a life like this," Tika began. "I mean, I've been to VIP sections before but never had my own. And the way these waitresses keep catering to me. Boop! This is the life."

Tika lifted her glass in the air and bounced her booty to the beat. The camera man, finally told her his name was Andy, did not miss a step when it came to catching all the action. When dudes tried to step to her, he was right there to catch it. Once this aired, she just knew that she was going to a hit. InstaPic had served her well. If anyone said that social media didn't pay, then they needed to talk to her, because if it weren't for that platform and a very good photographer, she never would have met Kyle.

"Look alive. You have company approaching," Andy screamed to Tika.

A tall, average looking dude made his way toward the VIP area. He swerved a few times and bumped into a few people who mean mugged him.

"Bruh is already tipsy. I don't want him over here," she said to Andy.

"Yooo, what's poppin'?" He asked.

"Nothing much. May I help you?" Tika asked.

Dude reached for the clasp on the velvet rope.

"Wait, what the fuck are you doing?"

"Oh, he's with me," Shante said, sliding up next to Tika. "I told him he could come chill with us."

"The fuck? Bitch your ass ain't even supposed to be here. This is my motherfucking section and the last time I checked; I didn't invite you."

"First of all, hoe, don't be calling me out my motherfucking name and my homegirl, Larissa invited me. She's part of the show too. This ain't just about you."

"I said what I said. This drunk nigga ain't welcome in this section and if you wanna be with him so bad tonight, take your broke ass out there with him."

Andy maneuvered his camera closer so that he could catch the entire argument. He wanted the sound crew to be able to filter all the noise out during edits.

"Don't be disrespecting my woman like that," the drunk guy said. "She'll molly whop yo' ass."

"Nigga please. You and this bitch need to get the fuck out of my section right now."

Without warning, Shante' hauled off and smacked Tika in the face and pulled her hair. Andy stepped back so that he would not get hit but there was no way he was going to miss all this action. Security rushed to the fight, breaking the girls up.

Shante' was still swinging and kicking as one lifted her in the air and carried her away.

"Where the fuck is Larissa. I'm ready to go."

She looked around and did not see her homegirl anywhere.

"Fuck it. Let's go."

Without waiting to see if Andy was following her, Tika grabbed her clutch from the sofa and hightailed it out the club. This night had not gone the way she planned, and a fight scene was the last thing she wanted to air on the show. Especially one that she lost.

CHAPTER 6

Sick and Tired

DO YOU REALIZE THAT I am sitting on top of the world right now?

"Actually, you're sitting on top of my dick, so shut the fuck up and take this shit."

The dude grabbed Larissa by her waist and with strong hands, began to lift and slam her down on his stiff meat. His thrusts were aggressive, and she winced with each jab. Her pleasure was no longer a concern of his. Not that it ever was.

"Ow, Trill. This shit hurts. Take it easy." She placed her hands on his chest and tried to get off him, but he held her firmly in place.

"You ain't going nowhere, bitch. Does it look like I'm done?" He reached behind her back and tugged hard on her twenty-six-inch weave.

She hated when he got like this. Lately, it had been happening quite frequently. Whatever was wrong, she hoped he would straighten it out, and fast. Because she did not think that her woman parts could handle the beat down that he gave them.

"Babe, I gotta go get dressed. We filming again. Rhona already told me I was skating on thin ice after the club fight and me being late to shoot twice. Shit, I need this money."

"Correction, hoe. We need this money."

Larissa rolled her eyes. "You tried it. Stop, nigga. We can pick this up later."

"Fuck, naw. I ain't stopping 'til my dick empties or I get tired. Whichever comes first."

Without freeing her from his dick's hold, Trill spun her around so that her back was facing him and rolled her over. While she lay flat on her stomach, he eased in and out of her.

"Baby, please. I'm gonna be late."

A low growl escaped past his lips.

"Uhn," she said, feeling the pain of his punch to her head. To protect herself from the blows that she knew were coming, Larissa grabbed a pillow to cover her head. She flinched, blow after blow, as he pounded his fist into her head.

"I said, shut the fuck up and let me finish."

Sex with Trill was becoming more and more combative. She should have left him alone after he leaked the sex tape that the two of them had made. Correction, she never should have fucked him in the first place. You see, Trill was her homegirl Shante's man and baby daddy. Larissa only fucked him out of spite because Shante' had landed a coveted role in music video that she really wanted. Hell, she wouldn't have even known about the video shoot, had Larissa not told her about it. To make matters worse, the video was Breeze's label mates, SKY-Hi and he was a featured artist on the song, which meant he was going to be in the video as well.

Even though she wasn't in the video, she was still Breeze's girl at that time, and he allowed her to be on set. It was there between a take that she saw her so-called "bff" pushing up on her man.

"You know you want these lips wrapped around that dick. Come on. I'll do you in the dressing room," Larissa had heard Shante' say. Steam burst through her ears and her nostrils flared. Causing a scene was the last thing she wanted to do because Breeze would not like that at all. So, she decided to pay the bitch back.

During that time, she and her baby daddy had been arguing a lot more than usual and she was over it and him. Admittedly, she knew that fucking her friends' man was wrong, but she didn't care. This was more about revenge than sex and Trill was nothing more than a pawn in her vengeful game. She orchestrated a meet-up with Trill at an upscale location but at the last minute, he changed things. That should have been a red flag right there.

Once she got to the motel, Trill had all the tricks and treats that she loved from Molly to Nose Candy to Patron. By the time they got to the fucking and sucking, she was so lit, she did not even know her own name. But she was coherent enough to know that his big dick felt good in every hole and it was something she wanted to experience time and again.

Things between her and Breeze were already bad. But after he saw that sex tape over his friend's house, he was enraged. He came home, threw all her belongings in a garbage bag, and kicked her out, ending their relationship without a second thought. To this day, she still wondered how her man ended up seeing the video but Shante' never did.

A hard slap across her ass brought her back to the present quickly. The sting tingled and she wanted to scratch that spot, but she dared not move the pillow, for fear that he begin to hit her again. She was not sure how much time had passed before he finally nutted and left, but by the time Larissa got in the shower, she was already an hour late.

"Fuck! That bitch, Rhona is gonna kill me. Ugh, I hate Trill's ass."

As much as she wanted to take the time to apply her makeup, she thought better of it. Making a good impression on the powers that be was the important thing for her to do. This was the first legitimate gig that she had had in ages and she wasn't trying to mess it up.

She fanned the eyelash that she had just applied glue to and waited for it to become tacky enough for application.

"I ain't giving them full face today, but I never leave home without lashes," she said to her mirror.

There was a knock at her door and then it opened.

"Mommy, I hungry," Brely said.

"Go tell your uncle to fix you some cereal or some shit. Can't you see I'm getting ready for work?"

The little girl's bottom lip began to tremble, and tears pooled in her eyes.

"Jerry at 'cool," she said.

"Don't be trying to pull that baby ass act on me. Grow the fuck up, little girl. Your granny will cook for you when she wakes up."

Brely shook her head. "Ganny gone."

"Gone? The fuck. She knew I needed her to watch you today and why in the hell did Jarell go to school? Damn. Who am I going to get to watch your ass?"

"I go with Daddy?"

"Your daddy? Bitch you done lost your ever-loving mind. Come on."

Larissa grabbed the little girl by her hand and hauled her into the bedroom.

"Wait here. I'm going to fix you something to eat."

The little girl nodded and sucked her thumb.

Five minutes later, Larissa returned with a tray of food for her daughter.

"Thank you, Mommy," the little girl said as she hugged her leg.

"You're welcome. Mama got you some cheese, crackers, apple slices and juice. All your favorite things. Now," she sat the child on the bed and placed the tray on the nightstand next to her. "Mommy wants you to sit in this room like a big girl and do not leave out of it okay. Uncle Jarell will be home this afternoon and he will feed you again, okay? And don't eat all this food at one time either or else your ass will starve, 'cause I ain't coming back no time soon."

A pair of big brown eyes stared at her. "Don't go, Mommy. I scared."

Whoosh. Larissa's hand flew toward the little girl's face so fast, it sounded like wind in the air. Slap. The noise resounded in the room when her hand connected to the skin.

"Oww," the baby squealed.

Angry, Larissa snatched her up, squeezing both of her arms tightly. She shook the little girl and then spit in her face.

"If you don't shut this shit up, I'm really going to give you something to cry about. Do you hear me, hoe?"

The little girl stopped crying immediately, only whimpering, as she tried to quiet down.

"Good. Now don't leave out this room. You be a good little girl and Mommy will buy you some snacks from Dollar Tree later."

Without looking back, Larissa walked out the room, down the stairs and out the house, leaving her two-year-old daughter in the house alone.

Thankfully, she was able to sail through the lights and when she got to the set, the first person she saw was Tika.

"Hoe, where you been? I had to cover for your ass."

Larissa hugged her tightly.

"Thanks, boo. This nigga I was fucking didn't want to let me out the bed. He got all abusive and shit."

"Is it that same nigga you been telling me about? The sex tape bum?"

"Yeah. One in the same."

"I'm still trying to figure out what you see in that nigga. Ain't no way I would still be fucking a nigga who tried to cancel my meal ticket."

Larissa didn't respond to that. Her friend did not know that it was Trill in the video, and she was not going to tell her. Somehow, his head managed to get cut off by the camera while it was taping. When Larissa asked him how that had happened,

he had shrugged his shoulders and told her that he didn't know.

"Technology ain't always up to par," he told her. She knew that to be true, so she believed him.

To change the subject, Larissa said, "what have I missed here?"

"Believe it or not, nothing. For the past two hours they have been running around like chickens with their heads cut off, trying to figure out what in the hell is going on with the power. It keeps going out."

"Damn. That's fucked up. Why were they asking for me?"

"They wanted us all on the soundstage, but I'm not sure why. Rhona's assistant asked where you were, and I said you were in the bathroom. Right after that, the power went out and I ain't seen her since."

"Thank you, baby Jesus. I'on need no more negative attention brought to me."

"I know that's right."

A young woman driving a golf cart, rolled to a stop in front of them.

"I'm glad that you two are together. They've fixed the power issue and you're wanted on soundstage three."

Larissa looked at Tika and smiled. God was looking down on her.

Rhona, Andy, and a few of the production crew team, were inside, waiting for all the cast to join them.

"Have a seat, ladies," Rhona began. "We apologize about the power issue. That was out of our control, but Georgia Electric has assured us that the issue if fixed. Unfortunately, that puts us behind schedule. I want us to finish up some confessional tapings and then we will call it a day."

Rhona's phone rang. She put her index finger up, signaling that she needed a moment and walked out of everyone's earshot. When she returned, she had a smile on her face.

"Ladies, great news. That was Keyon Steele of Man of Steele Records. He said that Grammy-Award winning, Platinum artists, SKY-Hi are having an album release party tonight and he said that I could film and gather footage. It will be free publicity for him and us. He has asked me to send him over your names to add to the guest list."

The ladies cheered. Larissa was excited because her baby's daddy was going to be there, and she could not wait to see him.

"Bitch, I gotta make sure I am looking like a million bucks tonight."

"For sure, Rissa. This is your opportunity to stunt on all those hoes you know will be checking for your nigga."

"Yep."

"Listen up. One final and the most important thing. Keyon is like family and I will not, I repeat, I will not be embarrassed by any of you or your ghetto ass behavior. Got it?"

She looked at Larissa. All the women nodded their heads.

"Now let's get to work. We've wasted enough time as it is."

For the next few hours, everyone did exactly as they were told, and they wrapped for the day. Before they left, Rhona gave them all a final warning.

"Remember that we are trying to get this show picked up. It's going to take all of us doing our parts for that to happen. You all are stars in the making. Govern yourselves accordingly."

This was it. Everything that Larissa had ever dreamed about was finally coming true. She drove home feeling as if she were floating on a magic carpet. Her joy did not last long because as soon as she walked in the door her mother laid into her.

"Larissa Rochelle MacIntosh. Why in the fuck would your dumb ass go off and leave your motherfucking baby in the house by her damned self?"

"Damn, can a bitch get in and take her shoes off first before you start with the bullshit? And the last time I checked she's my damned child and this is my got damned house. I can do whatever the fuck I want."

"Bitch, who the fuck you think you talking to? I will gut your disease packing ass like the slimy fish your pussy smells like, hoe. You better check yourself."

"Whatever, Laquanda. She was alright. Why you didn't tell me you were leaving?"

"Hoe, I'm grown. I don't answer to you."

"I know that, Mama damn. You could have at least told Jarell to stay home. His ass didn't need to go to school today."

"You's a dumb hoe. Don't your ass know that shit done changed? It's not like how it was when you were in school. He can't just kick it at home and fuck all day like you used to. If he don't take his ass to school, them people will call the cops and children's services and shit. I needs my food stamps and a bitch ain't trying to keep going to jail. Breeze gives you enough money to pay for a sitter. Put some of that money somewhere other than up your nose."

Unbeknownst to them, Jarell and Brely at the top of the staircase and he was recording the entire argument. When it became obvious that the fussing was over, he stopped the recording and slid his phone in his pocket.

"Shhh, let's go watch television." He took the little girl to his room and together they sat in the bean bag chair and watched cartoons.

Larissa and her mother walked into the kitchen. Her mom lit a blunt and passed it to her.

"Guess what, Ma? The cast was invited to SKY-HI's album release party tonight. They put all our names on the list."

"Awe, shit. Get it, bitch." Laquanda began to twerk around the kitchen.

"You know Breeze's ass is gonna be there. I'ma make my move on him tonight."

"It's been a year since y'all broke up and I know his fine ass ain't showing up alone. How you plan on coming between him and his new chick."

"He ain't like all these other artists. For real, dude is the settling down type. A one-woman man and I know he ain't serious about no other bitch because he would have told me."

Laquanda side-eyed her delusional daughter.

"Well, have fun. I'm going out tonight. But check this out, if you have my son watching your baby, you need to break him off. He not gon' keep doing shit for free."

"I'll take care of him. Promise."

True to her word, Larissa gave her brother five-hundred dollars before she left for the evening. Something told her that tonight was going to be like no other and she was feeling very good. Nothing, not even the dealership calling to tell her that she was late on her lease payment, was going to screw up her mood.

The valet had a big grin on his face when she pulled her 2019 Maserati Levante in front to the club. He opened the door for and gushed.

MEAL TICKET$

"Hello beautiful, welcome to Club Intensity."

She handed him her hand and he kissed it before helping her out the car. Long legs gracefully stepped out the car, barely covered by the short skirt she wore. Her top left very little to the imagination as it was a see-through lace halter with nipple covers. Her new ass was prominently on display under the form fitting material.

"Take care of her now, and I just might take care of you later," she said to the valet, walking off toward the door.

There were two lines, one for VIP guests and the other for the nobodies. As she passed the nothing ass bitches waiting to get in, she snubbed her nose at them.

Tika and a couple of the other cast members were at the front of the line, huddled in a small group.

"About time your ass got here," Tika said. "Come on y'all."

They walked to the bouncer. He was easily almost seven feet tall and well over three hundred pounds.

"Damn. He looks like a lineman for the Atlanta Kings," Joya, a footballer's baby mama said.

"His ass looks like he swallowed two regular sized niggas," Tika agreed.

"Welcome ladies." His deep voice washed over them like warm water. "I.D.'s please."

Joya handed him hers then Tika and another cast mate. He handed them to a hostess who checked their names off the list. Larissa had to dig hers out the bottom of her clutch.

"How in the hell you lose an I.D. in a bag that's not bigger than a minute?" Joya asked.

"It ain't lost, hoe. Here it is." She handed it to the hostess.

The hostess scanned the first page and flipped to the second page. Then the third. Then the fourth. She kept flipping and then started over again.

"I'm sorry, ma'am. Your name is not on the list."

"The fuck you mean, it ain't on the list? My producer sent Keyon a list of all our names."

"Don't start no shit, won't be no shit," the bouncer warned.

"You need to look again. It must be a mistake."

"I've check twice already. I can read."

"Ain't nobody ask you to be getting smart and shit. A bitch ain't said nothing about you not being able to read, but you do wear glasses so maybe you just can't see."

The Baller Babe's looked at one another then turned to go inside the club.

"Wait, I know y'all not gon' leave me out here by myself, are you?"

"Look, Rhona said no shenanigans tonight and I'm not trying to get caught up in whatever is about to go down right here. The drinks are free and I'm VIP." Joya chucked up the deuces and went inside. The other lady followed suit.

"Fuck them, bestie. We can go somewhere and have a good time by ourselves."

"You can. I'm going in. Later gator."

"Ooh." She stomped so hard, her heel broke. "Fuck!"

"Step aside for invited guests," the hostess said.

Larissa turned to walk toward the valet stand. The girls that she snubbed earlier were being admitted to the club. They laughed at her.

By the time she got home, her blood was boiling. Her brother had fallen asleep with every light on inside the house. He and her little girl were fast asleep in his bed. She walked in and eased the little girl from under his arm and took her into her room.

"Wake your bitch ass up," she said, shaking her. "This is all your damned fault. But I got something for your ass. If I can't be in the club tonight, then neither will your daddy's ass. And you bet not tell him about this. It's our secret."

Larissa got a syringe that she used to administer medicine and grabbed a bottle of Syrup of Ipecac. Filling the tube, she shoved it into her daughter's mouth.

"Swallow this shit."

She squeezed the little girl's cheeks until there was a small opening and she forced the medicine down her throat. The little girl began to cry.

"Shut up before I smother you."

She threw the syringe down and poured the liquid down her throat.

It did not take long for Brely to begin to vomit.

"Perfect."

She grabbed her phone and dialed Breeze's number.

"What?" He snapped.

"Babe, little Bre is vomiting again. The medicine that the doctor gave me before is gone. She's so pale. Can you please come and take us to the hospital? I'm too distraught to drive?"

"Fuck," she heard him say over the loud music in his background. "I'm on my way."

Before he arrived, Larissa made sure that all traces of the emetic were gone and that her baby was cleaned up. She walked into her brother's room and shook him gently on the shoulders.

"Breeze is downstairs. We're taking Brely to the hospital."

He rubbed his eyes. "What happened? She was fine before you came home."

"Well, she ain't now, bastard. If I ain't home 'fore Mama, just let her know what happened."

She took her time going down the stairs to open the door for him. When she did, he snatched his baby from her and walked quickly to the car.

"Why is my baby sick, Larissa?" He grilled her.

"She's our baby and I don't know. Just get us to the hospital without having a wreck."

They argued the entire ride.

For a Friday night, the emergency room was packed with children. Because of Brely's symptoms, she was seen immediately. None of the tests that the doctor's ran indicated any type of virus.

"Mister Coleman, the good news is that all the tests were negative, which means that this may be a simple bug. The bad news is that we are not sure what type of bug, so to be on the safe side, I'd like to admit her and watch her overnight. If she does not vomit anymore, it is safe to assume that it was a bug that passed, but if it persists, I may need to run more tests."

"Thanks, doctor. I appreciate all you have done."

A nurse came in and asked Breeze to come with her. There was a not so small matter of putting a method of payment on file and filling out other paperwork.

Larissa was walking down the hallway toward the desk, with Brely's things in her hands as he walked back toward the room, she was in.

"Where are you going with my baby's stuff?"

"You heard the doctor, he said they are keeping Bre overnight. I'm going home."

He did a triple take. "You're going where?"

"Home. Come on. You can stay with me tonight and when they release her, we can come back." She rubbed his chest. "My pussy is so wet for you, Zaddy. I can't wait to feel you all up in these guts."

"Get your hands off me," he said through clenched teeth. "If my baby is staying here, so am I. If you wanna leave, take an Uber."

"But babe," she whined. "I need your big dick in this ass. I've missed you."

She rubbed her hand over his crotch. He grabbed her hand and squeezed it tight. Her palm began to turn red.

"Larissa, I would not fuck you in any hole with somebody else's dick. Stop coming at me like that. This is the last time I will tell you. Now, if you want to go, leave. I'm staying here."

She stumbled slightly when he released her arm abruptly and stormed off, leaving her standing alone. There was no way that she was going to take an Uber home, so she decided to stay. Plus, if Tika asked her what she did tonight, she would say that she stayed the night with Breeze. For once, she would be telling the truth.

CHAPTER 7

Ammunition

BILLS WERE PILED UP on the roll top desk that sat in the eat-in kitchen at the Grave's home when Aisha walked in. Normally, she would not intrude in her parent's business and look through the mail, but something inside told her to go through it. Just this once. With her mother in the hospital, the family was down a considerable income. Her father, who was a very skilled mechanic, had begun working on cars after work as a side hustle. So far, he had a steady stream of clients, but the money they paid him still was not enough to cover the mounting hospital bills their mother received.

She was beyond frustrated because although she and her siblings still lived at home, she was the only one working to help around the house. Her sister had a job at a customer service center, but she quit because they wouldn't give her the time off to attend the NBA All-Star weekend. Her brother didn't work either. He and his friends rode around the city all day, doing nothing but smoking weed and chasing chicks. Both were older than her and she was the one who was making all the effort to help. As hard as it was, she had even withdrawn from the University of Georgia so that the family could save money. Even with financial aid, she still was not able to afford the tuition without both of her parents help. Almost grudgingly, she enrolled in a junior college instead and went part-time, attending classes around her work schedule.

The first bill she picked up just so happened to be from the hospital and it was already open. She pulled the paper out of the envelope and looked at it. Her eyes got as big as the bill. The amount owed was well over thirty-thousand dollars and it was already past due.

"What's up, chick?" Her sister, Sandra said.

"Just looking at all these bills. We have got to do something."

"We? Why you over there speaking French? None of those bills have my name on them." She grabbed some chips off the fridge and began eating out the bag.

"They're not mine either, but we all live here. The least we can do is help pay the mortgage and utilities. Damn, Sandra."

"Pssh, don't your man play for the Kings? And didn't I just read that he got an endorsement deal with Nike? Shit, you better get some money from him. His ass can afford it."

"This isn't Malik's problem," Aisha said.

"Welp, it ain't mine either," she said.

She sat there staring at her sister's back, watching her walk out of the kitchen. No sooner than she returned her attention to the remaining bills did her brother come in. She smelled him before she saw him.

"What you doing?" He said, grabbing a bottle of water out the fridge.

"Trying to make sense of all these bills. You didn't go into your interview like that did you?"

He smacked his lips. "Man, come on. I'm not stupid. The homies came through and swooped me. We had to put a lil' sumthin', sumthin' in the air to celebrate me getting the job."

"Oh, wow. Congrats, big bro. I'm happy for you."

"Thanks, Sis. Now I'll have some money to start doing my share."

"Amen. These bills are piling up, but with all of us chipping in, we can get it under control."

"Bills? I'm talking about doing my share when it comes to studio time. We're trying to get this music done. As soon as our first single is released, we know we're going to blow up. Our shit is fire."

"While I am happy that you got a job that will allow you to live your dream, this household needs you and Sandra's help. Neither of you seem to care that our dad is buried in bills."

"Shit, I care. Why the fuck you think I told Dad to get some business cards made for his mobile mechanic business. Because of me, the old man is able to parlay money out of that and use it for his bills."

"We all eat, sleep and bathe here, Clifford. You could at least pay the water bill when able."

"I'll think about it. My music comes first."

"Ugh," she said in frustration. How could their parents have taught them all the same things and yet, she seems to be the only one who learned anything?

As she went through bill after bill, the financial situation got bleaker. How was her father going to come from under all this debt? It was not clear at that time what she was going to do to help further, but Aisha was definitely going to do something. No matter what she said to her brother, there was no getting through to him. He tuned her out and fixed him the biggest bowl of cereal he could find and sat down to eat without a care in the world.

"What are you doing, going through my mail?" Her father walked up behind her and snatched the bill out of her hand. The soles of his shoes were soft, and he stepped lightly.

"Dad, I didn't hear you come in," she said.

"Obviously. Now answer my question."

"Well, uh. With mom in the hospital, the household is kinda feeling the missing income. I was just looking at the bills to see where I could do my part."

"Didn't nobody ask you to go snooping through the mail, little girl. I got this all under control."

She shook her head. "But Dad, you have been working so hard. When you are not at work, you're working on somebody's car and then you're at the hospital. You hardly sleep and you barely eat. We don't need both of y'all in the hospital."

"I said I got it," he snapped, causing her to jump a little and her brother to look up from his bowl.

Her father seldomly raised his voice like but when he did, one could assume he was not playing. Edward Graves was typically the strong, silent type. However, today, he was anything but. He looked at his little girl and immediately softened. She was the youngest of his three children and the only who truly helped him and his wife.

"I'm sorry, baby girl. I know that you're only trying to help, but this is not your problem. Your old man still has a few tricks up his sleeve to get us out of this crunch."

"I know, Daddy. I just want to help."

Clifford rolled his eyes. He loved his sister, but sometimes, she acted like such a goody two shoes. Like she was perfect or something.

"You've done enough as it is. Going to that rinky-dink school was above and beyond any sacrifice a child should make."

"There's nothing that I wouldn't do for you and Mommy," she said genuinely, walking over to give him a hug.

He stepped into her arms and welcomed her embrace.

"And we know that. But really, baby. I got this. Now, come over here and let me whip you up some of my famous pancakes."

Reluctantly, she walked to the breakfast bar and took a seat. Although her father assured her that he could handle things, she was still worried. She attempted to perk up and not let on that she was still thinking about their bills. Her dad looked so happy mixing the batter. He hummed an old Temptations tune and danced around the kitchen as he did so. Soon, his mood became infectious, and she and Clifford got up out their seats and began dancing.

The three of them grooved to the beat until the food was ready. After they ate, they cleaned the kitchen and sat at the table to talk. Her brother was the first to speak.

"Pops, thanks for putting in the good word for me with Frank down at the job. I am going to enjoy working alongside you."

His dad slapped him on the back. "No problem, Son. We make a great team."

Aisha smiled. "Yeah, Dad. Cliff was just saying how he's going to enjoy finally being able to help around the house."

Her dad gave her a side-eye and then pointed to his son.

"This dude said that? I find that hard to believe. All the money he ever gets goes toward his beloved mix tape." Their father stood up. "Never thought I would be the father of a forty-year-old rapper. I hope it all works out for you."

"Awe don't sound like that, Dad. I am going to help around here. I just need to hit a lick so I can pay bills and still afford studio time."

"Do you, Son. I'm going to lie down for a little while." Mister Graves' shoulders drooped with weariness and the light in his eyes dimmed. On his way out the kitchen, he leaned over to kiss his baby girl on the top of her head.

If her brother cared about their dad's plight, he certainly didn't show it because as soon as their father was out of sight, so was he.

Over the next few weeks, things around the house seemed to improve. With Clifford working and chipping in on the bills, their father didn't have to work as hard. Things were going well for her brother on the job. He was in charge of purchasing the parts for the school district's vehicles that her father worked on. After almost two months on the job, Clifford started bringing in more money. So much so that he was able to help pay off half of the hospital bill and the mortgage for two months. Even Sandra contributed when she could. Their father was happy and so was Aisha.

"You're looking good girl," Malik said to her one evening at dinner.

"I'm feeling good, babe. Things are going well at home. You know Cliff got a good job and so did Sandra."

He took a bite of food. "So, they're both helping your Pops out now?"

"Yes, finally. Cliff paid almost fifteen grand on one of the hospital bills."

"Damn, he's doing it like that? They paying hella good."

"Yeah, they pay good, but not *that* good. Something else is going on there."

"What else you think he's doing?"

"I don't know. But something is telling me it's not for the right thing." Aisha shrugged her shoulders. "Tell me about this endorsement deal your agent is working on for you."

Malik set his fork down and told her about the deal.

Meanwhile, across town, Cliff was making deals of his own.

"Check this out, Frank. You see all these parts? I have people lined up ready to pay top-dollar for each of them.

Especially these catalytic converters. Shit, we get'em for pennies on the dollar and sell each unit for hundreds. Now you tell me who's winning?" He shoved a piece of paper in his boss's face that had various auto parts listed.

"Are these people like the ones you sold to before? They broke bread," the man said.

Cliff nodded. "Yo', these people got more cheddar than Wisconsin. Let's get this sh'money."

"Well," the man rubbed his beard and hesitated answering. "I'm all for making money. But let me ask you this. You don't have a problem forging your father's signature, authorizing the purchase of all these parts?"

"Hell naw. Some of the money that I have been getting, I've used to help him out around the house. Shit, this is a team effort."

"Humph. If you like it, I love it. Let's get it. At some point though, we're going to have to wrap this up. It can't go on forever."

And it didn't, but for the next month things were peaches and cream. Cliff and Frank continued to make bogus orders for car parts, getting them at an extreme discount using the district's account, then selling them on the streets at inflated prices. They were making money hand over fist and their operation was on a roll. Then it came to a screeching halt.

The three men had walked into work that morning laughing and in good spirits. Now, neither one of them were smiling. Especially, Mister Graves. He sat in Frank's office, next to his son and his friend of over twenty years, as the auditor, who sat behind Frank's desk, poured over the department's purchasing receipts. Page after page, she handed the older man signed purchase orders.

"Hmm, this one is quite interesting. Why would you need to buy fifty, Dodge Ram 2500 catalytic converters when the district only owns five trucks like that, Mister Graves?"

"My handwriting hasn't always been the easiest to read, but I'm pretty sure I only ordered five," he defended.

"I know how to read, Sir. Here, see for yourself," she said, handing him the paper.

He took it and noticed that his son looked away.

"Eh hem," Frank said, scratching his chin.

When he looked down, he saw it. Fifty catalytic converters. There was a zero, that wasn't his handwriting next to the five he had written. He knew that writing well. Had seen it change grades and falsify signatures on behavior reports in school over the years and now this. Instead of looking at his son, he held his head up and spoke.

"I remember this purchase order. If you look at the supplier, you will see that they were a new company and they only sold in bulk. Compared to the price we had paid in the past; we can see a considerable cost savings."

Out of the corner of his eye, the father could see his son exhale out of relief.

"Well, you're the expert here. I'm just a numbers cruncher," the woman said.

For the next hour, she questioned Mister Graves about similar purchase orders, but he gave her the same answer, which she appeared to accept. On the outside, Edward Graves smiled and nodded pleasantly, as if nothing were wrong. But on the inside, the old man was dying. It was obvious that his son and his best friend were up to no good. He did inventory every Friday before leaving the warehouse and he had never seen that many auto parts on the shelves.

"Well gentlemen, I think that's all my questions, so you all are free to go, but Frank, I'll need your desk for a few more minutes. I need to send these reports over to my boss."

Frank scratched his head and blinked rapidly. "Your boss? Aren't you the one in charge of this investi-, I mean, audit?"

"Oh, no. I'm merely a worker bee. My boss is the one who will double check my numbers and then compare you all's spending record to the approved school district budget. I don't have access to that."

"Wait, what does that mean, compare to the district budget?" Cliff asked.

"That means, Son, that when they get this report she ran, they will look at the amount of money the district gave me to spend on parts and materials and see if I'm over budget. If I am, that means we will have to make budget cuts in this department, starting with jobs. Mine will be the first position eliminated."

"So, what are you saying, Dad?"

Frank spoke up, in a low voice. "He'll lose his job."

The auditor stood and closed her briefcase. "I'm afraid he's right. I'm all done here. You guys have a great day."

The smell of her perfume lingered in the office moments after she had gone, only to be overpowered by the hideous stench of deception.

"Frank, Cliff. What have you two done?" Mister Graves asked.

"Eddie, I'm sorry. I lost some money in a bet and needed to repay it. Fast. When the opportunity presented itself, I took advantage of it. I should have stopped after it was paid off, but it seemed so easy, that I, uh." Frank's voice tapered off and he hung his head.

"Twenty-years. That's how long we've worked together. Not one minute in all that time did I ever think that you would do anything like this. And you," Edward Graves turned to face his son. "My own, son. My flesh and blood, has just single-handedly signed my termination papers."

"Pops, I'm sorry too. I wasn't thinking. But don't talk like you're going to lose your job. You have to speak positive like you're always telling me."

"Are you crazy? Don't you know what you did is called embezzlement? Did you think about anybody but yourself? Did you take into consideration that it is this jobs insurance that pays most your mother's medical bills? No, you didn't. And to hell with my pension, right? I may as well hang that up."

The older gentlemen walked slowly to his desk and sat down.

"Pops, my bad. What can I do to make things right?"

"The audit will continue. There's nothing you can do about that. But you can go clean out your locker. You are fired, Clifford."

"Fired! Man, what the fuck for?"

Mister Graves palmed his face. "Aye, aye, aye. Dude, theft is grounds for immediate termination. If you were not my son, I would prosecute you. Frank, the same for you. Both of you clean out your lockers and leave the building immediately."

Edward Graves combed over the documents that the accountant had left on his desk. She had taken all the copies she needed. With his wife being sick, the last thing he needed was to lose his job and health insurance. At his age, finding another job would prove difficult. It was going to take a miracle for him to keep his job.

"Lord, please cover me," he said, and he bowed his head to pray.

$$$

The accountant had barely walked into the office and sat at her desk when her boss began buzzing her.

"Yes, Misses Jeffries," she said.

"It is about time you returned. Bring the files to my office."

Defiantly, the young woman rolled her eyes at the phone and stuck her tongue out at it.

"Damn, you could have at least said please."

Not wanting to incur anymore of her boss' backlash, she took the files into the office and gave her superior a brief rundown of her findings.

"So, you saw the overspending as well? Good job. I'll go over what you found and reconcile it to what I have here in my system. I appreciate your hard work. You can leave for the day."

She was surprised to hear her boss compliment her. "Thank you, Misses Jeffries. Have a great evening."

Eloise Jeffries had been watching the spending for the school district for quite some time. This was her pet project, and she was determined to keep them on budget. Doing so, would result in her getting a hefty bonus at year's end and she was not going to allow it to slip through her fingers.

"Let's see what's going on here," she said, putting her glasses on.

For the next hour, she reviewed each financial statement, line by line, highlighting discrepancies. By the time she finished, she was about ready to call the police and have everyone in the transportation department arrested. It was so obvious that they had been over ordering and most likely selling off the excess parts for personal gain.

"Who's the head of this department?" She asked herself.

She reached across her desk and got the personnel folder, leafing through the papers until she found the managers' profile.

"Hmm," she said. There was something familiar about the manager. The corners of her mouth turned up, slightly and light filled her eyes.

"Could it be? There's only one way to find out."

Eloise grabbed her cellphone and dialed her husband.

"Hello honey, I have a quick question. Doesn't Aisha's father work for the school district?"

"Yes, he does. Why?"

"I'm auditing the school's budget and I thought I saw Edward Graves on one of the files. Isn't that his name?"

"Sure is. Are you coming home soon?"

"Yes. I'm leaving now. Thank you. Yes, Lord!" She yelled.

It didn't take a rocket scientist to see that the signatures on the invoices did not match with Edward Grave's, so Eloise was pretty sure he was not the one swindling the parts. But because he was over the department, he was the one who would take the fall. She didn't know who did it or why, and frankly, she could care less. All she knew was that with this information, someone had unwittingly given her the ammunition to get that trailer park cast-off of a girlfriend out of her son's life, once and for all. Her prayers had been answered.

CHAPTER 8

Personal Foul

THE TELEVISION SEEMED LOUD in the quiet room and it made his head throb. Kyle muted it and hung his head low. He had just gotten home from basketball practice. A few of his teammates wanted him to hang out with them at a local sports bar, but he needed some alone time.

Tap. Tap. Tap. Exhaling, he looked at his front door. Not in the mood for company, he simply sat there.

Bang. Bang. Bang. "Bro, I know you're in there. Don't make me use my key."

It was his sister, Kayla. Since she had a key, he figured he would let her use it and remained seated. A few moments later, she was seated next to him on the sofa.

"What's up baby bro? You don't look too good."

"It's this shit with Tika. I have reporters hounding me before and after practice. People calling me and shit. It's bananas."

Just then, a picture of him flashed across the television screen and he unmuted it.

"It seems that Georgia Heat, center, KJ Hudson has experienced a personal foul. The star basketball player may soon find himself in court instead of on the court. Social media model and reality star, Tika Adams, has filed a contempt action for failing to pay child support against him. We were able to obtain the court documents that allege, Mister Hudson fathered the InstaPic sensations, six-month-old daughter. Yet, according to the complaint, he has not paid one dime in support since her birth."

"Well, Ms. Adams will be raking in the dough soon enough. It is rumored that the network may pick up the new reality show, Baller Babes, and give her a main role on the show."

"Good for her, Dan, but bad for Kyle. All this attention may prove to be too much during basketball playoffs."

The co-host nodded his head. "Absolutely, Rachel. But the Hudson's are not strangers to negative media attention. If you recall, KJ's sister, Kalia Hudson, was the one indicted on the infamous 'Head Doctor' case that broke over a year ago."

"Dan, I remember that case well, but never put two and two together. Wow, it's a small world after all."

An angry Kyle threw the remote toward the television. It hit the center like a bullseye leaving a gash in the screen and broke into pieces when it hit the hardwood floor.

"Do you hear this shit, Kayla? These clowns got me all messed up with this chick and now they're associating me with that whorish ass sister of yours."

Kayla exhaled. "She's your sister, too. But why are you watching *A-Tea-L Live* anyway? You know this is nothing more than a gossip television show."

He rolled his eyes. "I thought you were going to take care of this?"

"Unfortunately, my firm can't help who you're related to and the press can report anything as long as it's not libelous. However, we got you covered with the paternity suit and Tika will be served with a gag order soon."

Kyle was taking care of the little girl; he just didn't give his ex-girlfriend the amount of money she demanded. He was beginning to fall in love with the baby. Malia. The little girl was beautiful and innocent in all this. All he wanted to do was make sure she was his before he invested his heart and so much more of his money into it. But Tika was playing games and wouldn't submit to a paternity test. He had scheduled several different testing dates, but his ex-girlfriend never showed up to any of the appointments. Then a few weeks ago, she hit him with an inflated petition to modify his child support, asking for more than thirty-thousand-dollars monthly.

"How are we going to settle this crap without her allowing us to do a DNA test? That's the baffling part to me. She is the one who filed the support case but now won't comply with all the conditions."

"Don't sweat that. She's will also be served with a court order demanding she submits to testing. If she doesn't, she will be in contempt of court. No judge with a legitimate degree in law, will allow the case to move forward without one."

"Okay. But what if she still doesn't take it?" Wrinkles creased his forehead.

"Simple," Kayla shrugged. "She'll land her pretty ass in jail."

Kyle burst into laughter. It was hard to envision his bougie ex, looking like a broad from Orange Is the New Black. As amusing as the thought was, he sobered quickly. He didn't need this distraction. The playoffs were a week away, and he really needed to get his head into the game. His team was counting on him.

"Look, if Malia is mine, you know I'm going to be in her life the way she deserves. I just need to be sure, Sis. Tika was wild and I know for a fact that I wasn't the only dude she was smashing."

"While that may be true, bro, you're the only man she named in the paternity suit, so you need to step up to the plate.

Start spending more time with that beautiful baby. It's possible that she is not your baby but then again, it's possible that she is. I'd rather you operate like her father now than not to and end up regretting it later. It's not only about spending a few bucks on her. You need to spend some quality time with her as well."

He hung his head in despair. "I spend time with her when I can. But let's face it, I am not ready to be a daddy."

His statement angered her.

"Well, you should have thought of that shit before you fucked somebody you barely knew without a rubber. What the hell were you thinking? Don't you know that a baby is not the worst thing that can happen from having unprotected sex? Did your black ass forget about HIV or AIDS?"

"Damn, I'm your brother. You're supposed to be on my side. And we were together for five months."

"I am on your side, but geesh. You know better. Come on man. Stop acting like a spoiled, entitled athlete and start acting like the man who mom and dad raised. And real shit, five months isn't enough time to truly know anyone."

"You're right," he said, standing to his feet. "I've been tripping. This isn't me. Malia deserves better than what she's been getting. From both of us."

Shaking his head, he reached into his pocket and pulled out his cellphone. After pressing a few keys, he put the phone to his ear. It only rang once before it was answered.

"Hey, Tika. It's me. I want to come get Malia. It's time she met my par-, her grandparents. Are you cool with that?"

"Of course, I am. She needs you in her life. She needs her entire village." Tika grinned like a Cheshire cat, glad that KJ could not see her face. This was what she had been praying for.

"Great. Can I come get her now? Kayla and I were on our way to see my parents."

"Sure. You can get her anytime you want. I would never keep you from her."

"Cool, cool. Are you filming Baller Babe's today?"

"No. We just shot the pilot and a few other scenes. I'm praying that the network is going to pick it up."

"Hmm, well good luck with that."

"Thank you, baby."

The two of them talked a few more minutes and Kyle decided that he was going to keep her for the weekend.

"Don't pack her anything. I'll buy her whatever she needs."

"Okay then. I see you. Well, she'll be ready when you get here."

After they hung up, Kayla shook her head in disbelief.

"That went so much better than I expected."

"Honestly, me too. But I'm not going to look a gift horse in the mouth. Come on."

In Buckhead, Tika squealed in delight.

"What's got you so happy, bitch?" Her friend asked.

"That was, KJ. He's coming to get Malia for the weekend."

"You mean, he's actually acknowledging her?"

"Damned skippy. And he's taking her to meet his parents, too. I'm in there like swimwear."

The friends gave one another a high-five.

"Get it, bitch. You made it over one hurdle, what's next?"

"First, I'm gon' stack some dough."

"And then what?"

"Then I'm gon' stack some mo'."

"And then what?"

"Throw my Gucci in the back of the Benz, as my nigga eat me out while I'm suckin' his friend."

Laughter erupted as they chanted a rap, they made up based on Young Jeezy's lyrics.

"But seriously, I'm gonna show him how much I have changed and get him back. My mission will not be complete until I marry his ass. This child support lick is cool, but a bitch like me wants the benefits associated with being wifey. Plus, this will be a helluva story line for Baller Babes."

The two women continued to chat as Tika got the baby together to leave. Malia deserved everything that her father was about to bestow upon her. Kyle was a good dude. Tika kicked herself daily for cheating on him and especially taping it. That was low. But regardless of who she fucked; she was sure he was her baby's daddy. Well, she was twenty-five percent sure. The other seventy-five percent doubt stemmed from the fact that she had indeed cheated on him within the window of conception, with three separate men, two of them at the same time. All without a condom.

When she messed with rapper, Baby Boy, she thinks they had used protection, but she could not remember because she was sloppy drunk. Again. It was because she was so out of it, that she didn't stop him from taping their sexcapades. And then he showed the tape to his homies one night at his house. Kyle just happened to be one of the guys in attendance. That night, he stormed home, packed all her stuff, and put her out. She had hurt and embarrassed him. Getting him back was going to be a challenge, but Tika was determined to get back with Kyle. By any means necessary.

In Kyle's car, on the way to get his daughter, the conversation was almost like Tika's thoughts.

"So, do you, think the two of you will ever get back together?" Kayla asked.

"Hell naw, to the naw, naw, naw," he sang. "That ship has sailed, Sis."

"Hmmm, I'm sure she will try any and everything to change that."

"No doubt, she will. However, hell will have to thaw, after it freezes over before I give her another chance to break my heart."

"You really liked her, huh?"

"Yeah," he admitted. "She was so sweet and cool when we first met. Different, you know? But I guess that was all an act to get pregnant and use me. Shit, twenty grand a month in child support and now she's asking for ten more? Malia don't need all that. Tika is using that money to fund her lifestyle."

"I agree. But don't worry. Dad and some other officials are working together on some new legislature for Georgia regarding child support. You know how California is always the first to set a precedent and then the rest of us, follow suit?"

He nodded and she continued.

"Well, if all goes according to plan, Georgia is going to be the first on the map with a new child support law."

"Dad's working on something? Good for him."

"Yep. He started working on it after the last visit we had. It's going to be great for non-custodial parents. Come on. Put the pedal to the metal. "Let's go get this baby and see your girlfriend."

"Grrr," he growled, side-eyeing her.

It didn't take long to drive from his southside home to Buckhead, where Tika lived. Her townhome was located near Phipps Plaza, the mall where she spent most of her time and his money.

"Damn," Kayla said. "She's living like this?"

"Yep. Thanks to me." He shook his head. "Come on."

MEAL TICKET$

Admittedly, her home was quite impressive. The three-story townhome was over five-thousand square-feet and came equipped with a three-car garage. The private, gated community had an Olympic sized swimming pool with upscale clubhouse, four tennis courts and two playground areas for the children. Inside, she had five bedrooms, a media room, chef's kitchen, and a butler's pantry.

"This place is bigger than my house and I'm a fucking lawyer."

Admittedly, it was almost larger than his home as well and he was the one who busted his tail on the court night after night to make it happen. All he could do was shake his head and laugh as he was getting out of the car.

"I know. And she doesn't even have a job. C'mon."

The siblings walked up the steps and stood on the porch. Kyle raised his hand to ring the doorbell, but the door swung open before he pressed it.

"I was starting to think you weren't coming," she said. "Come in."

Kyle and his sister stepped inside and stood in her foyer. "You know I keep my word. We stopped to fill my tank and hit a small pocket of traffic. You know how that goes."

"I do. Well, she's ready but she's asleep. Come help me get her things."

Kayla sat down in the living room, across from Tika's friend.

"Hmph, so you're a lawyer?" The woman asked.

"Yes, ma'am." Kayla was already becoming annoyed by the woman with pink and purple hair.

"What made you wanna become one?"

"I have a great appreciation for the law, and I wanted to help people. I also wanted to be able to live a comfortable life."

"Hmph. Well, you and I both live comfortably. Only difference is that I don't have a shit load of student loans to pay back. Guess I got the better deal."

"If you say so." Who was this broad? Kayla thought. "I'm Kayla Hudson. You are?"

"Larissa Macintosh. I have a little girl by Breeze Coleman."

Recognition must have appeared on Kayla's face because she continued and said, "yeah, I live a very good life. He takes hella care of me and his daughter. Just like your brother's about to do for my homegirl and god-daughter."

Kayla simply smiled in response and looked at her watch. What was taking her brother and Tika so long?

Upstairs, Tika caressed Kyle's chest as he held the sleeping child in his arms.

"Lay her back in the bed for a second," she asked him.

As soon as the little girl was placed comfortably on her pillow, Tika dropped to her knees.

"I missed you, baby. Let me show you how much."

Skillfully, she pulled his basketball shorts down to his knees, freeing his hard dick, before wrapping her wet mouth around the head. Looking up at him, she bobbed back and forth, getting the tool wet with her saliva.

He threw his head back and placed his hand on the top of her head, thrusting in sync with her ministrations.

"Shit," he said between clinched teeth.

Her jaws tightened around him, and she caressed his heavy nut sack. Slurp. Slurp. She sucked him like a popsicle on a hot Atlanta day.

"Fuck, I need to be inside you," he said, pulling her to her feet and spinning her around. He bent her over at the waist, moved her panties to the side, and slid his hardness in her with one thrust. His hips bucked a couple of times. She felt so good, so tight around him. This is what he missed. A few long, steady pumps and then, he hurriedly pulled out, and came on her back.

"You should have come in me. Let all that heat flow inside. Why you pull out?"

Tika wiped the cream from her back and licked it from her fingers.

He looked at Malia sleeping peacefully. "Her. I'm not trying to get you pregnant again and I don't have any condoms."

She was disappointed and wanted to scream at him, but that wouldn't do anything but anger him. He needed to see that she was changing.

"I understand, babe. But you're still a little hard. I can't let you leave out of here like this." Without delay, she dropped back to her knees and sucked his dick until he released every bit of the milky sensation in her mouth. "There. You're good to go."

Kyle was shocked that she didn't make a big deal out of him pulling out. He knew how much she hated him doing that when they were together.

"That's all you have to say?"

"What do you mean?"

"When we were together, you always cussed me out when I would pull out. What gives?"

"Having Malia is changing me, believe it or not. I want to be a good mother and a better person for her. Arguing with you is not going to do either of us any good. Plus, you're right. Our baby is just six months old. We don't need to be having another baby so soon."

"Wow, you surprise me. Thanks for topping me off. I really needed that. It's been a long time."

"Since you've had your dick sucked?"

He remained quiet.

"You haven't been with another woman either?"

"Not since I was last with you."

Flattered, she smiled from ear to ear.

"Hmm, well, you know where I live when you need a tune-up. I got you. No strings attached." She stood on her tip toes and kissed him on the cheek. "Grab, Munchkin and come on. Your sister is probably downstairs wondering what's taking us so long."

With the diaper bag over his shoulder, he picked the baby up and made his way downstairs. When he got to the door he turned around.

"I'll call you when I get ready to bring her home."

"No worries. Have a great time and give your parent's my love."

"Will do."

In the car, Kayla started in on her brother after the infant was secured in the car seat.

"I hope your ass wrapped it up this time. Leaving me downstairs with that damned girl while you were up there fucking."

"I wasn't fucking. Well, I did stick it in for a minute, but I didn't nut in her or nothing."

"All it takes is a minute, idiot and there is such a thing as pre-ejaculation. That's how you got into this predicament in the first place. You're gonna have more babies with her if you keep this up. Hell, I won't be surprised if she is pregnant again. You have to be careful."

"Not this time. She swallowed these babies," he said.

"Eww. T-M-I" she said, swatting his arm. "I'm telling Mom and Pops how nasty your ass is."

"Snitch."

MEAL TICKET$

Kayla was right. He did have to be careful. Tika was always down to break him off. That was one thing he liked so much about her when they were together. But now, he knew he could not afford to fall between her legs again, especially unprotected. The last thing he needed was another paternity suit on his hands. He barely managed to escape her turkey basting trap. Nah, he couldn't fuck Tika or any other woman without protection ever again. If he didn't have a wrap, he would not fall into the trap.

CHAPTER 9

Cut

FUCK THE BABY. It was all about the bag. And for Larissa, the bag was loaded. It was the fifteenth. Child support payment day. At eight in the morning, the day had not even begun before she called Breeze about her payment.

"Dude, where is my money?" She snapped.

"First of all, take all that motherfuckin' base out ya' voice. I ain't one of those lame ass niggas' you be fucking with. Secondly, don't call me about no damned child support check. My accountant will make sure it's directly deposited into your account today."

Larissa was a cold piece of work. She was sugar and spice on the outside, but pure venom inside. Unfortunately, the latter was something Breeze discovered after she gave birth to their daughter. She spent very little time with the child, but just enough to retain full custody. With his schedule being what it was right now, it was highly unlikely that any judge would grant him custody of his little angel, but he had some moves he could make that would help him with that.

"Whatever, nigga. You know they cast me on the show Baller Babes? We've already started taping the first season. Once it airs, we just waiting on the word from the network letting us know if they are going to pick the show up or not. I know they will because me and Tika are dope as fuck and honestly, we make the whole motherfuckin' show."

"Yeah, I heard. I do wish you much success with that."

"Awe. You are so sweet, baby daddy. For real though, why can't we be together and raise our daughter as a family? I know you miss this."

"We have been over this before, Larissa. We are not together because you cheated on me and made a sex tape that all my homies saw. You are not honest and frankly, I do not trust you as far as I can throw you."

"Fine. I don't need your ass no way. You just make sure my money is straight." Click.

Larissa shook her head. She did not know why she asked Breeze that question because he always gave her the same answer and it always infuriated her. Stevie Wonder could see that she fucked up and no one, especially her mother, would ever allow her to live it down.

"I'on understand y'all young hoes these days. God blesses y'all with a good man, but you never satisfied. Just so quick to hop on the next niggas dick. One day you'll learn. Breeze was the best thang you ever had."

He was a good man to her and when she allowed him to be, a great father to Brely. But it was hard for Larissa to co-parent with him, still loving him the way she did. It hurt her when he came to get their baby but left her behind.

"That's why I'm gonna get him back by any means necessary. Me and Brely are a packaged deal. He can't have one without the other."

A jam from Faith Evan's first records came on the radio and she turned the volume up. Brely, stirred in her sleep. Larissa picked the brush up and stood in her full-length mirror and began to sing at the top of her lungs.

"Soon as I get home, I'll make it up to you. Baby, I'll do what I gotta do."

Adding her own ad libs, she continued to sing loudly until her little girl woke up completely.

"Morning Mommy," she said sweetly.

"Good morning, Suga plum."

Brely sat up in the bed, stretched and said, "I eat, Mommy?"

Smiling, Larissa said, "I knew you were going to be hungry when you woke that's why I was ready."

She walked to her dresser, picked up a tray and walked to her bed. After, setting the tray in front of her daughter, she sat next to her and pulled the tab off the can. The tab was a bit resistant and when it snapped off, it caused her to knock the crackers she had off the tray and onto the floor.

"Shit." She snapped her fingers, leaning to pick the food up off the floor. A ball of hair was stuck to one of the crackers.

"It's dirty, Mommy."

"Girl if your ass don't eat that shit. God made dirt and dirt don't hurt. Here."

She threw a plastic fork on the tray and went back to the mirror.

Brely turned her nose up at the food and moved away from the tray.

"Yucky. I don't want that. I like cereal."

"Oh my, gosh," Larissa screamed. She walked to her child and hit her in the top of her head with a wooden brush.

"Clink," the brush sounded after hitting the plastic ball in her head.

Tears began to well in her eyes, but Larissa cut her eyes at her sharply.

"I wish a bitch like you would start that crying."

Quickly, she sucked it up.

"Sniff, sniff." By now, she was learning what would happen to her when she made her mother mad.

"Now look here, little bitch. I'm not gonna keep putting up with all this bullshit. If you don't sit your hot ass down and eat those sardines and crackers right now, you won't get shit else to eat or drink for the rest of the day. With your ungrateful, spoiled ass."

The radio deejay played hit after hit and she sang along, applying her make-up until she felt picture perfect.

Honk. Honk. A horn sounded outside. Larissa snatched her housekeys and handbag from the chair and hurried down the steps. She stopped in her tracks and stared at the matte black on black Lamborghini. One of her neighbors was returning from a run and slowed to see who was inside.

"Ain't nothing to see here hoe so keep it moving," Larissa said neighborly. Not.

The woman smirked and jogged on.

"That wasn't nice," the man said, stepping out to open the door for her.

"I know, but damn. Bitches need to mind their damned business.

He helped her inside and lightly tapped the butterfly door and it closed.

"She was just trying to see a nigga like Con. Don't hate. But since you used your mouth to be so nasty, then you can use your mouth to be so nasty."

She heard 'zzzppp' and before she knew it, she was bobbing on his dick. He pushed her head down, holding it in place as he pumped his hips at the red light.

"Awk," she gagged with each thrust.

"Take this dick. I'm about to bust."

The car turned off the road and slowed as he drove through the parking lot. By the time he parked, his eruption began.

"Ah, shit. It's coming," he panted, pressing the button to recline his seat.

Able to relax a bit more, he used both hands and cupped her head like basketball, bouncing it until he made the shot. His breathing was heavy, and his heartbeat loud enough for her to hear it. Her eyes were watery, and she had a bit of come on the corner of her mouth when she sat up. Feeling sexy, she leaned in to kiss him. He put his palm in her face and pushed her head back.

"The fuck you doing? I don't kiss hoes after they swallow my shit. That's like me swallowing my own nut. Pssh," he said. "Let's go. We got work to do."

Slightly embarrassed, she adjusted her clothes, looked in the visor mirror and made sure that she did not have any evidence of foreplay on her face.

The studio was full of dudes that she recognized from around Atlanta's hip-hop and music scene. There were a couple of girls there but neither of them was as beautiful as she was. She pranced around the studio to show them that she was the top bitch there. Con, whose stage name is Conduit, gave the fella's some dap and introduced Larissa to them.

"Yo, peep. This is Shawty I was telling y'all about who got the reality television show, Baller Babe's. She got a baby by that nigga Breeze."

"Oh, is that right?" One of them said. She wasn't sure which one spoke. The smoke from the blunt that they just lit began to circulate around the room quickly and it was hazy.

"Fa show. So, check this out, Larissa. Vonda right here, wrote a song called 'Life's a Breeze', just for you. Read over the lyrics and listen to the track. When you feel like you can do a lil somethin' then you can get into the booth. Got it?"

"Yeah, I got it."

The beat was hot, and the lyrics were fire. It was as if this chick, Vonda knew exactly what was going on between she and her baby daddy because it was all on the table. Inside the booth, Larissa gave it her all and sang with passion.

"Why can't we be together? You promised me forever. Knowing you would not deliver, now I'm the taker and you're the giver. Now I'm living life just how I please, while you sit and watch me… life's a breeze."

"Damnnn, did you get all that?" Con said to the engineer.

"Yeah, man. This is a one hitta quitter. Baby girl is the truth."

He signaled Larissa to take the headphones off and come out the booth.

"Do you realize what you just did?"

"No, what did I do, Con?"

"You just did the damned thang."

"Eek," she squealed when he lifted her off the ground and spun her around.

"We got that in one take. Now all we have to do is add the background vocals and clean up a few things on our end and you've got yourself a single. What's even better is that you're on this show and it will help catapult this record to the top of the charts like that," he snapped.

It was music to her ears. For the next couple of hours, she sat with Vonda and watched this woman right song after song, simply by her telling her what was going on in her life.

Later that evening, Larissa met her friends at a posh Buckhead restaurant. She Tika, Joy and Shante' all sat in a booth, discussing her new music and career.

"Bitches, I can hardly believe that I have been in the studio all day with Con. He said I'm about to shoot to the top."

"Con?" Joy asked. "As in Conduit the rapper?"

"Yep. He has been amazing."

"Hmph, I bet he has. He is a wonderful producer and has a great team but watch out for that nigga though. He fucks all his artists and if they don't want to, he makes them regret it."

"I ain't worried about none of that. His ass is fine, and he can get it any way he wants it from me. No cap."

The ladies looked at Larissa and simply shook their heads.

"Not to sound cliché, but nigga's ain't turning hoes into housewives. That shit only happens in the movies."

"Fuck you, Joy. I ain't no motherfucking hoe, bitch and mark my words, I will get married. Shit, see if I don't snag Breeze's ass. He'll be on lockdown before you know it."

On the other side of the booth, a couple quieted their conversation so that they could listen to the ghetto girls on the other side.

"Did one of them mention Breeze? Isn't that the singer?" A man asked.

"Yes. I think that's his daughter's mother speaking. I should have known."

"Isn't she on your show, Rhona?"

She nodded. "If that's her, then yes."

He clutched his invisible pearls. "Oh, my gawd, your show is going to be in the toilet if she is associated with it."

She exhaled. "I was thinking that myself. I have an idea."

Quickly she jotted a small note on a napkin, pulled a fifty-dollar-bill out her purse and waved a waiter over.

Whispering she said, "please follow these instructions. Here's a tip for your trouble and my number if you want to be on a new reality show."

The waiter's green eyes lit up as he hurried to the beverage station, returning quickly with Cosmopolitan drink. He slowed as he approached the booth.

"Excuse me. I usually don't do this, but I am over here fanning out. Aren't you Larissa McIntosh from Baller Babe's?"

"Yeah, that's me," she said. "How did you know? The show ain't aired yet."

Rhona mouthed, "fuck" on the other side. But the waiter was quick on his feet.

"I saw a trailer that was leaked. Girl you are more beautiful in person. Those cameras don't do you justice. But anyway, this is for you. It's on the house. Enjoy, gorgeous," he said, waving as he walked away.

The girls squealed in excitement. Rhona and her friend, Barrett, covered their ears.

"Bitches get ready. This type of shit is about to start happening all the time. I gotta piss. I'll be back." Larissa stood.

"I'm coming with you."

"Me too."

"Joy, we'll be back," Tika said.

Barrett peaked around the booth.

"They're gone girlfriend. Let's go before they come back and recognize your ass."

Rhona signed the receipt and the two of them exited the restaurant in haste. Joy was looking at a menu when they passed and did not bother to look up.

Moments later, the ladies were back at the table, munching on appetizers.

"You know," Tika began. "If you release this single as planned, your musical career launch will give you another story-line on the show for another couple of seasons and you know what that means don't you?"

They smiled at one another knowingly. Joy and Shante' looked confused.

In unison Larissa and Tika said, "no mo', broke hoe, thanks to, this show."

All four of them laughed and took a swig of their drinks.

Larissa exhaled.

Things were quickly getting back on track for her. Although the bank had sent a repo man to come get her leased Maserati, the future still looked bright. She parked the car in Tika's garage until she caught up on the payments next Friday, which was payday. She could hardly wait.

In typical Larissa fashion, her money was already spent, and she hadn't even received it yet. There was a Gucci bag and a pair of red bottoms on her list of 'must haves' but first she had to figure out a way to deal with all those other inconsequential bills she had, like her rent and utilities. All were past due, and she was on the verge of being in the dark and possibly evicted. But she wasn't tripping too hard about that because she and her landlord, Mister Obatunda, had an 'arrangement. It was only when his wife called to collect the rent that she had issues.

"Did you hear us, hoe?" Tika shook Larissa.

"My bad. I zoned out. A bitch starts thinking about money and becomes oblivious to everything else."

"Well snap out of it and let's go. I have to go get my baby."

On the ride home, Larissa stared out the window quietly.

"You alright over there, bestie?"

"Yeah," she said and turned her head. "Do you like being a mother, T?"

"At first I didn't. I think that's because I really didn't know what I was doing and a part of me was scared. But Malia is such a sweet baby and now that I have calmed down, my mother is more active in my life and helps me a lot. Why? Do you?"

"Not really. Brely looks so much like her dad that it's hard for me to look at her. Because I'm mad at him, sometimes I take it out on her. Hell, all the time really. I be beating her ass. Sometimes... I hate her."

"Damn, girl. You need to cut that shit out. They locking people up and throwing away the key for child abuse."

Larissa shrugged. "I whoop her on the bottom of her feet and hit her in the head when she has those balls on. The shit hurts her but don't leave no marks."

"Hmph. That's smart."

Tika pulled in the driveway.

"I know. Thanks for everything, Bestie. I'll call you later. Bye."

Over the next few days, Larissa dealt very little with her child. The day after she and her friends had dinner, Breeze called and asked if he could spend time with her, so she let him. If she really wanted to get him back, she was going to have switch some shit up. Be sweet and accommodating, like her mother told her.

"You're going to be on the road for the next few weeks and she needs you, so come get her," she had told him.

Now was the time for her to work on her plan.

"This is 'Operation Get My Man Back'. By the time I'm done, he is going to think I am a different woman."

Thursday evening was Laquanda's date night, so Larissa had to leave.

"Ain't this some shit? Getting put out my own house." She walked to her mother's room where she saw her putting finishing touches of make-up on. "Mama, where Jarell at? It seems every time Bre leaves, his ass disappears."

"Hell do you blame him? Other than school, his ass stays cooped up in this bitch, babysitting. But to answer your question, my son's out there taking care of his business."

"Jerry is hustling now?"

"Yep. How the hell you think he be buying all that new shit?"

"I thought he was stealing it."

"Naw, boo. You can't get no receipt for hot shit."

"It's about time. I know you happy."

"Hell yeah. My little nigga is hard."

Larissa giggled. It was difficult to imagine her little brother being hard, but no one could deny his hustle. A horn sounded outside.

"Well, have fun. That's Tika. I'm staying with her tonight because we have to meet at the studio tomorrow."

The next day, Larissa woke up singing with the birds. It was a beautiful morning until...

"Fired? What the hell you mean?"

"I mean exactly what I just said, Larissa. You are fired. This was not a decision that I came to easily. I toiled long and hard," she said in a dry tone. "If I want the show to be picked up, it has to go in another direction. You are not a good fit for the new vision. Here is your final check."

Rhona slid an envelope across the desk.

Larissa opened it up. It was a check for fifteen-thousand-dollars.

"The fuck is this? This ain't enough for all the episodes that'll air with me in them? Do you do direct deposit or something?"

"Mmm, about that. We are editing our footage and removing you from all of it."

"What! You can't do that? You need me," she stomped.

"As bout as much as I need a hole in my head. Have a good day, Ms. McIntosh or should I have Atlanta police escort you out?"

Red-hot tears burned her face. A vein throbbed so hard in her neck she felt it and Rhona saw it. As much as she wanted to lay hands on the producer, she thought better of it. That woman would not hesitate to throw her in jail and from the amount of that check, she did not have bail money. Instead of making a scene, she exited the office, called an Uber, and went home.

Breeze pulled up as soon as she got out the ugly ass Ford Focus.

"What happened to your car?" He asked.

"Someone side swiped me. It's in the shop. They gave me a loner, but Mama needed it. Bre sleep?"

"Yeah. I'll take her in. I can't stay. Keyon called a meeting, and I can't be late."

"I understand. Maybe next time I can cook for you. I remember how much you liked my meatloaf."

"Yeah. It is delicious."

They walked toward the door. Silently Larissa prayed, "please let the housekeeper be finished." Her prayer was answered.

"This place is spotless and smells so good," he observed walking toward the stairs.

"I cleaned up before I left this morning."

"Nice. Where's Jarell?"

"Uh, with his friends." Hell, she had no clue.

Gently, he laid his baby down on the pillow and kissed her chubby cheek. "That's daddy's baby right there."

Larissa smirked and rolled her eyes behind his back.

"Can I get a hug before you go?"

He did not want to, but since she let his daughter spend time with him, free of charge, he obliged.

"Sure."

He wrapped his arms around her, and she held on a little longer than she should have. Before he had a chance to push her away, she stepped out of his embrace.

"Thank you for everything. Have a great tour. We'll see you when you get back."

Caught off guard, he looked out his peripheral at her.

"Thank you. See you soon."

She locked the door after she walked him out. This was the first time in ages that she had been home alone. It was quiet and she needed time to think. She was going to have to formulate a plan to get her single done and released without Con finding out she had gotten fired off the show. That's the only reason he agreed to work with her. Fired. Just thinking of the word made her angry all over again.

All the pent-up frustration needed to be released so she went in search of something to help her do that. Brely's playroom was next to the kitchen and Larissa walked in there. It was a pool noodle sticking up from the toy box so, she snatched it and swung it hard. Whoosh, whoosh, whoosh, it sounded. Tears came. The more she swung, the harder she cried. Sad, angry and frustrated, she went upstairs and saw one of the objects of her discontent lying in her bed.

"I hate you," she yelled before swinging the pool noodle at the toddler.

"Mommy," she cried. "Ouchee."

Thump. Thump. Thump. Whoosh. Whoosh. Whoosh.

Brely pulled a pillow close to her body. Larissa snatched it and grabbed her by the hair, shaking her.

"Stupid!"

MEAL TICKET$

She released her abruptly and the little girl fell to the floor. The pool noodle began flying again. Fifteen minutes later, an extremely tired Larissa plopped down on the bed and stared at her baby who looked like a roly-poly. Beating Brely hadn't changed anything. She was still hurt. She was still angry. And she was still fired.

CHAPTER 10

Flag on the Play

DIZZINESS AND NAUSEA WERE her constant companions. She wasn't sure if it was the stress of maintaining both a full-time job and school schedule, but Brandi was not feeling well. Things on the home front were not too good either. Although neither said anything, something was going on between her father and brother. When the two of them were in the same room, they barely said two words to one another. Whatever was going on between those two, she would surely find out later, but right now, she needed to concentrate on herself.

Malik was on his way to pick her up. They were going to visit her mother in the hospital and after that, lunch. Football had been keeping him very busy and she expected that. She even expected a bevy of girls to always throw themselves at him once he got into the league. But what she didn't expect was that his mother would be trying to hook him up with the daughter of her best friend.

Every game, every family dinner or outing...anything. She was there. Aisha could not stop his mother from inviting her. In fact, she believed that the only reason she did have her around so much was because she was trying to get rid of Aisha. Her and Malik had been dating since she was a junior in high school and he a senior. During that time, she had never heard

Selena Bowie's name mentioned. Now, since the draft, that's all she hears.

The sound of a heavy bass filled her room and she peaked out the curtain to see Malik pulling into the driveway. She stood there and watched him groom himself in the visor mirror. Looking good was of major concern to him but he wasn't vain. Well, maybe just a little. A soft laugh escaped past her lips as she released the curtain to head toward the door. Before he could ring the doorbell, the door swung open.

"Hey, handsome," she said, holding the screen door open.

"Hey yourself, beautiful. How did you know I was coming?"

"I heard you before I saw you."

"My bad. I'll turn the volume down next time."

"Don't trip. Let me grab my jacket and we can leave."

On the way to the hospital, the two lovers talked about what was going on with Aisha in school. She stole a few glances at him while she talked. He always gave her his undivided attention even when he was concentrating on the road. Her lips curled, showing all her teeth.

"What are you over there cheesing so hard for?" He asked.

"I'm just thinking about you and how blessed I am to have you. I love you so much."

"I love you, too. But I'm the blessed one. Since I got into the league, I have seen some treacherous women. And I'm talking about the ones that the players are dating, not the groupies. Shit, look at my cousin Kyle who plays for the Heat? He's going through child support and baby mama drama as we speak. I don't envy him at all."

She nodded. "Yeah, I read about that. But you can't believe everything that you read on social media. That's awful."

"Tell me about it. That's why you are so special to me. I know you are here for me and not for what I can give you or do for you."

"Of course not. I love you baby whether you play football or make them. This is us," she pointed between the two of them. "We are in this together no matter what."

"No matter what."

The traffic light turned red, so he seized the opportunity to kiss her. It was supposed to be just a peck on the lips but when he leaned into her, he immediately got turned on and wanted more. If it weren't for the car honking behind them, he would have undressed her right then and there.

"Wow. You have my woman parts over on fire over here."

He pointed to the bulge in his pants. "What do you call this problem right here. I can't go see your parents like this."

"I don't see a problem. I see an opportunity."

Aisha unzipped his pants and freed his hard dick that was already beginning to poke out the hole in his boxer briefs.

"Tell me how you like it daddy," she said before wrapping her mouth around the head.

"Soft and wet." His voice croaked. "O-o-oh. Thank God for tinted windows."

It took all the strength he could muster to drive like he had some sense but somehow, he was able to drive them around until he shot his load into her mouth. She sat up, wiped the corners of her mouth, and smiled.

"Problem solved."

He pulled into the hospital parking garage.

"When we leave here, I am going to return the favor and then some."

As expected, her father was in the hospital room, reading the newspaper to her mother. He stood to hug his daughter and to shake Malik's hand.

"Hey baby girl," he said.

"Hey, Daddy. Hey Mom. You're looking great."

She walked over and hugged her mother. Malik followed suit.

"You are looking fabulous, Misses Graves. How are you?"

Things are great. The doctors think I may be able to come home next week. They ran some tests and perhaps after this next round of chemo, it will be my last."

"Praise God," Aisha said.

"That's excellent news," Malik said, hugging her.

"I am excited. God is a keeper, and He never makes mistakes, even when we don't understand His plan."

A nurse came into the room with a lunch tray.

"How's my favorite patient doing today?" She asked.

"Just fine. Have you met my daughter and her boyfriend? She is the one I told you wanted to be an RN."

The nurse shook her head and Misses Graves introduced them.

"Awesome sauce. Nursing is a great profession and has many advantages. Did your mom tell you her exciting news?"

"She did. I'm so excited that I'm lightheaded. It's the best news I've heard in a long time."

The nurse pursed her lips and squinted her eyes. It happened so fast that had she not been staring into her face; Aisha would have missed it.

"Excitement tends to do that to us. I have some information at the nurse's station that you may be able to use in school if you wanna come grab it."

"Oh, wow. Thanks. I'll be back."

She followed the nurse down the hall to the nurse's station. The pretty brown skinned woman leaned down and reached into a drawer, pulling out a pink and white box, handing it to Aisha.

Confused, Aisha asked, "what's this for?"

"You. I think you may be pregnant. You said you were lightheaded, and looking at that fine ass man of yours, I know studying is not the only thing you're doing with him."

She blushed. "No. But, well, we do use protection."

The nurse placed her hand on top of Aisha's.

"Baby girl, no birth control is one-hundred-percent effective. Unless you're not doing it all, you are always at risk for pregnancy and STD's. Have you been feeling odd lately?" The nurse touched Aisha's stomach, below her navel. "Hmm."

"A bit nauseous and a little dizzy, but I haven't been eating the way I'm supposed to. It's midterms. Why did you say, hmm, like that?"

"Your tummy is a bit firm. But that could also you mean you are constipated. Let's not get ahead of ourselves. Take the test first. Here, put it in this." The nurse handed her a tampon box. "If anyone asks, just tell them you started your cycle, and I gave them to you. Trust me, no one will go in this box."

"Thank you so much. Do you mind if I get your number? I may need to call you for advice after I take this test."

"No problem."

After the nurse put her number in the phone, Aisha went back to her mother's room and finished her visit. They did not stay that long because her father wanted her mom to rest. That was fine with Aisha because it was getting harder for her to act as if nothing was wrong.

"I have a surprise for you," Malik said, once inside the car.

"Oh really? I like surprises."

"I know. And you're going to love this one."

They drove for twenty minutes and came to a gated community not too far from where Malik grew up. All the homes looked like mansions.

"Wow," she said breathlessly. Her eyes opened wide. "Oh my gosh. I didn't know we were coming to see one your teammates. I would have worn something better."

"Stop it. You look beautiful and we're not visiting anyone. You'll see."

He pulled into a cobblestone, circular driveway. The front entrance of the home had wrought iron and glass French doors. From what she could see, it looked like the home was three levels. Before she could question him, he hopped out the car and walked around to open her door.

"Come on, babe."

The doors to the house opened before she placed her foot on the first step.

"You are right on time." A regal black woman in her mid-fifties stepped out onto the porch.

Malik stood at the threshold, turned to face Aisha, and said, "My queen, welcome to our new castle."

Her jaw dropped but no words came out. He pulled her inside.

"Babe, say something."

She shook her head slowly. "I have no words. This is so beautiful."

"And it's all ours. I closed on it last Monday. I've been having some work done on it though."

The woman walked over and handed him some keys.

"I hope everything is to your liking. If not, please do not hesitate to call me. Thank you so much for allowing me to decorate you and your wife's home, Malik."

He closed the door behind her when she walked out.

"Your wife?" Aisha said.

"Girl stop playing. You know you are. So, do you like it?"

"I love it. She did a great job in here. All this," she fanned her hand around the living room she had just walked into, "are things I would have chosen. Same colors and all that."

"I know. I took pictures of your vision board and showed her. She did this according to your tastes. Come on, let me show you the bedroom. You're going to love it."

"I 'm sure I will."

He grabbed her by the hand and pulled her toward an elevator.

"You have got to be kidding me," she mumbled.

Upstairs, he escorted her to a room so huge, her parent's entire house could fit in it. The California king sized bed was draped in white silk sheets and a gray fur comforter. Just as she had imagined.

"Remember when I said, I was going to return the favor? What better place to do it than here?"

Malik laid her down on the bed and kissed her gently. Before she knew it, they were both naked and he was sliding into her. Making love in that bed was an aphrodisiac and she released all her inhibitions. He rolled onto his back and she straddled him, riding him into the sunset. Slap, slap, slap. The sound of skin against skin filled the air. Her juices coated his hard dick.

"Damn, Eesh. I love this shit."

Pfft. Pfft. Her pussy quiefed.

"Ohh," she groaned, bouncing on the dick.

"Fuck," he said. "I'm about to come."

She placed her hands on his thighs, using them to brace herself so she could grind on him and pull every drip of cum from his dick.

"Yesss, baby. I'm coming," she squealed.

Spent, she collapsed on his chest.

It was not until she woke up, did she realize they had fallen asleep.

"That was amazing," she said, kissing him on the lips.

"Imagine, we'll be able to do it like that every night. No interruptions."

"I like the sound of that. When are we moving in?"

"I was thinking that we could move on Friday. What do you say?"

"I say let's go get some boxes. We have some packing to do."

With all the excitement of the new house and moving, Aisha had completely forgotten about the pregnancy test that was hidden in her purse until a couple of days later. She was home alone and went into the bathroom to take it. Nerves were getting the best of her. Although she had to pee, it would not come out to get on the stick. She had to turn the faucet on to get it to come out.

"Aisha," she heard her brother call her. "Where you at?"

The door was locked but she was still scared that he would walk in.

"The bathroom. What's up?"

"I just came home to grab my lyric book. Tell Pops I'm at the studio. Later."

She leaned back against the toilet seat and exhaled, laying the stick on the box. The timer on her phone was set for three-minutes. That's how long the instructions said results would take. She looked at the phone again. Only thirty seconds had passed. Time was moving in slow motion. A minute and a half later, a pink plus sign began to appear and it got darker with each passing second. She and Malik were going to have a baby.

They were supposed to be going to dinner later that night, but she would not wait to tell him. She grabbed her jacket, threw the stick into her bag and headed to his parents' house. When she pulled into their driveway, she didn't see his car.

"I should have called first," she mumbled to the mirror. Her cellphone sat in the holder and pressed speed dial.

"Hey babe," he answered on the first ring.

"Hey. Are you home?"

"Naw. I'm out taking care of something for my mom's. What's up?"

"I'm at your house. I needed to talk to you. How long will you be?"

"About thirty minutes. Talk to me."

"I'd rather do it in person. I'll wait in your room."

"Bet. I'll see you soon."

Malik's brother, Omari answered the door.

"What up, Sis. Your man's not here."

"I know. We just got off the phone. I'm going to wait here for him."

"Cool. That's a sweet ass spot he got for y'all. You know I'm going to be crashing over there as much as possible so have my room ready."

"Of course. You know Mi casa es su casa."

The click-clack sound of heels approached.

"But we all know that's not your house. It's my son's. You will be nothing more than his concubine."

"Don't start that crap, Ma. You know what Dad said. This is getting old. Fast."

"Aren't you going to be late for work?" She lowered her head and lifted her eyes to her son.

"Sorry, Sis. I do gotta run. Why don't you come back when Malik is here?"

"She will be no more welcomed then either."

Aisha sighed. "It's okay. Your brother will be here soon. Don't work too hard."

"Never that."

He left her alone with Eloise, whose nostrils flared each time she looked at Aisha.

"What brings you by?"

"Um, I just wanted to see my boyfriend."

Eloise touched her chest. "Good lord. What does my son see in you? Come, if you must wait, you can do it in here."

"He told me to wait in his room." She took a step toward the hallway.

"His house is down the street. I run this here. Now either wait in the living room or leave."

Giving in, she walked to the living area and sat down.

"I'm really baffled as to why he wants you to wait here when he is on a date."

"He's what?"

"On a date, dear. With Selena. He took her to lunch, and she went with him to help him pick some things out for his house."

Aisha could not believe her ears. They were going to be living together and he had never asked her to do anything like that.

"He's quite smitten with her you know. Soon he's going to come to his senses and get a woman of quality."

Unable to be in his mom's presence any longer, Aisha dug through her purse and pulled her keys out. She was moving so quickly, things fell out. Hastily, she grabbed them and shoved them in her purse. Tears had already began to form and she did not want his mother to see that she had made her cry. Neither lady said another word. Aisha started her car and took off. Eloise watched her speed down the long driveway and laughed.

"Good riddance." She walked into the living room and looked down. "I know she didn't leave her trash in my house. Oh my God. What is this?"

Eloise used a napkin and picked up the white plastic stick.

"That little hussy is trying to trap my son. Over my dead body. I have got to get her away from him before it's too late."

An idea popped into her head and she snapped her fingers. "Look at God."

She went into her home office and began to look up some information on her computer. Scrolling down, she found the file she was looking for and opened it.

"Aha," she said. "This is excellent."

She picked up the phone and called Aisha.

"Hello dear, I don't like the way you left the house upset like that. I'd like to apologize. Can you come back to the house? Thanks, dear." She ended the call and placed another.

"Malik, before you take Selena home, will you please take her to Bloomingdales to pick up her mother's dress? Thanks, dear."

The conniving woman rapidly typed a text to Selena.

Keep Malik occupied as long as you can. I have a plan that's advantageous for us both.

Consider it done.

In minutes, the Grave's home was only ten-minutes away from the Jeffries place but the difference in neighborhoods was lightyears apart.

"Come in," Eloise said sweetly. Too sweet if you asked Aisha.

"You wanted to apologize," she said naively.

119

"Not quite. I am sorry but not for anything that I said before."

"Then   why   did…"
Eloise put her hand up to silence her son's girlfriend.

"You dropped this when you were here."

Aisha gasped. "I, we."

"Hush, you little gold-digging trollop. You must think I'm a fool if you think I'll allow you to trap my son."

"Trap him? I would never do that."

"Absolutely not," she thrust some papers at Aisha.

"What is this?"

"It seems that your brother had been falsifying orders for auto parts and forging your father's signature. There department is overbudget and the parts are missing. I performed an audit and found the discrepancy. That's embezzlement you know. Your poor old dad could easily get ten, maybe fifteen years in prison."

There was no hiding the tears that ran down her face.

"My father is the most honest alive."

"Perhaps, but a jury will hear about his mounting bills and will believe that he robbed the school system. I will be filing a theft report in the morning."

"Why are you doing this? What has he ever done to you?"

Eloise shrugged. "I like your father. It's you I abhor. But…if you love your father and want him to remain free, you will take this check, abort that child, and get out of my son's life for good."

"And if I don't?"

"Well then, you'll be visiting two parents. One in the hospital and the other in prison. It's your choice."

"But we're supposed to be moving tomorrow."

"Oh, you're moving. Just not with him. Like I said, it's your choice."

Her father would die if he went to jail and her mother would, also.

"I'll leave him alone."

"Smart girl," she said, patting her on top of her head. "It's best if you leave immediately. Once you leave this house, do not attempt to contact my son again. If he calls you, do not answer."

Aisha's shoulders shook with each sob.

"And if you even think about crossing me, I will make you live to regret it."

Without another word, she left the house. Her father was home when she got there, and she told him all that happened. As much as he wanted to tell her to stay, he knew that Eloise meant every word.

Malik called her several times. Unable to ignore his calls, she blocked them all together. An hour later, she drove toward an uncertain future, leaving behind the only life and loves she had ever known.

CHAPTER 11

The Golden Rule

NEVER USE A HOE'S condom. That was the golden rule. A rule Kyle had violated time and again. He didn't know if he was dumb, stupid, or both. Either way, he needed to get his shit together. A month ago, he let Tika bring Malia to his house. Per usual, the baby was asleep, and he and his baby's mama took advantage of it. Sensations still ran through his dick as he thought about that night.

"How does your pussy stay so tight?" He pumped in awe.

"It's tailor-made for your dick, Zaddy. Mmm, fuck me good baby. Write your name on my sugar walls."

Tiny pulses of electricity coursed through his veins. His penis was more engorged than ever, the orgasm strained inside for release. Holding onto her hips tightly, he banged her pussy, skin slapping skin, until his toes started to curl.

"It's coming babe," he said through clenched teeth.

Tika reached around and rubbed his tight ass cheek.

"Let it flow, my love."

The orgasm was so intense that Kyle forgot his name, let alone that he was not strapped. Instead of pulling out, he spilled his seed in its entirety into his gold-digging ex-girlfriend. It wasn't until the other day that he realized the error of his ways.

The team was at the training center shooting some rounds, excited about being the Eastern Conference Champions. For the first time in over twenty years, The Georgia Heat was heading to the Ship. Kyle was riding on the Starship Enterprise. Head in outer space. He was so elated, that when Tika called, he didn't mind speaking with her. There was nothing that bring him down.

"I think I'm pregnant again, KJ."

Nothing except that.

He immediately recoiled like someone punched him in his chest.

"What did you say?"

"I said I think I'm pregnant," she repeated.

Suddenly, his legs began to shake so he sat on the bleachers before they gave way altogether.

"Fuck, Tika," he said a little too loudly. Team members looked his way. "Are you sure?"

"Why are you yelling at me? This is something that we both did." She smiled brightly on the other end, but feigned disappointment on the phone.

"My bad. You're right. You said you think, right?"

"Yeah. My period is a week late."

"Okay, cool. Being late, doesn't mean you're pregnant. Let's not get ahead of ourselves and panic. We need to get you a test."

Which brought him to his current situation. Sitting in his bedroom, drumming his fingers on the nightstand, waiting for Tika to finish peeing on the stick he gave her.

"What's taking so long?" He asked.

"Stop yelling. It's making my pee go back up."

"Fuck this," he said, jumping off the bed, charging through the bathroom door. He turned the faucet on, hoping the stream of water would encourage her to pee.

"Are you gonna just stand there and watch me?"

"Yeah, why? You got something to hide?"

She smacked her lips and rolled her eyes. "No."

A few moments later, she peed on the stick and slammed it on the counter next to him. After pulling her panties up, which is all she had on, she flushed the toilet and walked in front of Kyle.

"Here," she said, crushing the box on his chest. "Since you're so interested in this shit, read the directions and you tell me what it says when you finish. I already know what's up. My period is always on time, just like Jesus."

She sauntered out the bathroom calmly, yet ecstatic. It took every ounce of self-control for her to maintain her composure. Without a doubt she knew she was pregnant because in all her thirteen years of having a cycle, the only other times she had been late was when she got pregnant. Which was four times prior.

"Damn, my ass would have had fo' damned babies," she whispered, counting on her fingers how many abortions she had had before and after her daughter was born.

"It's starting to show something," Kyle yelled from the bathroom. "I think I see two lines."

Tika jumped up and down and screamed silently.

"Two lines means it's positive," she finally answered.

He did not reply. The quietness in the other room, disturbed her peace. She began to pace the floor.

"Yes!" She heard Kyle holler.

He ran into the room, picked her up and twirled her around.

"Oh my gosh, babe. We are so blessed." He squeezed her tightly.

"I can't breathe, honey."

"My bad. It's just that I am so happy."

She preened like a peacock.

"See I told you. I know my body. I'm pregnant."

"Huh? What are you talking about?"

"The test. You said that we were so blessed. I told you I was pregnant."

"You misunderstand. I said we are so blessed because you're not."

He handed her the stick and trotted off. She stared at the results. One dark pink line. The test was, indeed, negative.

"Fuck," she whispered and shook her head. This was not what she expected. How could she not be pregnant? Her body was beginning to show signs. First, the late cycle. Then, tender breast. Hell, she even felt a little morning sickness the other day. The test had to be wrong.

Kyle walked into the bedroom with Malia in his arms. She bounced and cooed when he lifted her over his head.

"You're Daddy's only Princess. Me and Mommy are not going to be careful anymore."

Tika plastered a fake smile on her face and walked over to rub her daughter's back.

"Daddy's right."

The little girl responded to the gentle rubs and laid her head on the strong shoulder of her father.

"This little girl stays sleepy."

"I know. If I didn't know any better, I would swear that she sneaks out at night and goes club-hopping or something," Tika said.

It did not take long before the baby entered a deep slumber. Kyle took her to the nursery he had designed for her and placed her in the crib.

"I never thought I would be a dad, T. The shit had me running scared, honestly. That's why I wasn't as present in her life as I should have been in the beginning," he said, pointing to his daughter. "But she's such an easy-going baby and I think she knows I'm her dad. She's the smallest person I love, and I would do anything to protect her."

"She knows who you are, which is why she responds to you the way she does. If you notice, she is not even like that with me. And I get it. I was like you too. After I first had her, I thought I was going to kill her or something because I didn't understand feeding schedules, diaper changing or any of that. But I wanted to be a good mother, so I stayed out the streets. When Mommy saw I was serious, she began to teach me things. Now, I am an old pro."

"Were you disappointed about the pregnancy results? You seemed certain about being pregnant."

"Not at all," she lied through her teeth. "The only reason I thought I was, is because I had tender breasts and a few other things going on."

Kyle looked down and noticed she was still topless. He leaned over and sucked one nipple, before moving to the next one.

"The reason your titties are tender is because every time I see them, I can't keep my mouth off of 'em," he said after lifting his head.

Tika gyrated her hips and latched her thumbs in the sides of her panties, easing them down slowly.

"I got something else you can't keep your mouth off of."

Naked, she turned around and grinded her ass into his pelvis, causing his pants to stretch.

"Come on, don't we have some celebrating to do?"

She took him by the hand and led him to his room, closing the door behind her with her foot.

"Lay down."

AVERY GOODE

Lying back, Kyle rested his head on a stack of pillows and enjoyed the show his baby's mother put on with her mouth. The way she kept her mouth perfectly round and wet was amazing. He loved the fact that she never touched his dick with her teeth or sucked to hard. Somehow, her sucking and stroking was always perfectly in sync. And when she swallowed? Oh, that was the Queen Mother of all sex acts for him.

Intense pressure was beginning to build for him. Tika recognized that he was on the verge of an eruption by the way his dick flexed inside her mouth.

"Let me ride this bronco, Zaddy," she begged.

Not waiting for his reply, she stopped sucking and eased her way up his body. Her hot box was poised over the tip of his dick but just before she put his sword in her sheath, he grabbed her hips and sat her to the side.

"Uhn, uhn. We can't have any more screw ups. Here."

He handed her a condom. Disappointed, she took it, until she remembered a trick.

"May I put it on you, love? I wanna show you something."

Kyle nodded in response.

Tika removed the condom from the foil packet. Turning it around so that the tip was facing her, she put it into her mouth, biting it slightly without him seeing her move her teeth. Then she leaned over him and slipped the rubber down his shaft.

"Damn that was the sexiest shit ever. Where you learn to do that?"

"Larissa."

"I should have known."

Pleased, Tika once again positioned herself over him.

"Hold up."

127

He reached over to the nightstand and grabbed another rubber. This time, he put it on himself. "Just in case."

Satisfied and ready, he picked up her roughly and slammed her down on his dick, bucking and pumping until sweat drenched both their bodies.

Although she was angry that Kyle had thwarted another attempt at getting her pregnant, she could not deny the immense pleasure he brought her with his lovemaking. It was like his dick understood who she was inside, and it knew what she craved.

"Oh, yes. Please don't stop," she said.

And he didn't either. For the next hour and a half, he had Tika's legs up, down, and all around his bed. His dick had entered every hole on her body. It wasn't until his own body was empty that he rolled over.

"What the hell was that Kyle?" She asked.

"I call that, my victory lap," he said, pulling her into his body.

The two of them remained on the bed until their breathing steadied.

Tika ran her hand down Kyle's body and rested it on his penis, which was still covered. She began to tug at it.

"I'll flush this for you, babe. I gotta pee," she volunteered.

"Nah, I got it," he said, rolling out of bed, heading toward the bathroom.

She was hot on his heels.

Kyle removed both condoms and dropped them into the toilet. Tika looked over his shoulder when he leaned over and picked something up from the side of the commode.

"What are you doing?" She asked with interest.

He held up a white bottle with a blue lid.

"Oh, this? My cousin, Malik told me to do this for security."

She looked on in horror as he poured an entire gallon of bleach into the water on top of the rubbers, killing any sperm she could have used for insemination. When he flushed the condoms down the toilet, he flushed her dreams of getting pregnant again right along with them.

"The whole gallon my nig?" Malik said, doubled over in laughter.

"The whole motherfuckin' gallon." Kyle shook his head. "I have had one too many near misses with her, man. I mean don't get me wrong, Malia is beautiful, and I know our kids would be dope as fuck, but on the real, I ain't trying to have a basketball team of my own running around here."

"Shit, I feel you. Me and this one shorty were about to get busy when she said I didn't have to use protection because she was safe. I told her ass unless she had her tubes tied and I was there to witness it, she was a threat to my livelihood."

The cousins gave one another high-fives. A pretty waitress came up to the VIP section where they sat in the club with another bottle.

"May I get you either of you anything else? And I do mean anything.

"Hmph, nah we good, Ma. But thanks though," Malik said.

"This is a crazy life we live, fam. For once, I would like to meet a woman who is not impressed by none of this shit."

"Yeah, I had one of those."

"Aisha? Have you heard from her?"

"Nope. But I don't wanna talk about that. This is our night to celebrate. Next week, you all will be the NBA Champions."

"From your lips to God's ears."

"Salute," Malik said, raising his glass.

"What are we saluting?" Breeze asked before sitting down and picking up a glass.

"This ship, KJ and the team are about to bring us."

"Now I will most definitely drink to that."

The three friends threw the drinks back. A slight burn trailed the back of Kyle's throat.

"What the hell is in this drink?"

"Hell, if I know," Malik shrugged. "The bartender is a homegirl from school and she said she was sending me one of her special mixes."

"This shit will take all the hair off your chest," Breeze said, rubbing his.

"Chest, nuts, all that shit."

They laughed and took another swig, adjusting slowly to the potent potable. The DJ cranked the music up and people swarmed the dance floor. Kyle sat back, tapping his foot to the beat. Their VIP section was on the second level, so he had a great view of the entire club. His gaze traveled to the entry of the club, just as the bouncer stepped aside, allowing two women inside. One he recognized but was unsure where from. The other, he was certain had never seen before.

"Damn," he mouthed. His foot stilled and he stood to see where they headed within the club. It was hard for him to follow them through the throng of people.

"Hey, do you guys mind if my lady joins us for a second? She's here with friends and won't stay long."

"Shit the more the merrier."

"Thanks, Malik. What about you, KJ? You cool?"

Kyle turned around, took his seat, and shrugged.

"No, peezy."

Pulling out his phone, Breeze typed a quick text and then stood over the railing so that the security guard could see him when Caresse got there. A few minutes later, the three-hundred fifty pound, six-four bodyguard, turned his head as Caresse pointed her man's way. Breeze nodded and the man let the women passed.

As soon as she stepped onto the landing, Breeze hugged his girlfriend.

"Hey, you," he said, kissing her.

"Hey, yourself. Hello everyone."

Malik gave them a head nod and Kyle waved. But then he saw her. The girl from downstairs.

"Fella's this is my girlfriend, Caresse and her cousin, Sunrise. Ladies, this is Malik Jeffries of the Atlanta Condors and Kyle Hudson of the Georgia Heat."

"It's a pleasure." Caresse smiled.

"Nice to meet you both," Sunrise said.

"Um, sit us with drink and have a down." Kyle stumbled over his words.

"The fuck you just say, dude?" Malik laughed.

"I meant, sit down with us and have a drink."

This was not like him. Kyle was a smooth talker and always had the right words to say in any situation. But there was something about this woman that had him all discombobulated. Once he regained his composure, things flowed smoothly.

Sunrise. That was her real name. Apparently, she and Caresses' mothers were into unique names. Although he had only spoken with her for an hour, her name was befitting. This lady had thoughts in her head that did not consist of shoes, clothes, whips, or handbags. She was different.

"Would you like to dance?" He asked when a slow jam began to play.

"Sure."

He escorted her downstairs to the dance floor and stepped closely to her. Too close. She placed her hands on his chest.

"Give us a little room, please." She was polite and asked nicely.

He did what she said but by the time the song reached the bridge, he was feeling it and her. His hands pulled her closer and gripped her ass.

She responded with a "Whap!"

A few heads turned and a bouncer was upon them in seconds.

"You good, KJ?"

Kyle nodded. "It's cool. I overstepped my boundaries."

"He damned sure did. I know you're used to a certain type of woman, Sir. But let me assure you, this ain't that. I don't care what you have or who you *think* you are, you need to know who *I* am. And a jump-off ain't it."

The bouncer did not budge.

"You are right. Please accept my apologies. Disrespecting you is the last thing I want to do," he said sincerely. "Forgiven?"

"Those damned puppy dog eyes of yours. Smch," she smacked. "I guess. But don't do it again."

"You have my word. We're good here, Tank," he said, giving the big man permission to leave.

Upstairs, the two settled into their seats again and Kyle refreshed their drinks.

Sunrise put her hand over the top of her glass.

"Whoa, there buddy. That's not enough for me."

"Okay. I am sorry about earlier. May I ask what you do for a living? I haven't been chastised like that by anyone except my mother."

"I'm an engineer. As a woman in a male dominated field, I have to be stern," she said.

He laughed. "Of course, you are."

"I'm being honest. Caresse, tell this man I am an engineer with the City of Atlanta."

Caresse nodded.

"I believe you. I said you reprimanded me like my mother. She's a teacher."

Before two in the morning, Sunrise and Caresse left, but not before Kyle got her number.

"'Member when I said I wanna a woman who wasn't who wasn't impressed by me or this life?"

Malik and Breeze nodded.

"I think I found her," Kyle admitted.

The next day, still reeling from a great night, he got even better news. He had just gotten out the shower and dressed when his doorbell rang.

"Hey, Sis," he said to Kayla, hugging her.

"What's going on? Why are you so happy?"

"I met the woman I am going to marry."

"Oh, Lord. Here we go, again."

"Naw, for real. She's different."

"How? Her ass is big and real?"

He stopped and scratched his chin.

"You know, come to think of it, I don't know how big her ass is."

Kayla felt his forehead. "Are you sure, you're, okay?"

"Yeah. I mean, I tried to touch it when we danced but she cussed me out when I did."

"She did? Oh, wow."

"Kay, she calls herself a blerd. A black nerd. She's smart, funny and sexy."

"Hmph, so which porn star does she look like?"

He shrugged. "None. She looks like she could be KeKe Palmer's twin. Everything about her is so dope."

"That's great, bro. Well, allow me to add a little more joy to your life. The gag order that I worked on has been signed off by the judge. Tika is not allowed to mention you, Malia, child support, dead beat or any other phrase to any media outlet or friend. If she does, she will be in contempt of court and will face a large fine or jail."

"You are the best, Sis."

"I know. And the coup de grace, is that the order is retroactive, and we also served Rhona Stewart Elder, Baller Babe's Franchise and ATL1 Network. They will not be allowed to air anymore footage of her talking about you."

"Damn. When she realizes what the ramifications are of this order, she is going to hate me. I may not be able to see Malia again."

"I know. But when we go to court, the judge will grant you visitation. I'm shooting for joint-custody."

"I pray we are victorious. 'Cause if she's mine and we don't win, I stand to lose a lot more than money."

CHAPTER 12

Dollars and Bills

ALL EYES WERE ON Georgia as the state's decision makers grappled with the new child support legislature, that would undoubtedly cause a whirlwind of backlash from opposition. Everyone was talking about. Especially the news outlets.

Atlanta's ABC Affiliate WCB- TV was all over it.

"This is Sara Jane Lindley reporting from the newsroom. Our field correspondent, Robin Robertson is coming to you live from the state capital. Robin, can you tell us what's going on right now?"

"Absolutely, Sara Jane. Right now, the Governor is signing off on Braden's Bill, which is a comprehensive bill that places stringent limitations on custodial parents who receive child support payments."

"Is the bill that was introduced by State Senator Gayle Halpern?"

"Yes, it is. If you recall, Senator Halpern's son, Braden Halpern, was the starting quarterback for the Giants for three years. He allegedly got a young woman pregnant, and she filed a child support claim against him. The court granted her over fifty-thousand dollars a month."

"Phwwwwwhht," Sara whistled. "That is a mint. I'm a mother of three and I know that children are expensive, but they are not that expensive."

"Exactly. The young lady took Braden to court to ask for an increase in support. The judge was going to grant but ordered a DNA test. It turns out, Braden Halpern had been paying support for a child that was not even his. What's worse, is that the child never saw a dime of that money. He was living with his grandparents in another state."

"That's awful, Robin. So, what does Braden's Bill mean for Georgian's?"

"A few substantial things. For starters, DNA tests will be mandatory for every child support case. No exceptions. If the plaintiff in the case refuses, the case will be denied. In addition, the custodial parent will have to provide receipts to an independent, court appointed accountant, that shows how all child support payments are spent."

Kyle could not believe what he was watching. Usually, he hated watching the news, but this was worth it. When his dad called him twenty minutes ago and told him to tune in, he had no clue this is what he would see and hear.

"Amazing. The implications of this bill are vast."

"Indeed, they are, Sara. Finally, any amount over $1500 per month of a child support award is to be held in a trust for the child until they reach the age of majority. It cannot be accessed by either parent except in the event of the child's untimely passing."

A smile was plastered on Kyle's face. Was he dreaming? He pinched himself to make sure that he wasn't. His phone vibrated loudly on the glass table next to him.

"KJ my man. It's a beautiful day in the neighborhood," Malik said.

"Very beautiful indeed, fam."

"You know California is usually the one who would set a precedent for something like this and then the rest of the world would follow suit. But shit, now the world has to follow us."

"You're right. This is epic."

The cousins chatted briefly and then ended the call. Kyle returned his attention to the television. A few minutes later, his phone rang again.

"Bruh, are you seeing this shit?" Breeze asked his friend.

"Man, hey. This is some next level shit right here. These gold-diggers are about to get their come-uppance with this bill."

"You ain't never lied. Larissa is going to shit bricks when her attorney tells her what the deal is."

"On the real, bruh. This is a blessing for the kids and us. I mean for real; it doesn't make sense that we have to foot the bill for a lifestyle that these broads did not have before they got pregnant. Shit, setting up a trust for the kid can be used as a college fund or money they can used to start their life when they grow up. They shouldn't be broke because their mamas don't know how to save."

"Facts on top of facts. I'm about to get back into this studio. Just wanted to call and chop it up with you for a minute."

"Right on. Hold up though, are you still going to ask baby girl to marry you?"

"Hell, yeah. Now more than ever. When you see your Pops, tell him I said thank you. We owe him."

"Sure thing. Later."

The reporters were still discussing the bill. Kyle watched as the camera slowly panned the room, stopping at the podium. A man walked up, shuffled some papers, and cleared his throat.

MEAL TICKET$

"Governor Abraham has signed off on Braden's Bill and it will be enacted into Georgia law, effective July 1."

The camera moved back to focus on the reporter.

"There it is Georgia. Braden's Bill is the new, necessary legislation."

"Robin, thank you so much for reporting this. You have been our eyes and ears inside the Georgia General Assembly for months now, since they first introduced the bill."

"To clarify, Sara. This bill was co-authored by Senator Gayle Halpern and Representative Kyle Hudson, Sr."

"Interesting. This bill should come in handy considering his son is facing his own child support battle."

Kyle shook his head and grabbed his remote.

"Here they go with this bullshit," he mumbled, turning off the television.

But no amount of gossip reporting would spoil the happiness that he felt. His father was always looking out for other's. Yes, this bill would help Kyle, but it would also help so many people like him. He did not mind taking care of his daughter. If she was really his. But he did mind, getting Tika's hair, nails, and feet done every week. None of that helped the baby in any way. The money she got from him each month had upgraded her lifestyle considerably. When he first met her, she was living in a cute, two-bedroom apartment in Buckhead, but she had a roommate. And although she drove a Mercedes, it was a few years old, and it was paid for.

Even though she had Malia, she did not need that big ass townhome. It was located off West Paces Ferry, which was in the heart of Billionaire Buckhead, as people called it. She drove a new convertible, Mercedes GT which was barely big enough for Malia, let alone her car seat. Every dime she received was used to fund her lavish lifestyle and Kyle was sick of it. This bill would change things drastically for Tika.

If she had to start reporting where she spent the money, there were going to be a few places that she would have to omit from her daily routine. Knowing her and her scheming ass though, she would probably try to give the accountant bogus receipts.

"I hope she's smarter than that. Those people will be calling to verify authenticity. Oh well," he shrugged. "That's on her."

Kyle grabbed a towel off the shelf and headed to his home gym in the basement. With all the happy endorphins floating around inside him, this was the perfect time for him to pump some iron. He adjusted the weights on the bar and lie down so he could bench press for a while. Thirty-minutes into his workout, his phone rang. He had just finished a rep, so he carefully lowered the barbell onto the bench. By the time he got to his phone, it had stopped ringing. He pressed the picture of the phone and it redialed the last caller.

"Hey, you," a pretty, soft voice said.

"Hey, yourself. What's going on?"

"I just finished watching the news. You know your dad is the G.O.A.T. right?"

"Hell yeah, he is. I'm grateful. This is good news for us all."

"I thought so, too. What are you doing? Do you feel like some company?"

"If the company, is you, then yes," he said.

"Great. See you soon."

Since most women were slow, Kyle figured that 'see you soon' meant at least an hour so he returned to his workout. Twenty-minutes later, his doorbell rang. He picked up his phone, tapped the security camera and saw that it was Sunrise.

"Damn. She wasn't playing."

Wiping the sweat from his forehead, he ran upstairs to let her in.

"That was fast," he said, kissing her on the cheek.

"Kyle, I only work ten minutes from here."

His eyes dropped in shame.

"My bad. I'm so used to women taking a long time. I thought I would have time to finish my workout and shower before you got here."

"I keep asking you to stop comparing me with all these other females you know. What do I keep telling you? She pointed to herself.

"This," he said.

She pointed away from her.

"Ain't that," he finished.

"Now do you get it?"

"Yes, ma'am. You wanna work out with me? Kayla has some stuff over here you can fit."

"That would be great, but I keep a gym bag in the car. I'll be right back."

When she returned, he was in the gym, running on the treadmill. She dropped her bag and went toward the weight bench. After removing a few dumbbells, she laid back, and began to bench press. Watching her, Kyle lost his footing on the treadmill and almost fell. He grabbed the sides immediately to hold himself up. Sunrise replaced the barbell and burst into laughter.

"I just got so weak. My arms are like noodles now thanks to you making me laugh like this."

He switched the treadmill off and walked over to her.

"You know you're the sexiest woman in this gym?"

Sunrise bit her lower lip. "Oh yeah. You think so?"

"I know so," he said. "Come with me."

"Wait, I haven't worked out yet."

"Oh, you will. Trust me."

They walked upstairs to the master bathroom, where he turned on the steam shower. The two of them got in once the water was hot and they bathed one another.

"This water feels so good," she said.

She was about to say something else, but Kyle kissed her, muffling her words.

He nibbled on her neck, pushing her against the warm ceramic tile.

"Mmm," she moaned sensuously.

His hands gently kneaded her breasts and caressed her stomach before cupping her center. The heat that came from her had nothing to do with the water.

"You're so damned hot, Sun," he said, inserting a finger into her wet pussy. He kissed her and finger fucked her, as she moaned into his mouth.

"I've waited so long for this," she admitted.

The water started to cool. Kyle shut it off. Steam had filled the room. He stepped out onto the heated ceramic floors and lifted her into his arms, carrying her to the bedroom. Gently, he laid her down in the center and spread her legs.

His tongue flicked at her clit, making her jump.

"Ooh," she squealed.

Skillfully he licked and sucked her pussy while simultaneously fingering her. Sunrise didn't know what to do with her hands. She didn't know whether to rub his shoulders, pull his hair or what. The sensations that coursed through her body had her mind scattered into a million different directions.

"Slurrp."

MEAL TICKET$

The sound of him sucking on her drove her wild. Tingling sensations began to form in the pit of her stomach and worked their way up her spine. A strong orgasm was on the verge of forming, but he stopped what he was doing and looked up at her.

"That's not how I want you to come."

He got to his knees and her eyes traveled down the length of him. She admired his sleek, athletic body. Strong arms, a muscular chest, and lean, solid legs. Her eyes lingered on his manhood and she blushed slightly. Unlike many of the other women he had been with before, Sunrise did not have that much experience with men. But she was smart enough to gauge that her man's dick was a good eight or nine inches. And it was thick.

Kyle positioned his dick right at her opening. She felt the head poke her lips.

"Ha, ha, ha," she giggled nervously as he held his dick and rubbed it up and down inside her folds.

She clenched his shoulders tightly when he eased inside her. He stilled briefly, allowing her body the time to adjust to his size before he began moving.

"Ahh," she exhaled.

To urged him deeper, welcoming him home as she spread her legs wider.

He looked into her natural jade green eyes and the passion was undeniable. Like magnets, they held his gaze. Only when her lashes fluttered was the trance broken. Instinctively, he lowered his mouth into hers. Their tongues swirled and wrestled erotically. With each stroke, her warm center began to heat up. Soon, she was hot and ready like a Little Caesars Pizza and her juices began to flow, saturating his condom covered dick.

"Sun. Coming. Shit," he mumbled incoherently.

In response to his staggered announcement, she cupped his ass and pulled him as far as he could go inside her. She grinded beneath him until she gave him every ounce of her nectar.

Spent, he collapsed on top of her, breathing heavy, and his heart pounding.

"Damn," he said, rolling onto his back, pulling her with him to lay on his chest.

"Exactly."

It felt so natural, so right to have Sunrise lying in his arms like this. The two of them had been kicking it tough since they met, and he was enjoying learning about her. She was so different from any woman he had ever met since he had been the NBA. It was not often that a man found a woman of substance like this. Whatever he did, he could not fuck this up.

"I hear those wheels turning inside your head," she said. "What are you thinking about?"

"You. Us. This. I'm happy about the way things are going with us and the direction this relationship is taking."

She raised herself up on her elbow.

"Seriously?"

He nodded.

She lay back on his chest.

"I thought I was the only who felt like this."

"I'm not trying to sound like a pansy or nothing but... where do we go from here?"

"We identify a lane that we want to be in and travel it. Together."

"Hmm, what if there isn't a lane for us?"

"Well babe, God was smiling on you. As a civil engineer with a dual degree in city and regional planning, if there isn't a lane for us, I will build us a highway."

"You are so motherfucking dope."

"Thank you."

She lay quietly against his chest, stroking it lightly, listening to his heartbeat.

"Sun, when it comes to this thing between you and I, I find myself at a loss for words sometimes. You make me think in a way that I never have and since we have been together, I have re-evaluated what's important."

Her fingers stilled. Did he mean to say that? Together? As in a relationship?

"Um, babe. Are we together?"

He sat up and looked her square in eyes.

"Yes. What do you think we've been doing?"

She shrugged.

"Honestly, I don't know. I just thought we were kicking in."

He shook his head.

"The night I met you in the club, I had just finished telling the fellas that I wanted a woman like you, then God answered and voila. There you were. I'd be a fool to let you slip away."

Sunrise sat up and kissed him.

"I love what we are developing and if you're willing to see where this goes, so am I." She giggled.

"What's so funny?"

"Do you realize this was our first-time making love?"

"Wow, you're right. Well, it won't be the last. As a matter of fact, it's time for round two."

Kyle eased on his back and pulled Sunrise on top of him, positioning her at his ready tip. Her gaze penetrated his soul and hypnotized him. Before the night was over, he was sure of a few things. One, he would never fuck Tika again. Two, smart girls were freaks. And three, he was in love with Sunrise and wanted to marry her.

CHAPTER 13
Don't Wake Me...I'm Dreaming!

BREEZE WAS NERVOUS. Caresse hadn't noticed. She was too busy chatting away about Sunrise and Kyle and how the two had been spending so much time together.

"Babe, I think she really loves him, and he seems to feel the same way. I hope this works out for them."

"So, do I. They're good people."

A waiter walked up to the table and set a dessert in the middle of the table. Breeze looked at the plate, smiled and took a deep breath.

"Caresse."

She kept chattering away.

He placed his hand over hers and squeezed, getting her attention.

"Caresse, you know how I'm always calling you my wifey at home?"

"Yes," she said.

"I want to do that everywhere we go, starting today."

He pushed the plate in front of her.

She mouthed the words on the plate. "Veux-tu m'épouser. Breeze when did you learn to speak French?" She whispered, tears filling her eyes.

Slowly he moved from his seat and kneeled next to her.

"The moment I fell in love with you." The lid from the black box snapped open.

"Will I marry you? Je fais. I do."

Her face leaned into his and he kissed her long and hard on the mouth, oblivious to the onlookers in the restaurant.

A few tables over, a woman was taping the entire scene as it unfolded.

When Breeze paid the bill and he and his new fiancé left the restaurant, the woman made a quick phone call.

"You are not going to believe what I just taped. I'm going to send it to your email because the video is almost six minutes long. The audio is as clear as the video."

She tapped a few keys, and the video was delivered into the hands of those who were about to make things very difficult for Breeze, Caresse and his daughter, Brely.

The woman who filmed Breeze and Caresse at the restaurant was a blogger with *A-Tea-L Live*. Their kiss, the ring, him on bended knee; she had caught it all and it aired on the show last night during *Tea-Time*, the hot topics segment. Today, it was all over the internet. He loved his fiancé and was not ashamed of her in any way, but he knew that this would not bode well with Larissa. She already made it hard for him to see his daughter, but now she may try to make it damned near impossible.

Breeze exhaled. "I hate this damned gossip show. They are always in people's business, not realizing that what they report can damage somebody. This is fucked up."

"Maybe she didn't see the show," Keyon said.

"Pssh," he began. "That's her favorite show and she believes everything that they report. She even believed that crap about Obama and Michelle living in Bankhead back in the day."

Keyon tilted his head and his mouth opened in disbelief. "Damn."

"Right. I'm sure she is going to have a lot to say."

"Give her the benefit of the doubt. She may not even care," Keyon offered. But he didn't believe that himself.

As soon as he finished his sentence, Breeze's phone rang. He clicked the speaker button, and the rant began.

"Oh, so your ass is getting married to some bitch named, Caresse and you didn't even have the common courtesy to tell me? I'm your motherfuckin' girlfriend."

He rolled his eyes in the top of his head and exhaled loudly. "First of all, Caresse, is not a bitch and secondly, you are not my girlfriend, she is. You are only my daughter's mother."

"Whateva, nigga. So, you be having that bih- um, chick around our daughter without my permission? That's fucked up, man. I ain't never had no other dude around her."

"Were you not just at Lake Lanier on a family vacation with our daughter and a dude who plays for the Jets? And didn't I see you the other day sitting courtside with some unknown nigga who was holding our daughter? You can miss me with all that, Larissa. Your ass doesn't even fuck with our baby like that. What was she, a publicity stunt for that damned show you're on?"

She inhaled sharply. He didn't know she had gotten fired, and she was not going to volunteer the information.

"I swear you got me so fucked up. How many times I got to tell you that we are a packaged deal?"

"What the hell does that mean?"

"Whatever the fuck you want it to mean. You make me sick. I hate you so much right now."

"Listen, we can talk about this. Just let me-,"

"So now you want to talk? Man fuck you and your dumb ass fiancé. Me and my baby are good this way. She doesn't need you and neither do I. Just keep those fat ass checks coming, trick."

Beep. Beep. The call ended as abruptly as it began. Breeze stood staring at the phone as the time flashed on the screen. In three minutes and twenty seconds, he knew that his life had changed.

"You're going to need a good attorney."

"I got one, Keyon. Yours. He is already on the case. I have three more stops on the tour and then we are headed to court."

The two men gave one another some dap and Breeze left the Man of Steele office. Court was something that he wished he could avoid. Not because he didn't think he had a good chance of winning, but because his daughter, no matter the outcome, was the ultimate loser. She was going to be the one caught in the middle of name calling, being pulled back and forth between her parents. If there was any way he could avoid that, he would.

Once he got into his car, he called Caresse. He had texted her while in Keyon's office to let her know that Larissa was on a rampage and he was sure that she was concerned. The phone rang several times before her voice mail picked up. Breeze frowned at his phone before dialing her number again. It was not like her not answer when he called. The next time, the phone rang twice before she answered.

"Hel-lo," she said. She was out of breath.

"Hey. What were you doing the reason my phone call went to voice mail?" His words were rushed and his voice a little higher in pitch than normal.

"Whoa. I get that you're upset with Larissa and all that's going on, but please, don't take that out on me."

"I'm sorry. I didn't mean to come at you like that. Forgive me."

"Forgiven. Are you okay?"

"Not really, but I'm going to be. I have the Los Angeles and San Francisco dates this weekend, then Seattle." He lowered his voice. "After those three performances we will be back here to go to court."

"Going to court makes you sad, huh?" She asked intuitively.

"Yeah. This is not really what I want but I know it's the only way that I will be able to spend time with my baby."

"I know. Concentrate on driving and come home. We can talk more about it when you get here. I'll have dinner ready."

"Thanks, babe. I love you."

"I love you, too. See ya' soon."

"Who the hell do you think you are?" Larissa shouted to the hanging picture of Breeze. "Answer me!" Her fist punched through the drywall.

The picture fell to the floor and shattered on the hardwood floor. Scared, her little girl began to cry.

"You wanna cry, little bitch? I'll give you something to cry about."

Larissa yanked her by one arm and slammed her to the floor. The little girl tried to crawl under the bed, but she was not quick enough. Her mother pulled her, bumping her head on the bed frame.

Boom! Boom!

"What the hell is going on in there?" Laquanda yelled.

"Nothing, Mama damn. This hoe fell out the bed. Stay out my fucking business."

"Don't get your ass kicked, bitch," her mother said through the door. "I'm going to get Jarell from the station. He's back from his class trip."

Clip. Clop. Clip. Clop. Larissa heard heals on the floor fade as they walked away from her door. Brely whimpered.

"I hate you," she yelled as she swatted the bottom of the little girls' feet with a wooden ruler. "I wish you were dead."

She picked up a pillow and covered her baby's face until the little girl was quiet.

Caresse was standing at the door, waiting and as soon as Breeze walked in the, she wrapped her arms around him. In response, he hugged her tight and held on for a while. He needed the transfer of positive energy that she was allowing him.

"Better?"

"Much. You take such good care of me, Bae. What would I do without you?"

"You would live a blessed and prosperous life, just like God designed. Go wash up and let's eat."

The couple sat down and ate in silence for a few minutes. Caresse did not want to bombard her soon-to-be-husband with questions, although she was anxious to ask him what happened. After he text her earlier, she searched the internet for the clip that the gossip show had posted about them but considering that it was the number one trending topic, it didn't take her long to find it.

Breeze set his fork down and wiped his mouth with the cloth napkin, then cleared his throat.

"Larissa is on a rampage. The call in Keyon's office was just the beginning. After she called me, she phoned my parent's and told them that thanks to me, they would never see their grandchild again. You know that pissed my mother off. She cussed Larissa out. I am pretty sure that's not the response that she was expecting from a grandmother."

"Clearly she doesn't know Misses Margaret. That woman is a fighter and does not play about her kids or grandkids."

"Not at all. What am I going to do?"

"I think you should talk to her. Call her up and ask her out to lunch. If you talk with her in a public place, she may behave more civilly."

"That's a good idea. I'll call her in the morning…let her sleep on things tonight. Cool off a bit."

She nodded her agreement. They finished dinner and washed the dishes before heading upstairs to bed. That night, instead of making love, they held one another closely. Breeze rubbed Caresses' hair until she fell asleep and then he dozed off shortly thereafter.

When he did call Larissa, he exercised every bit of restraint that he had because she was testing his patience.

"What, nigga?"

He exhaled. "Good morning, Larissa. How are you doing?"

"I've been better. Why you calling me?"

"I want to talk. Will you meet at Plates today for lunch at noon?"

The upscale restaurant in Atlantic Station was the meeting place of Atlanta's Who's Who and one of her favorite eateries. He asked her there to appeal to her vanity. She always wanted to be seen in public with him and would not want to do or say anything that would get her banned from getting into that or any other popular establishment.

"Sure. I'll see you then."

"Um, can Brely join us? It's been a minute since I've seen her."

"Your woman ain't gonna be there is she? Cause if she is, then the answer is hell fucking naw."

"It will be just us."

"Yes. Our family. No outsiders."

"Great. See you then."

The restaurant, which was typically crowded from the time they opened until they closed, was surprisingly empty. That didn't stop Breeze from asking the Maître d', for a private table. The last thing he needed was reporters from A-Tea-L Live filming any more of his private moments. He had just sat when a hostess escorted Larissa and their daughter to his table.

"You both look beautiful." He stood kissed her on the cheek and picked up his daughter.

"Of course, we do," she said.

"Daddy," the little girl said.

"Hey, Princess. Shall we sit?"

Larissa rolled her eyes and sat across from him, placing Brely in the middle of the booth. He opened his mouth, but she put her hand up to stop him.

"Before you say shit, lemme get this off my chest. It's fucked up that you didn't think you could be honest with me about having a woman. That shit hurt like hell seeing you on your knee, asking another bih- I mean, chick to marry you. All my homegirls were at my house watching it and they clowned the shit outta me. Thanks for nothing."

"Regardless of what has happened between us, Larissa, you know I would never do anything to hurt you intentionally. But lately, I can't talk to you because you fly off the handle. You and I will forever be connected because of Bre. She is the best thing that has ever happened in my life and I have you to thank for that. But I am in love with Caresse, and I chose her to be my wife."

"Mch," she smacked. "Who names their baby after a bar of soap?"

"Don't start. Just know that she is a great woman and that no one will ever come between me and my baby."

"Yeah, alright."

They took a break from talking to enjoy lunch. To Breeze's delight, things were going quite well. Larissa did not cause a scene at any time and she was agreeable to suggestions he made regarding co-parenting.

"I heard you were back in the studio. How's that going?" He asked.

"Pretty good. I didn't realize how much I missed it until I was back in there. Working with Con has been interesting."

"Right on. I'm happy for you. You have a beautiful voice. Don't let it go to waste."

"Definitely not." Her phone vibrated and moved on the table. "Sorry."

She picked up the phone and read the text message, smiling as if nothing was wrong.

Larissa, it's Miles from Atlanta Bank and Commerce. ABC has recovered the 2019 Maserati Levante. To redeem your vehicle, you must pay the past due balance on the loan plus any repossession, storage, and attorney fees, if applicable. Please remit payment of $9,853.85 by cash, *cashier's check, or certified funds only. No checks or credit cards will be accepted. A letter explaining your rights of redemption will be mailed within five days.*

"Everything alright?"

"Oh, yeah. It's good. Fine. It's the mechanic saying that the part they needed is on backorder. I'm going to find me a nice, cheap American made car and leave all those foreign ones alone."

"That's smart."

"Potty, Mommy."

Perfect timing. She felt like she was suffocating and needed to come up for air. She and Brely walked to the restroom. Once inside, she sat her daughter on the toilet, then called Tika immediately to find out how the repo man was able to get the car out of her garage.

"Hoe, what the fuck? I just got a message that my car was repo'd. How is that possible?"

"Baby Boy saw it in my garage and wanted to take it for a spin around the block."

"You let that nigga drive my car? Oh my, gosh," she slapped her forehead. "I can't believe this."

"It ain't shit. Just pay the bill and get it back."

"I ain't got ten stacks, bitch. If I, did it wouldn't have been in your garage. Fuck!"

"My bad. I'll call you later. I gotta go pick him up because he was in Douglasville when they took the car and now, he's stranded."

"I thought you said he was only going around the corner. That's forty-minutes from your house."

"Yeah. We'll talk later, chica. Bye."

"Mommy I'm done."

Larissa was livid as she helped her daughter fix her clothes.

"A bitch can't win for losing."

She shook her head in disgust. The car was a status symbol for her. It got her into more clubs than her name ever could. When she pulled up in front of any establishment, people tripped over themselves to help her. That car made her somebody. Now that her baby's daddy was moving on, she really didn't have shit.

Shrugging, she said, "Oh, well. We ain't got shit else to live for, Bre."

The little girl took her thumb out her mouth. "Huh, Mommy?"

"You remember how Mommy asks you to keep a secret?"

Brely nods.

"Well, soon, you won't have to keep them anymore. It'll all be over. Let's go."

Breeze stood as they approached the table.

"I was beginning to think I was going to have to come in after you guys. What took so long?"

"Tika called. She's having a crisis with Baby Boy."

"She's still messing with that clown?" Breeze knew all about Baby Boy. Afterall, they were label mates. But the rapper was bad news. Rumors circulated about his active involvement with gangs and drugs, and he was on the verge of losing his contract with Man of Steele. "Oh, well. Some of us learn the hard way."

"That, or we don't learn at all," she said sadly.

He heard something in her voice but could not pinpoint what it was. Was it regret? Disappointment? He wasn't sure.

"Did you take an Uber here? I can give you two a ride home."

"Thank you, but no. It's a beautiful day. Me and Bre are going to walk to the Children's Museum. It's just across the bridge."

"Are you sure? I don't mind."

"I said no," she snapped.

A few heads turned to face them. Breeze turned his head and side-eyed her.

"Where did that come? I thought we were moving in another direction."

"We were. But me and Bre are going someplace you're not."

She started walking toward the exit.

"Where's that?" He said, walking fast to catch up to her.

"Tell, Daddy good-bye Brely and that you love him."

"Bye-bye, Daddy. Love you."

"I love you too, munchkin. Larissa, wait."

She walked through the door. The waiter caught Breeze by the hand.

"Your bill, Mister Coleman."

"Fuck, man. Just take the damned card. Have them bring my car up, too. Now."

By the time he got his car, Larissa was a block away.

Traffic was thick at Seventeenth Street. Disrespectful drivers who did not want to miss another green light, pulled into the middle of the street, creating gridlock. He could not move.

"Larissa," he called.

She kept walking.

He leaned on his horn.

"Get out the way, dammit."

Traffic began to move slowly.

He turned the corner and was stopped by another red light. The speed from the cars traveling on I-85 North and South, made the overpass tremble.

"Larissa, please. Let's talk."

This time, she stopped and turned toward him. She stood on the sidewalk of the bridge and waved to him.

"Rissa!" He screamed at her when she picked up their baby.

She hoisted the little girl on her hip and climbed onto the concrete wall that was only three and a half-foot tall.

Onlookers parked and got out their cars.

"Stop her," a woman screamed.

Larissa looked down at the oncoming traffic. An eighteen-wheeler barreled down the highway.

Breeze shifted the gear into park. His legs felt like led as he jumped from his car and ran toward her and his baby.

The truck got closer.

Breeze was within a few feet.

A police cruiser had pulled up.

"Daddy," Brely yelled, reaching out for her father.

His fingers touched hers just as she went over the edge. The tires of the diesel screeched as the driver attempted to break. Brely hit the windshield like a bug at high velocity and blood spattered everywhere. The bed of the truck jack-knifed, hitting the car next to hit. Larissa's body landed on the pavement but was run over by a car.

Screams pierced the air. The loudest one, belonging to Breeze.

"Nooooo!" He cried in anguish. Hot tears ran down his face.

Soft hands touched his body but soon became forceful.

"Baby. Baby, wake up. You're having a bad dream."

Breeze's eyes flew open, and his head moved side to side frantically. His heartbeat loudly in his chest. Panting, he reached out to Caresse and felt her arms.

"It's okay, honey. I'm right here. It was just a bad dream."

Slowly he sat up.

"That was more than a bad dream. It was a prophetic nightmare."

"What was it about?"

"Larissa. She's going to kill Brely."

CHAPTER 14

Hide and Seek

NO MATTER WHERE HE searched for Aisha, Malik hit a dead end. It was like she had vanished into thin air.

Eloise stood in the threshold of her dining room and watched tears stream down her son's face. There was light in her eyes from the joy she felt inside from having got rid of that trailer park trash her son dated. Although she did not like to see her son hurting, she figured that it was only temporary. He would get over the raggedy trollop, sooner or later. With her help, it would be much sooner. She straightened her dress and turned her smile upside down, so she could pretend to care about what her son was going through.

"What's going on, Son?"

Malik looked and wiped his eyes. "Mom, it's not looking good. I can't find her anywhere."

"How long has it been now? Three…four months since she has been gone? I thought you would be over her by now."

"Over her? How can I get over the only one I have ever loved? Don't do that. Not now, Mama. I'm not in the mood."

"Cheer up, baby. It's going to be okay," she said, rubbing his back.

He shook his head. "I just don't get it, Mom. What would make her leave me? We were about to move in together. Had been talking marriage and the whole nine. Things were going so well with us."

"Apparently not as well as you thought. Women are complex creatures, and we are known for holding things inside. Perhaps, she was becoming overwhelmed with being the girlfriend of such a high-profile man. I mean, it's not like she has ever been on your level before and since you've elevated your status, well, she had been acting strangely before she left."

"Aisha did not care about any of that stuff, and she is on my level. Yeah, she may have been acting differently but that's probably because I hadn't been able to spend as much time with her as I once did."

"You can make all the excuses in the world for that girl, Malik, but the bottom line is this. If she really cared about you as much as you claimed she did, then not hell or high water would have made her leave."

It was a bitter pill to swallow, but Malik knew she was right. If Aisha cared about him, she would have come to him to talk over whatever problem she had. But no, instead she chose to leave him alone, with no explanation. Just a bullshit ass note. She was the one person he thought would always be here. He thought wrong.

"I've got to figure out what's going on. I'm going to call Watson McCoy, a private investigator and have him find her. I heard he can locate a needle in a haystack."

Alarmed, Eloise motioned for him to stop.

"No!" She blurted out.

He looked at her quizzically.

"Um, I uh. Son, you have so much on your plate right now and your focus should be on your career. I'll tell you what, I don't know the Watson man, but I have a friend who's a private investigator. Let me get with him and have him work on finding her, okay? That man can find anything and anyone."

"Really, Mom?" He said, perking up. "You would do that for me?"

"Of course, I would. I want you to be happy."

He stood and bear hugged his mother and kissed her cheek.

"You're the best. I have to run. The team has a meeting in an hour. If I'm late, I'll get fined."

She followed her son out the kitchen and watched him leave. Shaking her head, she returned to the kitchen where she began to prepare dinner.

"That boy must think I'm a special kind of stupid if he thinks I'm going to invite trouble back into this household. Thank God he doesn't know about the baby. The heifer probably got knocked-up by someone else and then planned to pass that bastard off as my son's. Hmph, not today, Satan. Not today."

By getting rid of Aisha, Eloise had effectively 'taken out the garbage' so to speak. That girl was nothing more than trailer park rubbish, looking for a free ride. How dare she try to trap her son. To make sure that the gold-digging, baby-trapping, poverty-stricken tart did not try to contact her son, she would indeed hire a detective to find and keep tabs on her. But she would never tell, Malik. He was better off without her. Men like her son needed a woman of substance like Selena, on his arms. Yes, she would give it a few weeks, pretend to look for the skank and then put Malik and Selena together, once and for all.

$$$

Aisha and her father unloaded the last of the boxes from his truck. Thankfully, her new apartment in South Georgia was on the ground level. The place was quaint, but cute and very affordable. With a part-time job, she would be able to handle the rent, utilities, and still afford to attend the University of West Georgia. Living without Malik was not going to be easy, especially with half of him growing inside her, but she had to do what was best for her family. Even if it meant sacrificing her own happiness.

Inside, her father looked around her new place.

"Phewww," he whistled. "This is a really nice place, baby girl. Are you sure you're going to be okay all the way down here?"

"I'll be fine, Dad. Plus, it's better than being in Wacko, Texas with Aunt Wanda."

"It's Waco."

"You say tomato, I say tomato." She shrugged. "Semantics, Daddy."

Her father looked away, then turned to face her again.

"Having you in Texas was torture for me. I'm so used to seeing you every day."

"Awe, Dad. It's okay. You are only an hour away by car and even closer with a phone. Don't worry about me."

"That's easier said than done. I miss you."

She stepped near her father and hugged him tightly.

"Same here. Um, Dad? We have never talked about this but why didn't you tell me what was going on?"

He sat on the brown, green and red plaid sofa that came with the semi-furnished apartment and exhaled.

"I didn't find out about Cliff stealing until the audit. I was just as surprised as you were."

She shook her head. "I cannot believe that your son would put you in such a precarious situation. Is he on drugs?"

"Other than weed?" He shrugged. "Don't know."

"That's really jacked up, Dad. Has he said anything to you? Apologized even?"

Her father wiped tiny beads of perspiration from his forehead.

"Not at first. I think he was too embarrassed. But now he won't stop saying how sorry he is."

"Hmph, he sure is sorry. I knew something was going on between the two of you because things were so tense around the house."

"Yeah. They were very bad at first, however, you know how me, and your mom are always telling you kids to forgive one another, so I had to take my own advice."

"That's good. Cliff is a knucklehead, but I don't think he meant to harm you with his scheme. He probably didn't think he would ever get caught."

"No, he didn't think he would get caught but he claims that that was going to be the last time he did it. Frank was getting too nervous."

She shook her head.

"What are the odds that Misses Jeffries was the lead accountant over that job?"

"God has a way of bringing things to light and He will use anything and anyone to do it."

"And she couldn't wait to use this as ammunition against me. Anything to get me away from her precious son."

Aisha rolled her eyes and stomped to the kitchen and began unpacking the few dishes she had bought, slamming the drawers and cabinet doors.

"The truth will come out, Baby Girl and when it does, she may regret what she did."

"You're right, Dad. God don't like ugly and He ain't too fond of pretty either."

"Amen. That audit cast such an ugly light on our department. Everyone is walking around on pins and needles now that Frank and your brother are gone."

"Poor Frank. I know his wife is angry at him for losing his job. I pray that she forgives him."

"Speaking of forgiveness," he paused. "You know that you are going to have to forgive Eloise and Malik, too."

"Malik? I'm sure he had nothing to do with this. It's her evil ass who orchestrated this."

"Watch your mouth and yes, you will need to forgive them both. Her, for creating such an evil plan to keep you and Malik apart and especially for paying to have her grandchild killed."

"But why him?"

"Because he didn't fight for you, baby."

Tears welled in her eyes. Her father walked to the kitchen and stopped in front of her.

"I know that's his mother, but he should have put her in her place long ago. She should have never been able to talk to you or treat you the way she has over the past few years. I used to see your tears, Baby Girl. None of y'all have ever been good at masking your emotions."

She stepped into her father's arms and he wrapped them around her. He gave her the tightest hug that he could.

"It's going to be okay. I promise you that."

Sniff. Sniff.

"I let you and Mommy down. I can't believe I'm pregnant, unmarried and no education to fall back on."

"Stop it. Your mom and I are proud of you and you will finish college. That's why you are here. You are doing what you believe is best for you and my grandbaby. Mark my words, God is going to set things right."

"Thanks, Daddy. I always thought Sandra would be the one to have a baby first. Her or Cliff."

The mocha-colored man with salt and pepper hair laughed.

"Honestly, so did we."

The two continued to talk and unpack until things were manageable for her to finish the rest on her own. Once they were done, they went to grab a bite to eat at a cute diner near her apartment. The aroma coming from inside made both their stomach's growl.

Misses Vi's Place was charming diner that was reminiscent of one she had seen on television. It had the all the retro designs of the sixties, but the technology was current. The jukebox in the corner was Bluetooth compatible and had selections by just about every artist, from Aretha to ZZ Top. Aisha was not sure who the last group was until the waiter said it was a rock band. They had a hit song called La Grange that Misses Vi, the owner loved.

Once they had placed their orders, they played a trivia game on the tablet that sat on the table. Of course, her father won because he was knowledgeable in many subjects.

"Dad, I did not know you were so up on pop culture."

"I wasn't before you kids came along. To keep up with you, I had to know what was hip and happening."

She leaned down and peered over the top of her glasses that she had put on to read the menu.

"Hip and happening? Aye, aye, aye."

The waiter and a pretty woman headed their way with trays, bearing their food.

"Here you are, Suga's. I'm Misses Violet and I would like to personally welcome you first timers to my diner."

"How did you know this was our first time?" Mister Graves said.

"Honey child, La Grange is small. I know everything that goes on in this town."

The waiter and Misses Vi laughed, and Aisha and her dad nodded.

"Just kidding. You all told Tyler," she pointed to their waiter. "And he told me. I just wanted to come out here and introduce myself. You know, give you a personal welcome."

Mister Graves asked Misses Vi to sit and join them. She accepted his invitation and the three of them chatted as if they had known one another forever. Talking to her was easy. Even after Aisha told her that she was pregnant, the woman did not bat an eye. Instead, she offered the young girl her support.

"If you need anything, please do not hesitate to tell Misses Vi."

"I need a job that will allow me to work like this." She rubbed her tiny baby bump. "Can you help me with that?"

"You know, it just so happens that I can. One of my girls is leaving to return to Bethune-Cookman and I need to replace her. Can you come from training next Wednesday?"

"I sure can. Thank you so much."

"Well, I gotta get back to work. It was a pleasure to meet you Mister Graves and Aisha, I am excited to have you work with me."

She got up from the table and returned to the kitchen. Aisha pinched herself on the arm to make she was not dreaming.

"Can you believe that Daddy?"

"Yes, I can. Look at God at work on your behalf. He will never leave us nor forsake us, no matter how we terrible we get. Everything is going to work out for your good."

The first day of work came and went. It did not take her long to get acclimated with the menu and stations. The young lady who would be leaving was also named Iesha, but it was spelled differently. Misses Vi asked Aisha what her middle name was so that she could differentiate between the girls and so they would be able to know who she was talking to.

"My middle name is Michelle."

It did not take long for Misses Vi to go from calling her Michelle to Mimi. Over the next few months, the two women developed a relationship that more closely resembled sisters than boss and employee. Aisha worked at the diner until a week before she gave birth, at which time, Misses Vi and Aisha's mother, Vera Graves, forced her to take maternity leave.

"Mom, I am so glad that you are here with me."

"Baby, there's no place I would rather be. Soon, I am going to meet my handsome, precious grandson and I cannot wait."

Neither could the baby. Within a couple of hours, Aisha, her parents, and Misses Vi rushed to Grady South, where she delivered a five-pound-eight-ounce baby boy. Zion Sincere Graves. While the baby was in the nursery, everyone stood outside the glass, snapping photos of the adorable newborn. They were all so excited, none of them paid attention to the man who eased up next to them. He took pictures of the same child and they did not even realize it. After storing his camera back in its bag, he eased away as quietly as he had come.

Being a mother was a joy and a pain at the same time. Since she was back in school, Aisha found herself having to balance full-time parenthood and school with a part-time, yet demanding job. Thankfully, her mother stayed with her for the first two months of Zion's life and then when she was able, she put him into childcare.

Days turned into weeks and life slowly began to resume to a normal pace for her. One day at work, a handsome, well-dressed man came in to dine. He was obviously close with Misses Vi, as he had managed to monopolize the woman's time, but he was not too busy to try to shoot his shot, with Aisha.

"Had I known beautiful women like you were in La Grange; I would have come home to visit long ago."

She rolled her eyes before responding.

"Hello, I'm Mimi. May I get you something?"

"I'll take you on a platter please."

"Ugh, please stop it with those lame lines. Now, what may I bring you?"

Impressed that she blew him off and didn't try to get with him because of who he was, Quentin tried a different approach.

"I apologize. It was all fun and games. But I would like to get to know you. May I take you out?"

"Thank you, but no. I'm really trying to focus on school and cannot afford the distractions right now."

"I understand that. But I'm not going to give up. I'm opening a car dealership across the street. We break ground next week so I will be in town handling business. Misses Vi knows I eat here every day so get used to seeing this pretty face around."

She could not help but to laugh at him. But he didn't lie. Every day he came to the diner to eat and every day he tried his darndest to persuade her to go on a date with him. And every day, she turned him down. However, they started to talk like old bodies and for once, it felt good for her to have a man around to talk to.

Back in Atlanta, Eloise Jeffries smiled from ear-to-ear. Tonight, her family and the Bowies, were having dinner and then family game night. Since Malik had started dating Selena a couple of months ago, Eloise thought it best to include her family also. Afterall, it was her desire to have the two young people wed so interacting with her family often would make the transition from friends to in-laws much simpler.

MEAL TICKET$

While everyone was in the family room trying to guess what her husband was drawing, Eloise went to her office. She needed to lock up the latest report and pictures of Aisha.

She stared at one of the pictures.

"Hmph, he is an adorable little boy, and he does look a little like Malik," she said to the photograph.

"Who looks like, Malik?" Selena asked.

"Oh, uh, um, nobody," she said, stumbling over the lie.

Sooner than she could stop her, Selena grabbed a few baby pictures. The girl's eyes grew round like saucers.

"Damn, this baby looks just like Malik. I take it Aisha is his mother?"

Busted, Eloise sat down and the two of them had a very telling conversation. Before they returned to the living room, the two of them had formed an alliance. They were now partners in deception and board games were not the only games they planned on playing.

CHAPTER 15

Full Court Press

EVERY DOG HAD HER day and today was Tika's. Not that Kyle though of her as a female dog, but she had been acting like one lately. She continued to make it difficult for him to get the answer to the only question he has asked her since finding out she was pregnant; was Malia his daughter? Whether she liked it or not, soon he would know the truth.

As he dressed for court, a million questions ran through his mind. The most important one being, if the baby girl were not his, how would he feel? He had grown to love the cherub faced baby and even in a short while, could not imagine his life without her. How would his parents react? His father had even began spending more time with her, calling her his little "Pookie Pooh."

His mother believed that the child was his, regardless of the DNA results. She had pulled out all the photo albums of him and his siblings when they were babies and even some of her own. The resemblance between the little girl and the Hudson clan was uncanny. But still, he needed the scientific proof. Eerily, and much to Kyles's chagrin, Malia was the spitting image of his baby sister, Kalia.

Admittedly, Kyle got his just rewards with her and he knew it. Prior to getting played by her, he was the one doing all the playing – on and off the court. He was hard on women and did not always treat them with the respect they deserved. Hell, with so many women willing to do whatever he said just to be seen with him, why should he? They made it too easy for him and guys like him to be the rude, disrespectful, bastards, his sister, Kayla said he was behaving like.

"Baby brother, for all of you fellas who mistreat and disrespect women, Karma is going to bless y'all asses with daughters. Mark my words. One day you're going to sit back and remember this conversation and it's going to fuck you up."

His sister was right. If Malia were his baby, he could only hope and pray that she did not end up with a man like the one he used to be not too long ago. If God loved him like he believed, then maybe his daughter would be spared.

"Sins of the father, indeed," he whispered, adjusting his tie in the mirror.

Despite all the wrong he had done before; he could see that he was changing, and he owed so much of that to Sunrise. She was nothing like Tika, or any other woman he had gone out with for that matter. Ever.

"About time you grew up," his mother said, after she met Sunrise for the first time.

"Hmph, you have grown up, my guy. Good job. And you are looking quite dashing if I do say so myself." He turned to the side, tugged at his lapels, approved his finished look, and left for court.

When he walked inside the courtroom, Judge Lauren Latchet was seated at the bench and talking to someone's attorney. His and Tika's case was set for the ten-thirty docket. He could not wait to get things going either. He had been waiting for this moment for what seemed like a lifetime.

The judge banged her gavel. Kyle noted how beautiful the woman was, despite her furrowed brow and stern look.

"Listen," she said to the litigants before her. "I have the DNA results right here, but what we're not going to do is clown up in here today. My court room is not a circus, Ms. Lucas. You gave Mister Brown, reason to doubt if this child was his when you decided to lie down with two other men during the window of conception. There is so much more to you than what is between your legs. It's time that you focus on getting something between your ears. Are you picking up what I'm putting down?"

The woman nodded. "Yes, yo'wanna."

Oh yeah, KJ thought. *This judge is the truth.*

He stood in the back of the court, scanning to see if Tika or Kayla had arrived. He saw neither. The place was packed for it to be family court. Then again, he did not know what a normal day in this court would be like considering that he had never been before. Because of his schedule and Tika's reluctance to appear before a judge, both their attorneys had handled things from one of their offices.

The judge asked both parties to approach the bench and people began to chat quietly in the courtroom. Kyle was about to take a seat when the door swung open. A tall, buffed up dude walked in and stood next to him. Just then, Kyle's phone vibrated with a text message from Tika.

OMW. Traffic is bad.

Instead of replying via text, he dialed her number. The call went to voice message.

"Tika, I hope your ass is not planning on missing court. I'm already here. Bye."

The big guy next to him nodded his head and rubbed his chin.

"Oh, so you're the bitch ass nigga who 'posed to be Malia's daddy, huh? I been taking care of her since she was born and now you wanna try to step up?"

Angry, but still aware of his surroundings, Kyle spoke softly, yet firm.

"I don't know who the fuck you think you're talking to, but son, I'm not a bitch. Furthermore, I've been taking care of her, too. I'm here to find out if she is really mine."

"Grrr," the big man replied. "She lied to me."

Kyle rolled his eyes and smacked his lips. "Ya' think?"

"You don't understand. I've given Shawty almost one-hundred and fifty stacks for Lee Lee."

Stunned, his mouth flew open. His head did a triple take and brows shot up. Kyle could not believe what he heard.

"One-fifty?"

The big man nodded.

"Damn. That's way more money than I have given her. What the hell you do for a living?"

"Construction," the dude answered.

At the front of the court, the judge banged her gavel, getting everyone's attention.

"Court is in recess."

The people exited the room and stepped into the hallway. Kyle and the huge stranger made their way toward the window at the end of the hall. The man excused himself and went into the men's restroom. Several people who recognized Kyle, came, and asked for autographs. Once the man returned, he formally introduced himself.

"I'm Kyle Hudson," he said. "You can call me, KJ."

"Shit, I would have to be living under a rock not to know who you are. I need to shake your hand and thank you. That three pointer you put up with two seconds left in the game against the Bulls, won me fifty large."

"Glad that I could be of some assistance."

The big man scratched his head.

"Uh yeah, sorry about earlier. A nigga is just frustrated at all that is going on. The name's Dough, by the way." They shook hands. "I don't know if that baby is mine either, but I know one thing, my entire family loves her. Hell, they love all Tika's kids."

"All? What the hell you mean, all?"

Dough laughed. "My bad. All those nieces and nephews who live with her are hers. Bruh, T got six kids."

Shocked was an understatement on how Kyle felt. Pissed off was more like it. He sat down to process what he had just heard.

"Clearly, I don't know her as well as I ought."

"Nah. You don't know the half of it. She and her mom snort powder together. That's why they are always butting heads."

"Hold up. Her holier than-thou, Mama is on drugs and where are all the kids at most of the time? I've only seen them a few times."

"Jennifer, the oldest, lives with her dad. Jules and Janiyah…no they are not twins. They be with their people most of the time. Jaden and Jericho, not twins either, be with their people, and Malia is split between us and our people."

Kyle scratched his head.

"Wow, I had no idea. This is a lot to take in."

"Tell me about it. When she lost custody of Jenny, that's when she began to go down. Dude's child support for that one child, supported Tika, all the kids, her mother, and her sister, Quita and all eight of her kids."

Dough had been knowing Tika since high school and they messed around back then. The two reconnected a few years ago after she lost custody of her first daughter. She was devastated by the loss and that's when she began doing drugs. It was Dough who helped her get off drugs and get her act together again. Kyle also learned that the Buckhead townhome she lived in, was owned by Dough and she did not pay any rent.

"Well, if she's living rent-free, where is all the money going?" Kyle asked, stupidly.

Shaking his head, Dough said, "you do realize those Birkin bags can cost like fifteen stacks each, right? Ol' girl has eight. You do the math."

At first Kyle was cool when the other man began divulging the secrets, but it seemed that the more Dough spoke, the angrier he got.

"I do not believe this shit. If Tika is only twenty-seven and has six kids, then when did she start having them? Fifteen or sixteen?" Kyle's voice shook nervously. He dreaded the answer.

"Actually, she was fourteen when she had, Jennifer and her birthday is coming up. She's about to turn thirteen. Drago, her dad, is going to throw her a bash."

"The rapper?"

"None other. Listen, word on the street is that Shawty is gunning for you to be the baby daddy simply because your money is longer and stronger." Dough shrugged. "I'on know if the baby is mine or not but I'm going to get a DNA test either way and me and my attorney are using our own lab. Tika knows people who'll doctor things up and we ain't using shit she recommends. I suggest you do the same."

"Are you saying she will tamper with the DNA results?"

"If things don't go her way, hell yeah. Don't take no chances."

The elevator dinged and the doors opened. A tall, well-dressed man with salt and pepper hair stepped off, followed by Kayla and a few other people. Dough got up and walked toward the man. Kyle looked on in interest as the two men spoke. Whatever they were saying had to be about him because they both looked in his direction.

"Dang, that man must have some serious loot to hire Grayson Ryner," Kayla said, stepping next to her brother, motioning her head toward Dough.

"Who?"

"The man in the tailor-made Armani suit is Grayson Tyson – attorney to the rich and famous. He's like all of O.J. Simpson's dream legal team, Ben Crump, Perry Mason, and Matlock all rolled up into one. Dude must have a heavy wallet to retain him."

"Oh. His name is Dough and get this, he is here for the paternity case with Tika, too."

"I knew someone else was going to be here, but I don't think that's the name in my notes." Kayla sat down and opened her briefcase to check her files.

"Sis, check this out."

Kyle sat next to his sister and quickly ran down everything that Dough told him moments ago.

"It's not surprising that she was playing you both. My investigator discovered that she has a daughter with Drago, and she tried the same thing with him. Apparently, this is her come up. All her kids are by men of means."

"Have a baby by me baby, be a millionaire," he chanted.

"Exactly."

The bailiff stepped into the hallway and announced that the judge would be returning in ten minutes.

Grayson Ryner and Dough walked in their direction.

"Ms. Hudson," he began, extending his hand to her. "Gray Ryner. It's a pleasure to finally meet you in person."

"It's an honor, Sir. I'm a huge fan of your legalese."

"I feel the same about you. The way you finessed the win in the Brooks v. Reid Holdings case was very impressive. I could use a hot shot like you on my team." He handed her a business card. "Let's meet for lunch after this is all over and we can discuss it."

"Sounds like a plan. Until then, I think we should work together on this one."

"I agree. That's why we came over to speak with you. It seems both our clients have made considerable investments in this little girl, emotionally and financially."

"Yeah, and Malia could either of our daughter," Kyle said.

"Or neither," Kayla added. "My investigator identified a third party who has also been told he was the father. He's in Alabama."

"There's a fourth man in New York. A hockey player," said Grayson.

"Damn. So, basically ol' girl is going from state to state, nigga to nigga," Dough said angrily.

Grayson cleared his throat, forcefully and peered at his client. Dough hung his head and corrected himself.

"My bad. Man-to-man, running this scheme."

"Yes. Pardon my rudeness, Ms. Hudson. This is my client and my son, Dolan Ryner. Your client needs no introduction. K.J., it is a pleasure to formally make your acquaintance. You are as impressive on the court, as your sister is in the court. Your parents must be quite proud of you both."

Kyle shook hands with the attorney.

"Dough and I got acquainted before you two arrived. The things he told me about Tika made my head spin."

"I imagine so. Martika has not always been troubled. She came from an affluent family but when her father died suddenly, it left the family in financial peril and sent her into a downward spiral."

"Martika?" Kyle slapped his forehead. "Man, come on."

Frustrated, he walked away from the group.

"Please, excuse me. We'll see you all inside."

Kayla saw the shimmer of tears in her brother's eyes before one spilled over. She placed her hand on his shoulder and gave it a gentle squeeze.

"Hey, Bro. You okay?"

He shook his head. "Nah, Kay. I'm not. All my life I felt like I had all this game, on and off the court. I've been hoeing around, fucking women, whose names or faces I can't even remember now. It's by the grace of God that I don't have AIDS or HIV. I call myself being a player and now look at me. Played by someone who I never took the time to get to know."

"Don't beat yourself up. Us women can be cunning and crafty. Tika is just good at both."

"Yeah, maybe. Here I am thinking that I really knew this girl but as Dough was telling me shit, I realized that the only things I know about her are things she told me. Kayla, I never asked her anything about herself. All I cared about was what she could do for me."

"And all she cared about was all you could do for her. Both of you were operating with ulterior motives and your relationship was only superficial."

The familiar ding of the elevator sounded in the distance. Clip. Clop. Clip. Clop. The conversations around Kyle and Kayla stopped. All the men's heads turn to watch the beautiful woman who walked with intent, toward her baby's daddy.

"Hello K.J."

And this is how she got him each time. Every nerve in his body reacted to the sultry way she said his name. He looked down at the bulge in his pants. It never failed.

He turned slowly to face her.

"Glad you finally made it, Tika."

Kayla grabbed her brother by the elbow.

"Come on, let's go inside."

No sooner had they taken their seats, than the judge walked in.

"All rise," the bailiff said.

The judge rifled through some documents that were placed in front of her, before calling her next case.

"Lord, this is going to be a mess. Jeremy, call the next case."

The burly bailiff, called Kyle and Tika's case next. The judge was right. This was going to be a mess. Both Kayla and Mister Ryner presented facts to the judge, who read them over carefully. She questioned Kyle, Dough and the two other men, allowing them all the opportunity to express their doubts of being the baby's father.

"Mister Benjamin," the judge said to Tika's attorney. "Will you and your client please stand. It seems that you have been a very busy young lady, Ms. Adams. We have two potential fathers' here in court with us today and two via Zoom. That's three people too many."

The courtroom was abuzz with chatter and the judge banged her gavel to quiet them. If Kyle thought that the judge read the other young lady earlier, she really laid into Tika.

"Ms. Adams, it is evident that your father was not present while you were growing up. You have been looking for love in the faces of men who probably promised you the world but gave you a globe instead. The mere fact that you have six children at twenty-seven speaks volumes. Now, I'm not trying to judge you but honey child, you need to find another hobby. And don't get me started on you Mister Ryner. This is the third time you have been before me and frankly, I'm sick of it. If you don't invest some of that money you have in a condom, I am going to issue a court order for you to have a vasectomy."

"Can she do that, Pops?" He whispered to his father who simply shrugged.

Kyle snickered, but what did he do that for.

"Mister Hudson, just because you have not been before me doesn't mean much. Word of your escapades precedes you and you should know better. Y'all young people out here spreading your seed around like it's a game."

Censured, everyone involved in the Hudson, Jones, Norris, and Ryner versus Adams case, all hung their heads.

"During these proceedings, we have heard so much about each of you but not enough about Malia, and she is the only person who matters right now."

"Your Honor," Kayla began. "You are correct. We all have one goal here and that is to find out who the father of this beautiful little girl is. It is our hopes that you will order a DNA test for each of these gentlemen. Also, Mister Ryner and I have it on good authority that Ms. Adams has access to a few laboratories and may tamper with the test results to shift them in her favor. We ask that the court orders immediate testing, performed under heavy scrutiny, in an independent or court appointed lab."

Judge Latchet rolled her eyes and shook her head.

"It is evident that we need testing. Malia is almost nine months old. Although she is at an age where she won't remember any of this, it is imperative that we get the answers we need, immediately. We will adjourn for testing and I have notified the lab that I need a forty-eight-hour turnaround on the results. Attorney's, I need you all to be proactive with your clients and work on a custody agreement that is amicable for both parties. I want this resolved once and for all. Got it?"

All the attorney's and their clients nodded.

"Good. Court is adjourned until Thursday at one o'clock."

The judge banged her gavel, and each party was given instructions on where to go for their DNA tests. Dough was not playing about his results and hired an off-duty cop to monitor everything that went down with his test. Kyle also took extra precautions. He did not want to leave anything to chance.

"I know Tika had been trying to get pregnant by me purposely the last few times we messed around but thanks to you Sis, I avoided the trap. These next forty-eight hours are going to seem like the longest of my life."

"Probably so. We need to put a custody plan in place. What would you like to do if she is your baby?"

"If she is, I want full custody. I don't want to give that girl my money so she can blow it on shit, trying to keep up with the Joneses."

"Okay. We may have a fight on our hands, just so you know. I can't see her giving up her meal ticket that easily."

"Neither can I, but God will make a way. If Malia is my daughter, I want her raised right, how we were. I have a new woman now and I'm a different man. My child deserves the best and I'm not talking about material things either."

Kayla gave her brother a high-five.

"Alright then. Let's get it."

It took everything in Kyle's power from keeping him from going crazy. Had it not been for Sunrise, he would have lost it for sure.

"Calm down, babe," she told him, lying in his arms the night before court. "No matter what the results say, I am here for you. We can get through this together. I love Malia. She is a sweetie pie, and I will do all I can to help you with her."

He kissed her forehead. "I don't know what I did to deserve you, but I am so blessed that you are here with me."

"And don't you forget it either."

The next day, both Kyle and Sunrise prepared for court. This was an important day in her man's life, and she was going to be by his side. Together, they walked hand in hand into the courtroom and sat next to his sister until their case was called.

Judge Latchet's bailiff finally called their case. He took the remote from the table and clicked on the television Today, there was no one allowed inside the courtroom, except the parties involved. Kyle told the judge that Sunrise was his fiancé because that is the only way she could stay. He noted the look of sadness in Tika's eyes when he announced that to the judge. Although theirs was a toxic relationship and she had done much in the past to hurt him, he did not want to hurt her.

"I'm ready for the results. Jeremy, envelope please. These results were prepared by the DNA Diagnostic Center of America and they read as follows. In the case of Hudson, Jones, Norris, and Ryner versus Adams, as it pertains to Malia Adams. It has been determined by this court, Mister Hudson, you are the father."

Tika reached into her bag and pulled out a pair of dollar sign shades and slid them on her face. With a grin as big as Texas, she walked over to Kyle and said, "Cut the check, boo."

Now that he had his answer, Kyle was assured of one thing. Malia deserved the best mother he could possibly give her and Tika was not it.

CHAPTER 16

Judgement Day

LIFE'S A BITCH, and so is having a gold-digging, coke snorting, materialistic, wanna-be superstar for a baby's mother. And yet, that was Breeze's reality. As he sat on one side of the courtroom, all he could do was stare at the woman he once loved. She was even prettier than she was when they first met. Her looks had never been a problem. It was her attitude and drug use that ended their relationship and ultimately killed her career. If she were not so easily influenced by the wrong people, they would probably still be together, but her mother and friends stayed in her ear with negativity. He turned around in his seat and looked at Caresse.

Now she was a woman worth holding on to. From the moment that they met she had been down for him and showed him repeatedly where he stood with her. She was not impressed with anything that he had or what he could do for her. All she wanted from him was his love, respect, and trust. He gave her that. And in a few months, he was going to give her something more…his last name.

Judge Latchet sat on her bench reviewing documents that each attorney had submitted to the court. Breeze prayed that the judge would provide him with more visitation, especially now that he was engaged. Hopefully, that would show her that he was settled in his personal life, despite his public persona.

"Mister Drew and Miss MacIntosh, can you please explain all these visits to the emergency room for Brely?"

The attorney shuffled through pages on the table before him, trying to find the documents that the judge was looking at.

"Bailiff, hand this to Mister Drew so he can see what I am talking about."

Once he had the paper, he quickly scanned it and then turned to face Larissa.

"What's this all about?" He whispered to her.

"Shit, my baby gets sick. Don't everybody's kids? She don't got no regular doctor."

"Why not? Isn't Mister Coleman paying for her health insurance. You know what?" His brows furrowed and he shook his head. "Let me handle this. Your Honor. This is something that I should have received long ago from the plaintiff to ensure its validity."

"Mister Drew, the plaintiff had nothing to do with my office obtaining these documents. They came across my desk through referral from Child Protective Services. It seems that the doctors were concerned by the number of hospital visits that your client's daughter had."

Grayson Tyson, Breeze's lawyer, leaned closer to his client, smiled, and whispered, "did you have anything to do with this?"

"No, but I think I know who does."

Breeze turned and looked at his fiancé. Grayson nodded.

"She is definitely a woman worth having on your team. Don't screw that up."

He chuckled. "Trust me. I won't."

The judge drummed her fingers. "I'm waiting, Mister Drew."

"Your Honor, may we take a brief recess? I need to confer with my client?"

"Courts in recess for ten minutes." The judge banged her gavel and left the bench.

"Let's go," the attorney said angrily.

Like a lost puppy, Larissa followed her lawyer out the courtroom. He found an empty conference room down the hall and locked the door behind them once they were inside.

"Dammit, Larissa. You told me that there wouldn't be any surprises. Why in the hell has your daughter been to the emergency room over sixty times in a year?"

Larissa walked over to him and rubbed his crotch through his pants.

"Awe, Phillip, baby. You know Brely has asthma. I don't play around with that shit. Anytime I hear her breathing funny, I'm heading straight to the hospital."

The lawyer moaned and threw his head back.

"That feels good," he whispered.

"And I know how to make it feel even better."

Nimble fingers loosened his belt and unfastened his belt. Dropping to her knees, Larissa made quick work of freeing his member from the constraints of the silk boxers he wore, taking the engorged head into her hot mouth.

"Ah, yes," he moaned appreciatively as she began wetting it with her tongue and sucking gently. He needed this. And he missed this.

Phillip Drew had been fucking Larissa since the day she walked into his office four years ago, needing representation for a shoplifting case she had caught. It was a hot Georgia day, and she came in bearing it all. It just so happened that his secretary had called off sick that day and he was in the office alone. As she sat across from him, he could not help but admire the way her ample 36DD breasts rose and fell when she sighed deeply after telling him her story.

"You like what you see?" She had asked him. All he could do was nod. To his surprise, she got up, locked his door, and did a striptease dance for him right then and there. By the time she sat on his lap, her pussy was drenched, and his dick was rock hard. She rode him like a stallion that day. It was the beginning of a beautiful relationship.

Nobody sucked dick like her. His wife didn't even come close. So, it was in these moments that he reveled in having a client who had no gag reflex.

He pumped his hips back and forth, gently holding her head so that he could control his pleasure.

"Mmm," she moaned between slurps. "Come in my mouth, babe."

Her jaws clenched tightly around his shaft as she took more of him into her mouth. Soon, her nose was touching his stomach and only a bulge at the base of her throat could be seen.

"Ah," he grunted as the pressure of cum caused his testicles to tighten. With release only moments away, he pumped harder and faster.

"Here. It. Comes." His speech was staggered, and his voice shook.

Larissa leaned back on her haunches, careful not to let him slip out of her, tilted her head back, and swallowed the hot cream, allowing it to slide down her throat.

He helped her to her feet and fixed his clothes. In a flash, he was back to his professional self. He placed his briefcase on the table and began going over the papers the judge handed him.

"You must think I'm stupid. None of these records say that you took her in for asthma, Larissa. Headaches, dizziness, nausea, and vomiting. But no asthma. What's going on?"

"Hell, if I know," she shrugged. "Why do you think I go to the emergency room to find out? If I had the answers, Phillip, I would give them to you. But I don't."

He slammed his briefcase shut. "I hope you're telling me the truth about this, because having a CPS investigator involved in your custody hearing is as bad as it gets. Things may not bode well with you if they keep finding things like this and you cannot provide a good answer for their questions."

"Have I ever lied to you, Philly? Wasn't I honest when I told you that Brely could be yours or Breeze's baby?"

He nodded.

"What you and I have is different...special. Although we mutually agreed to abort the two babies you put in me, you are still my baby daddy, boo."

She wrapped her arms around his neck and licked his lips with her tongue before plunging it into his mouth. Fire coursed through his loins yet again and his dick sprang to life.

"Dammit, now look what you have done," he said, looking down at the torpedo in his pants.

"I got you."

Using no further words, she allowed her actions to speak. She hiked up her skirt, revealing her panty-less, round ass, and leaned over the table. The attorney merely unzipped his pants and pulled his dick through the slit in his boxers before ramming it into her ass.

"Oh," she whined. Having his dick in her ass didn't hurt that bad but because she wasn't lubed, it was not exactly comfortable either. So that she would not be sore, she fingered her pussy, taking the juices from it, and rubbing it on his dick as it came out.

"Yes. I like that," he nodded. In one quick motion he removed himself from one hole and entered the next. She rubbed her clit until a tingling sensation began to form in her toes and travel up her thigh. For the next couple of minutes, he alternated between her pussy and ass, finally settling in her ass. He released another hot load inside her while her own juices ran down her inner thigh.

Their heavy breathing was the only noise in the room. He handed her a wipe from his briefcase so she could clean up.

Zzzppp. He fixed his pants and adjusted his tie and was ready to return to court.

"I hope that helped you feel better," she said.

"It did. Thank you."

He walked to the door and placed his hand on the knob.

"Grayson Tyson is one of the world's most brilliant legal minds and he will uncover any hidden deception. I hope you're keeping it one hundred with me."

"Trust me, Boo. I am."

"Let's hope so. If you lose custody of your daughter, all that child support money you've been living high off the hog with is gone. And when the money is gone, so am I. Because unlike you, I don't fuck for free."

By the time what he had just said to her registered, he was out the door. Tears formed in her eyes but did not fall. It was evident that the only man who genuinely cared about her and did not want her money was the same man she was taking to court.

"Oh, well. Shit happens." She shrugged nonchalantly and left the room.

It was mayhem in the hallway after fans and reporters from A-Tea-L Live found out that Breeze was in the building.

"Why didn't we do this in the judge's chambers like we normally do?" Breeze asked his attorney.

"Your daughter's mother declined the closed conference. I think she wanted this media circus for attention."

Just then, someone called Larissa's name and she turned around to pose for the camera. Grayson rolled his eyes. "Don't worry. I'll keep your baby out the limelight."

"Thank you."

Judge Latchet resumed the court proceedings. When Larissa spoke, the judge cocked her head to one side and squinted her eyes, like she was struggling to understand what the young woman was saying. The look she had on her face when Larissa tried to lie about the frequent hospital trips was priceless.

"Miss MacIntosh. Clearly you do not understand that judges are lawyers as well. I have been on this bench long enough to tell when someone is not telling me the truth. Mister Drew, I suggest you advise your client to start telling the truth, the whole truth, and nothing but the truth, so help her God, before I have her locked up for perjury next time. Until then, I am granting Mister Coleman's petition for joint custody. Because of the new child support law this is in effect, Mister Drew, your client must gather all the receipts and documents showing how the payments were spent. This matter will be set to the August Docket so that the child support order can be reviewed fully. Today however, monthly payments will be set to $2000, effective immediately."

Larissa jumped to her feet and yelled. "Two-grand? What the hell am I supposed to do with that? That's not even enough to cover my rent."

"Well then young lady, I suggest you find a cheaper place to live," the judge said. She banged her gavel, signifying the end of the court session.

"Fuck!" Larissa snapped. "This is not what I need at all."

"This is only temporary, but if you keep up with these shenanigans, the judge will make it permanent."

The media and fans were still in the hallway, hoping to catch a glimpse of Breeze.

"Larissa, I have an engagement next weekend. Do you mind if I get Brely this weekend instead?

"I sure the fuck do mind. If you can't see her on your appointed days, then I guess you just won't be seeing her." And with that, she walked off. The exchange was caught on tape, but Larissa did not care.

She took the stairs to the parking garage, got into her car, and left. Once she got home, there was more drama waiting for her.

"Bitch," Laquanda began. "Did you smoke up my weed?"

"It was only one blunt left, Mama. Damn. I'll buy you some more."

"I'm sick and damned tired of you going into my shit."

"Your shit? Your shit? Woman this is my motherfuckin house and every got damned thang that's in here belongs to me. Please don't ever forget that. And if you have a problem with it, you can take your shit and your son and get the fuck out."

Like a bull, all Laquanda saw was red when she charged her daughter. A right hook caught Larissa off guard, knocking her off balance. She stumbled and tried to lunge at her mother but Laquanda was moving with the agility of a trained boxer. A one-two punch put her on her ass. Her mother looked down at her, breathing heavy.

"Check this out, little bitch. The next time you decide to battle me, come with your 'A' game. Dirty, hoe."

Ptui. Laquanda spat on her daughter as she stepped over her.

"Fine, Mama. Whatever. See if I give you any more money."

Jarell and Brely sat on the steps watching the entire exchange between mother and daughter. They had learned the hard way not to intervene when the two women went at it. Unfortunately for Jarell, his sister meant what she said about

191

not giving her mother any more money and his cell phone got cut off, which meant, he could not call Breeze when he or Brely needed anything. They would be in trouble.

It had been over two weeks since they went to court and just as long since Breeze had seen his daughter. He and Caresse lay in bed, talking.

"This shit is burning me up. I can't even call Jarell because his phone is off."

Caresse rolled over to the nightstand and handed Breeze a number.

"Put this number in your contacts."

He looked at the paper.

"Whose number is this?"

"Jarell's. I had my friend, who's a social worker, go visit him. When she saw him, she gave him the phone for me. He knows to keep quiet about it."

Breeze shook his head.

"I'm so tired of all these damned secrets. But if it weren't for him, I would never see my daughter. Thank you so much, baby. You keep proving to me time and again that you are down for me. That's why I am never going to let you go."

"You'd better not."

"Oh, I'm not. Believe that. As a matter of fact, we're going to go half on our own baby, starting right now."

CHAPTER 17

Rules of Engagement

A **PAIR OF PERKY** 36DD breasts, peaked from under the white silk sheet, giving Malik an instant hard-on. He rolled over and placed his hot mouth over a nipple and began to suck it gently. His left hand rubbed the other breast before slowly moving south. The beautiful woman lying next to him stirred in her sleep, parting her legs slightly, allowing his fingers enough room to find their destination. Moist heat covered them as he slid one, then two fingers inside.

"Mmm, good morning," she purred, reveling in the early morning foreplay.

He swirled his tongue around her nipple before mumbling, "good morning," and quickly returned to his pleasurable task. Wanting more from him, the woman pushed on his shoulders, attempting to get him to replace his fingers with his mouth but he didn't budge. She wanted to feel his wet tongue deep inside her pussy, but he wanted something else. His hard dick strained against the cotton material, begging to be released. A deep, throaty moan escaped his lips as he freed his member, positioned himself between her thighs and thrust home.

"Uhn," she gasped as his thick meat filled her up.

Electric pulses began to develop in her toes as his tender and steady strokes hit her spot. She felt tiny beads of sweat on his back as she caressed him. If a couple was going to make love first thing in the morning, this was the way to do it. A smile spread across her face as the beginnings of a powerful orgasm began to form. Just as she was about to experience her first quake, Malik pulled out, flipped her over roughly and lifted her ass in the air with his hands.

"Let me see this pretty pussy," he said, spreading her lips. "Yeah, that's it."

He smacked his lips in appreciation and then entered her once more. They were no longer making love, this time they were straight fucking. Squish, slap, squish, slap, boom, boom were the noises their bodies made as his dick created suction noises with her pussy, his thighs slapped her ass and her head hit the headboard.

"Shit, Malik. Take it easy," Selena said.

Instead of easing up, he fucked her more aggressively until he spilled his seed inside the latex condom he had slid on. Spent, he collapsed on the bed beside his girlfriend who glared at him, none too pleased.

"Why do you always do that?" She asked angrily.

He snickered. "Do what? Make that kitty purr early in the morning?"

"No. You start out making love to me and then you end up fucking me like I'm some bitch on the street."

He wanted to tell her that he doesn't make love to her because he wasn't in love with her, but he knew that would start the next world war. Instead, he chose a diplomatic approach.

"Sometimes I like it slow and gentle. Sometimes I like it fast and rough. Either way, I always make sure you get yours. Lie and say I don't."

"I didn't come this time."

"Okay, my bad. I don't ever want to leave you hanging. Gimme, a minute to rejuvenate."

With a wicked grin she pointed to his dick and said, "Let him rest. Use your other tool," and then spread her legs and lifted her knees.

Malik snapped his head and looked at her like she had grown two heads.

"I already told your ass you can hang that up. I don't do that shit."

Embarrassed and angry, she sat up in the bed and hit him with a pillow.

"So, I can suck your dick and swallow your nut, but you can't return the favor? That's fucked up."

"Here we go with this shit again."

Malik swung his legs to the side of the bed and stood up. He looked down and shook his head. His condom covered dick was standing at attention. If he wanted to, he knew he could take care of his hard-on. All he had to do was tell Selena a few words she wanted to hear, promise he would eat her out one day and slide right back inside her. But he was tired of the same old arguments.

Lately, he found himself giving in to arguments just to shut people up. Because of that, he ended up in a predicament that could forever change his life if he didn't put a stop to it soon. Thinking about it made his dick get soft and he walked to the bathroom. He removed the condom and dropped it in the toilet, leaned down behind the stool, grabbed a small bottle of bleach, and poured some on the floating rubber.

"Did you hear me talking to you? What are you doing?" She looked at him quizzically.

"Killing my sperm. I ain't trying to have any turkey basting babies around this camp. Y'all women are treacherous."

"Y'all women? I'm your woman and not just any woman either, I'm your fiancé. Remember?" She flashed the Emerald-cut Sapphire and pear-shaped diamond halo ring that sat in an eighteen-carat white gold setting, in his face. "Or did you forget?"

"Ain't nobody forgot nothing, Selena, damn." He wished he could forget though. No, what he really wished he could do was turn back the hands of time three weeks so he could redo the day he asked her to marry him. Thinking back, they had been arguing that day, also.

"We need to take our relationship to the next level. My parents didn't raise me to be a mere girlfriend. I'm wife material and you know it."

"I'm not ready to get married and be a husband."

"Hmph, but you don't mind exercising your husbandly duties, is that it?"

The couple argued all the way to the restaurant where they were going to dine with both of their parents. By the time they arrived, everyone had already been seated and Malik and Selena were not speaking.

"What's with the silent treatment, you two? Did you have an argument?" Selena's father asked.

"It's nothing like that, Daddy. Malik and I were just talking about getting married."

"What! My baby is getting married?" Malik's mother yelled. "Thank you, Lord."

"Wait a minute. Young man, did you propose to my daughter before asking me for her hand in marriage?"

"He didn't propo-," Selena started to say.

"Let your father handle this dear," her mother interrupted, patting her hand.

"Son, you know asking the father for permission is the proper thing to do," Malik's dad said.

"Huh?" *Malik was confused and unsure at what was happening all around him.*

"This is perfect though. We are all here. Malik, ask Mister Bowie for Selena's hand in marriage," his dad said sternly.

"Wait, what?"

"And get down on one knee, Son," his mother added.

"Where's the engagement ring?" Someone said.

"We can go ring shopping together tomorrow, Mildred. I know the perfect place. Selena, you and Malik are going to be so happy together," his mother said.

Before he knew it, Malik was on one knee with Selena's hand in his, asking her to marry him. It all happened so fast he was helpless to stop it. Now, he was engaged to a woman he only liked, while still pining away for the one woman he truly loved.

"Earth to Malik." Selena snapped her fingers, bringing him back to the present. "We will be married in five months. After we say, 'I do', you can throw those condoms away. I want us to start working on a family right away."

"I bet you do," he mumbled. Just then his cell phone rang in the other room. "Saved by the bell," he whispered before going to get it. It was his friend and teammate, Quentin.

"Yo, are you still riding to Lagrange with me today?"

"Yep. I was about to hop in the shower now. Pick me up in thirty minutes. I'll be ready."

The call ended and Malik made a hasty retreat to the bathroom, cell phone in hand, locking the door behind him.

"This conversation isn't over," Selena yelled through the door.

"This whole fiasco is about to be over, period," he said softly.

197

An hour later he and his friend were on 85 South, headed toward Quentin's hometown of Lagrange, Georgia, where he was opening a new car dealership. The whole ride there, all Malik heard about was his friend's future wife.

"Where you meet her?"

"She waits tables at this diner across the street from the dealership."

"Your new boo, is a waitress?" Malik guffawed.

"Man, honey is banging. Not only is she fine and stacked right, but she's also funny, sweet and intelligent."

"She can't be too smart bussing tables."

"No disrespect, but you sound just like your snobby mother, dude."

Malik winced at the comparison.

"Baby girl works at Misses Violet's to pay for school. Most chicks we know would take the easy way out and jump on a pole somewhere. As beautiful as she is, she would be the baddest chick in the club, but she chose to do this instead. My baby has a five-year plan."

Malik nodded but remained silent. Quentin's love interest reminded him of Aisha in a way. His ex-girlfriend was gorgeous and a natural-born comedian. She also had a five-year plan and had urged Malik to get one too.

"That's what's up. I dated a chick like that once."

"Oh, yeah? What happened?" Quentin asked.

"I don't know," Malik shrugged. "One day we were really happy, planning our future, and the next day she was gone. Straight disappeared on me. No one in her family would tell me anything either."

"Damn, that's fucked up. Well, all I know is, don't get any ideas about this one when you finally meet her. She's mine."

"Whatever man.

The two friends continued to talk until they arrived at the dealership. The large lot and grand showroom were bustling with activity. Large transportation rigs unloaded cars that were still covered with protective film. For the next hour Malik sat and watched Quentin give orders and handle tasks. By the time his friend finally joined him, Malik was starving.

"Yo, I'm so hungry my stomach is touching my back. Let's hit up that diner you been raving about."

"Bet." Quentin turned and faced an older black gentleman, who had salt and pepper hair. "Joe, hold down the fort. I'm headed to Misses Vi's and then back to the A."

"I got ya' boss," the man nodded.

Although the diner was within walking distance, Quentin drove them over since they would be heading back to Atlanta right after eating. From the outside, Misses Vi's Place looked like any run-of-the-mill diner but inside it was a different story. The hardwood floors and upgraded finishes made the small establishment look more like an upscale eatery.

"Hey Stan," Quentin said, giving the cook a fist bump. "Where's Misses Violet and Mimi?"

"It's Tuesday. Mimi has class tonight and Misses Vi is cooking at the nursing home."

Quentin slapped his forehead. "Damn. It slipped my mind. Well bro," he said to Malik. "You will have to meet the love of my life another time."

"They will both be here during your grand-opening," the cook offered.

"Great. Until then, whip us up some of your best steaks. We are wasting away to nothing."

The cook laughed on his way to the kitchen. It didn't take him long to grill two porterhouse steaks and he served them with side salads, baked sweet potatoes, corn on the cob and Misses Vi's homemade yeast rolls. After eating, Malik had to unsnap the button on his pants because he was so stuffed.

"This food right here," he pointed at his empty plate with the fork, "was on point."

"Told ya. Let's bounce. Later Stan. See ya' in two weeks."

On the drive back to Atlanta, Malik got the 'itis' and passed out. He woke up and wiped the drool from his face when he heard the engine die.

"What's going on?" He looked at his house. "Shit. I fell asleep."

"No shit, Sherlock. Get your ass out my car. I have to go meet my Tuesday night babe."

"Don't forget we have practice tomorrow while you're out hoeing around."

Quentin laughed and sped off, leaving his friend in the driveway. Malik walked to the front door and placed his hand on the knob and exhaled.

"This shit is crazy," he said to himself. "I don't even want to go in my own house."

Quickly, he punched in the code of his keyless entry and stepped inside. It was quiet, and apart from the light coming from his fish tank, it was dark. He headed towards his bedroom and jumped in the shower. It was almost eleven when he got in the bed, but Selena still wasn't home yet, and he didn't care either.

Over the next two weeks, he and his fiancé only saw one another in passing. Malik did any and everything to be gone when she was at the house. Until finally, the day of Q's red-carpet grand opening arrived. At five o'clock, both Malik and Selena were dressed to the nines, ready for their driver to pull up.

"I don't know why we are taking a flight from Atlanta to Lagrange. That's stupid and a waste of money," Selena griped.

"The event starts at seven-thirty. Traffic on 85 South is horrible right about now. I would rather take a twenty-minute flight than to sit in two- hour traffic any day. I would think a woman of your caliber would rather fly than drive anyway." His voice dripped with sarcasm. "Stop complaining and let's go."

When they landed at the airport, Quentin had arranged for a car service to transport his guests to the dealership. Georgia's elite and the sports industry came out in full force to support the grand opening. Cameras flashed, capturing images of the megastars who walked the red carpet.

Malik and Selena were among the last guests to go inside. This was not the dealership that he came to a few weeks ago. The showroom floor had translucent marble and recessed lighting surrounded each of the luxury vehicles, some of which sat on platforms.

"Wow," Selena breathed. "This is impressive."

"Q went all out for this, didn't he?" One of the players said.

"Yes, Sir," Malik agreed.

"They don't call me 'Showstopper' for nothing," Quentin said, walking up on the group.

The men gave each other some dap and talked a bit before being whisked away on a tour of the showroom and the outer buildings. Everyone was having a great time once the party got underway. Even Malik had allowed himself the chance to really enjoy himself with Selena. He liked her a lot, but he didn't love her the way he should have. The way he loved...

"Damn," he mumbled under his breath. No matter how hard he tried, thoughts of Aisha clouded his head.

The upbeat song ended and the D.J. made a surprise announcement.

"Please help me in welcoming Man of Steele's Grammy award winning group, SKY-Hi to the stage, singing their new slow jam, "All the Woman I Need.""

With another woman on his mind, slow dancing with Selena was the last thing he wanted to do. Especially to a song like that.

"You don't mind if I sit this one out do you?" He asked his fiancé.

"Actually, I do. You never slow dance with me. It's like you're scared of being close to me."

"Here you go," he said, shaking his head. "If I was scared to touch you, I wouldn't dick you down every night."

He snickered at his last comment and that angered her even more.

"That's just it, Malik. The only time you pay me any attention is when you want some ass. I'm not one of these groupies you're used to dealing with."

He smacked his lips. "Whatever, man. I don't know what you want from me."

"Your heart for starters. I'm about to be your wife."

Not knowing what to say, Malik turned away. Boldly, Selena put her hand on his cheek and turned his head back to face her.

"I'm serious. I want, no, I need your heart, Malik. Can you give that to me?"

"Look, now's not the time and this damned sure is not the place to have this conversation."

Across the room, Quentin raised his arms in the air and waved them at Malik, motioning for him to come over.

"Now's a good a time as any to find out where I really stand with you. Can I have your heart?"

Malik exhaled. "I'm sorry, Selena. It's not available to give right now."

Just then, Quentin walked up.

"Man, did you see me trying to get your attention?"

"My bad. Me and this pretty lady were having a conversation."

"Cool, cool. Well, I need to holla at you."

"Alright. Be right back, babe," he said, leaning down to kiss her.

She dodged him. "I'm going to the ladies' room." Her voice was peppered with venom.

Malik didn't care. He laughed as he walked away with his friend.

"Man, I ain't trying to be in your business bu-"

"Ah, shit. Here comes a lecture."

Quentin continued. "Ol' girl is bad news. Just because her parents got money don't mean shit. She has gold digging, opportunist written all over her face. You need to drop that zero and get with you a shero, like me."

Malik stopped walking. "You don't think she's any good for me?"

"Hell naw," Q shook his head. "I know that type, bruh. That's all I used to run into when I first got into the league. But my mama didn't raise no fool. That's why I don't have any children. I keeps it right and tight this way."

"Selena's cool. You just got to get to know her." The lie tasted bitter on Malik's tongue and he didn't believe it himself.

"I'm right and you know it."

The two walked out the dealership towards a golf cart.

"I'm taking you to meet my future wife. Now that's a real woman right there. A true goal digger. G-o-a-l," he clarified.

"Yeah, I'll be the judge of that when I meet this mystery woman. Last time I came, she wasn't at work. I'm starting to think that you made her up."

"You'll see."

The diner was busy with patrons who were trying to see the celebrities who attended the grand opening. A large crowd of people walked up to Q and Malik. Instead of asking for pictures and autographs, which surprised Malik, they offered congratulations to Quentin and expressed thanks to him for bringing more jobs to the community. The only person who paid any attention to Malik was a pretty, curvy woman who flashed a smile so big it showed all her teeth.

The crowd dispersed and Quentin walked Malik over to the woman to introduce them.

"Malik, I would like you to meet none other than,"

"No need for introductions. As much as you talk about her, I feel like I already know her. You must be Mimi."

"Eh, wrong," Q said.

"Suga," the woman began, "I'm flattered that you think I'm her, but I'm Misses Violet. Friends call me Vi."

Clearly Misses Violet had lived a good life because Malik was expecting to meet an older lady with graying hair. This woman looked to be in her early to mid-thirties. Not what he was expecting at all.

"Is Mimi here?" Q asked.

"She sure is. I'll get her for you."

"What? She really exists. I'm going to the bathroom; I'll be right back."

While Malik was gone, Mimi came from the back to greet Quentin.

"How did I know you would show up tonight?" She asked, giving him a hug.

"Nothing could have kept me away. You should be over there with me, on my arm. I don't know why you won't be my woman and let me take you away from this. We could have a great relationship."

"I'm flattered, but I'm not the one for you. You are an amazing man. There's a woman out there who will be everything you need and want. Unfortunately, I'm not her."

"We are two single people who need to get to know one another. Let me show you what I'm about."

Mimi giggled. "I'm single, but I'm not available."

"What does that mean?"

"That means, Quentin, that my heart belongs to someone else."

Malik walked up and stood behind Q. He looked over his friends' shoulder to see who he was talking with and his mouth fell open.

"Who does your heart belong to then?" Quentin asked.

Mimi looked up. Her breath caught in her throat. Tears formed in her eyes. "Him," she whispered and pointed to Malik.

CHAPTER 18

Up in Smoke

JARELL GOT OFF THE school bus, thanking God that it was Friday. All he wanted to do was pig out, play video games, and chill all weekend. He ran up the steps to the Buckhead townhome, unlocked the door, and rushed inside. It was fifteen before four and he figured his sister nor mother would be home. The sun was out and so were they. It didn't matter to him. He preferred it that way. His niece would be getting dropped off by the daycare bus soon and knowing her, she would be hungry.

He slung his backpack to the sofa and raced to the kitchen. When he opened the fridge, the light did not come on.

"Ah, man," he said. Slowly, he closed to the door and walked over to the light switch. He flipped it. Nothing. The electricity was shut off. Again.

It made no sense that his sister blew her money the way she did. She was so reckless and irresponsible.

"I'm more of an adult than she is," he mumbled in the quiet room. That morning when he left for school, they had power. There was no telling how long it had been off or how long it would stay off this time. Quickly, he prepped some sandwiches and put them in the temperature-controlled bag he bought from the grocery store the last time they were without electricity. The bag would keep the food cool for a few hours.

The last thing the twelve-year wanted was to spend his weekend in the dark. A few of his friends had asked if they could stay over with him. At first, he was considering it, but now he was happy he had turned them down.

"The entire school would have been clowning me."

Grrr. His stomach rumbled and he rubbed it. There was only enough lunch meat to make them two sandwiches each. His sister sometimes left money in her purses when she changed them. Hopefully, he would luck up on some cash to buy them something later.

As soon as the food was put away, he opened the blinds to allow natural light to stream in. When he opened the last one, he saw the daycare van pull up and he went to meet his niece.

"Jerry," the little girl squealed when he lifted her off the van and sat her on the ground.

"Hey, Bre-Bre."

The driver picked up a bag and handed it to Jarell.

"Misses Mann made y'all a plate for later because she cooked so much for lunch. It's just a little meat loaf, her homemade macaroni and cheese, yams, cabbage, and cornbread. She even put some chocolate cake in there."

"Thank you, Jesus," he mumbled, inhaling the delicious aroma that seeped through the bag. "Please thank her for us. You know how much we love her cooking."

"Sure thing. Y'all have a great weekend. See ya' Monday."

The van pulled off just as the little boy's eyes filled with tears.

"God, I know You are real because You always come through for me and my niece when we need it."

The two went inside and put her things away and then went to playground where they played until they were tired. Around seven that evening, his sister and mother came home, carrying doggie bags from Ruth's Chris Steakhouse. Jarell was happy because he and his niece had eaten the food Misses Mann had cooked already and he wanted to save the sandwiches for a late snack.

"Man, am I glad to see you guys. We are starving." He reached for his mother's bag and she quickly snatched it out of his reach.

"I'on know what the fuck you think you're doing, but this is my shit. If your ass was hungry, you should have fixed you something to eat."

His mouth fell open. "In case you have not noticed Mother, the lights are off."

"And? It's some sandwich meat in there."

Larissa brushed past her mother and went upstairs. Jarell could hear her opening and closing drawers because the house was so quiet.

"Ma," she yelled downstairs. "Hurry up."

Their mother walked away.

"Mama, where are you two going?" Jarell asked quietly.

"We going to a hotel and getting out of this dark ass house."

"Yayyy. Did you hear that Bre? We are going to stay at a hotel."

He jumped up and down with the little girl.

Laquanda turned her nose up. "Ain't nobody speaking French up in this bitch. Where you get this 'we' shit from? No, sir. Y'all bastards are staying here."

"In the dark, by ourselves?" He asked incredulously.

"Lil' nigga, y'all gon' be alright."

"B-b-but, you did not pay my phone bill. How do I reach you in case of an emergency?"

"If it's an emergency, don't call me, call 9-1-1. It works whether your phone is on or off."

Larissa galloped down the steps.

"Damn, stop harassing Mama. If you need to use the phone, go next door. Shit, you're supposed to be a hustler. Go hustle up on a phone. Here Mama," she said, handing her mother a bag. "I grabbed the bag that you packed. Anything we don't have; we can buy while we're out."

"When are you coming back?" He asked when they opened the front door to leave.

"Monday," his sister answered and walked out.

He shook his head and turned toward his niece.

"Well, at least we have a little more food," he said, looking at both bags of food on the coffee table.

A gush of wind blew into the room when the front door swung open once more.

"We almost forgot these," Larissa said, grabbing the food. "Peace."

This time when she left, she slammed the door.

"Mommy, gone?" Brely asked.

Jarell looked at the little girl, realizing that her mother had not even acknowledged her presence. He sighed.

"Yes, she's gone."

The darkness began to settle into the home.

"I scared," she whined.

He picked her up. "Don't be. I got you. I'm going to call Caresse and ask her to come get us."

"I like her. She is nice to me."

"So do I know."

Using the cellphone, she had given him, he called her up and she happily agreed to come get them. Twenty minutes later, there was a knock at the door.

MEAL TICKET$

"Bro, what are you doing in town?" Jarell jumped into Breeze's arms when he opened the door.

"The venue we were supposed to perform at flooded and the gig was rescheduled. Now I see that was God because He knew I needed to be here this weekend."

"How long has the power been off?" Caresse asked, stepping inside.

Jarell shrugged. "A few hours. They were off when I came in from school but were on when I left."

"See," Breeze began, turning to face his fiancé. "This is that bullsh-, stuff, I'm talking about."

She placed her hand on his chest.

"It's okay, babe. We're here now and we got this."

The judge had granted Breeze weekly visitation the last time they went to court. But with this new information he had, hopefully the judge would grant him full custody at the next hearing.

"Go get your PS4, Jarell. You can set it up in your room at my house."

The little boy didn't budge. "Um, my mama sold it so she could get her lashes done."

"What the eff." Breeze had to be mindful that his daughter was at the stage where she repeated much of what she heard others say. "Bump that. I'll get you a new one. Don't take nothing from this house. Anything you two need, we will get it. I don't care what no court in the world says, neither of you are stepping foot back in the house again.

He had never spoken more truer words.

A few miles away, Larissa, Tika, and a few other friends lounged at the day spa.

"Bitch, why won't you go out with us tonight?" Larissa badgered Tika. It's the Man of Steele and So Dope Artist Takeover at Club 404 tonight."

Tika side-eyed her friend. "Oh, so that's what this deluxe spa treatment is all about. Someone's trying to impress her baby's daddy."

"Impress him? No. Hell, he's on tour and won't even be there. I'm on to the next. Plus, this will be an opportunity to pass out my new single to the execs that will be there."

"If he did come, I'm sure his fiancé would be in tow," her friend Fatima said. "He takes her everywhere he goes."

Larissa rolled her eyes. "His ugly cow you mean?"

"That girl is far from ugly and she certainly isn't fat. She is my size."

"Exactly," Larissa said.

"Hoe I ain't fat," Fatima snapped back. "And even if I was, that didn't stop my man from putting a ring on it."

She flashed her left hand, showing off the large diamond.

"Cocky bitch," Larissa whispered.

She could not stand Fatima. Although they had been so-called friends for a while, they were always at odds regarding one thing or the next. Larissa swore that Fatima was jealous of her when she snagged Breeze and had his baby. But now, it was her turn to be jealous because not only had her friend got the baby and the bag, but she also got her bae, too. Her eyes squinted and she pursed her lips before relaxing the tension that had built in her face. She waved her hand at Fatima and turned her back to her.

"Anyway, Tika. I know you are not getting all this shit done just to sit in the house on a Friday night."

"I told you, no sitter. KJ is out of town and Mama is mad again so it looks like I am."

"Mch, is that all? Jarell will watch the kids. He got Brely and has already agreed to watch Shannon and Vonda's kids. One more won't hurt."

"It's on then," Tika smiled.

Fatima's eyes grew round, and she sat straight up. "Hold up. That's eight motherfuckin kids for an eleven-year-old to watch. Y'all hoes are crazy. Couldn't be me."

"Right," another friend chimed in. "Ain't no way, I'm leaving my two heartbeats with Jarell. He's a baby his damned self."

"Send Malia to K.J.'s mom's house, Tika," Fatima said. "She would love to keep her."

That was an option, but since she had been angry with K.J. since court and was taking it out on his entire family. Nobody could see her. Period.

"Nah. She'll be fine with Lil Jay. He is more responsible than some niggas we fuck with."

"Facts. Just send some money for pizza or pack her some snacks because he cannot cook." Literally, she thought.

After the spa, the ladies went their separate ways and met up later at Larissa's hotel room at the Intercontinental Hotel. The wet bar was fully stocked, and they took advantage of it. Laquanda had forgotten her heels so Larissa volunteered to drop all the kids off and grab the shoes while she was there.

"Y'all bitches be ready to roll when I get back. We gon' fuck the club up. Come on y'all," she said to the children, picking Malia up out her car seat and placing her on her hip.

She piled the eight kids in her rented Maserati Levante that looked exactly like the one that got repossessed. Only Tika knew that it was not her car, and they didn't need to know either. One of the bigger kids held Malia in her lap as Larissa sped along, breaking multiple traffic laws. Not one of them wore a seatbelt.

In the few short blocks to her house, she had run two red lights and blew through a stop sign, almost hitting a man and his dog. Back at the townhouse, she hurried the kids inside and used the flashlight from her phone to find her mother's shoe.

"It's dark in here, Miss Larissa. Will you turn on the light? Where is Jarell?"

"He and Brely are playing hide and seek. You guys can join in. Go hide and he will come find you," she lied.

The little ones scurried to find hiding places, leaving Malia alone on the sofa in the dark living room. Quickly, Larissa grabbed the shoes and made her way to leave.

"Jarell, watch these kids," she yelled. "I got something special for you when I get back." And with that, she was gone.

From the moment that Larissa and her friends stepped into the club, all eyes were on them. The VIP section that Vonda was able to secure for them was all that. Bottles popped, booties twerked, blunts stayed lit, and little white lines disappeared faster than tax refund checks. Club 404 did not owe the ladies anything that night.

Larissa was about to snort a line off the tray when her phone began to buzz.

"Who is that blowing up your phone like that?" Vonda asked.

"Nobody, but my damned nosey ass neighbor. Jarell and the kids probably making too much noise. I'll call him in a minute." She proceeded to sniff the powder and then relaxed against the sofa. "This is some good shit."

Her phone continued to ring.

"Damn, bitch. Answer that thang. It's starting to fuck up my high," Vonda said.

The request fell on deaf ears. Just then, Tika's phone rang.

"Not you, too," Vonda yelled over the music track that just started. Frustrated, she grabbed her drink and exited the section.

Tika looked at her caller I.D. It was KJ.

"Ugh. Hello?" She snapped. "What do you want?"

"Don't start the shit, Tika. I was just calling to see if I could come get Malia in the morning and take her to church with me and my family?"

"Nope. She's already going to church with me."

"Now you know damned well your ass ain't going up in nobodies church tomorrow or any other day."

"You don't know shit about me, nigga."

"Obviously. Hey, isn't Larissa's house off West Paces Ferry?"

"Yeah, why?"

"Some townhomes are on fire. It looks bad. I'm a few blocks away stuck in traffic. The fire trucks have the streets blocked off."

"Wait, what? Hold on." Tika leaned over and hit Larissa's arm. "Bitch, call your neighbor and see what she wanted. KJ said it's a big fire not too far from your house."

"Fuck. I'on wanna talk to that old hag."

"Hoe if you don't call her and find out what she wants, I'm gonna beat your ass right here, right now."

"Whatever." Reluctantly, she dialed the number.

Tika put her hand over her phone receiver to block out the background noise.

"Rissa is calling her neighbor now to see what's going on," she told KJ.

"Cool. The ambulance is coming and so are more trucks."

"So, when you gonna let me give you some more of this sloppy toppy?" His baby's mother asked.

"Never. And just so you know, you're on speaker phone and my woman can hear you. Say hello Sunrise."

"Hello," his woman said.

"Fuck you, KJ. I don't need you."

Just then, Larissa started screaming.

"What's wrong, bitch?"

"We gotta go. My neighbor said my house is on fire and she heard babies crying."

Larissa grabbed her purse and jumped up.

"What? No!" Tika wailed. "KJ, please get to Larissa's. That's her house on fire and Malia is there. Hurry."

The line went dead.

KJ was shocked.

"My daughter is in that fire? Fuck!" He yelled, banging the steering wheel. "I'm going to get my baby. When traffic starts moving, get as close as you can to Northside Drive. Call my family and tell them what's going on."

KJ jumped out the car and ran as fast as he could toward the orange glow in the trees. By the time he got on the scene, the firemen had just hooked the hose up to begin putting the fire out. He ran toward Larissa's and a cop held him back.

"Whoa, you can't go near there, buddy. It's too dangerous."

"Fuck that. My little girl is in that house." Anger gave Kyle hulk-like strength and he jerked away from the officer and darted up the stairs. Flames burst through the upstairs window and glass showered down on him. Children's screams poured from the house.

"Oh my, God. There are children in there. Someone please help them."

KJ kicked at the door until it gave way. Larissa, Tika, and their friends ran up as he disappeared inside. In a panic, Larissa grabbed a fireman's arm.

"Please get this fire out," she begged. "I just bought a new Birkin bag and it's not insured yet. All my clothes and shoes will be ruined. Jesus, no!"

The man turned his nose up at her and pushed her away from him.

"There are children in that house lady, and all you're worried about is a fucking purse? You disgust me."

"My babies," Vonda cried.

All the mother's leaned on one another for support, as they helplessly watched the house burn. Billows of gray-black smoke filled the night sky.

A fireman ran inside after KJ, pulling him out to safety, while another was able to locate the children and get them out. Paramedics immediately laid the children on stretchers and placed oxygen masks on their faces, before whisking them away to the nearest children's hospital.

It took thirty minutes to put the fire out that started in an empty unit next to Larissa's. Until an investigation was done, no one would know how the fire started.

Police had managed to redirect traffic, allowing Sunrise to maneuver closer to the scene but by the time she got there, KJ was gone to the hospital. She did get there just in time to see the police placing each mother in the back of a cruiser.

"Why are they going to jail?" She asked an onlooker.

"All those women left their children alone a house without electricity so they could go to the club?"

"Jesus, baby Mali was left alone. That is awful."

The neighbor shook her head. "It is terrible. My heart breaks for those precious souls. I don't think any of them survived."

CHAPTER 19

The Same Girl

AISHA WAS THE WOMAN Quentin had been talking about all along. Malik was stunned. Out of all the places she could have been, she was in Misses Violet's diner, in Lagrange, Georgia. The thick tension surrounded them. Q looked at his friend and saw unshed tears in the corner of his eyes then he looked at Mimi. Silent tears streamed down her face.

"Hold up, my Mimi is your Aisha? How is that possible?"

"My full name is Aisha Michelle, Quentin. When I started working here, there was already another Aisha here so Misses Vi, started calling me Michelle until she shortened it to Mimi."

"Day-yumm," he sang. "So, you're the shorty that broke my bro's heart? Hmm, it's a small world after all." He turned his head side to side, looking at the two of them, who stood there, staring, saying nothing.

"Indeed, it is," Malik said.

The trio stood in a quiet, awkward circle. Misses Vi walked from around the counter to the group.

"Mimi, are you okay?" She asked, concerned. Her voice was low but loud enough for them to hear her. The nosey diner patrons had stopped eating to watch the scene unfold before them. They wanted to see what was going to happen next, but she wasn't trying to have them all up in someone

217

else's business. The older lady looked at young girl who stood, crying silently. From the first moment the young woman stepped foot into her establishment, she had taken an instant liking to her and after almost a year, she loved her like the daughter she always wished she had.

Aisha wiped her tears and cleared her throat. "Eh, hem. I'm fine. Uh, I'm sure you know but this is Mal- "

"Q introduced us already," the older woman interrupted.

"Yes, ma'am, but this is my ex, who I told you about."

Awareness dawned on her. "Ohh, so this is Zi- "

Aisha shook her head vigorously before Misses Vi, let the cat out of the bag.

"Hmm, well, you guys obviously need some privacy. You are more than welcomed to use my office in the back.

Realizing that no further drama was going to pop-off, the patrons went back to eating and their previous conversations. Quentin and Malik followed the woman to her office with Aisha taking up the rear. Misses Vi pulled the door closed so that she could say a few things in private to her friend.

"Mimi," she said, placing her hand on the side of the girl's arm. "I know you're still hurting because of all that has happened. But this is your chance to set the record straight. Be honest. Tell him about Zion, baby girl. He has the right to know."

She nodded as the tears began again. Using the corner of her apron, she wiped her eyes, took a deep breath and exhaled, to compose herself.

"Here goes nothing."

No one said anything when she walked into the room. Malik's head was down, and Quentin was texting someone. Once he put his phone away, he looked back and forth at the star-crossed lovers.

"I can't be the only one with questions. It's time to get rid of the elephant in the room. Aisha Michelle, why did you leave without letting the homie know what was up?"

Malik's eyes squinted and his nostrils flared. His breathing became heavy and ragged. Aisha had seen this look many times before. So had Quentin. Dude was pissed off.

"I didn't want to stand in the way of his career," she said, not taking her eyes off her ex-boyfriend. "I'm sorry. I never wanted to hurt you."

"How the fuck you think you hurt me?" He snapped.

His bark was so loud, it brought Misses Vi back to see what was going on.

"Y'all good in here?" Lines creased the older woman's forehead, and she wrung her hands.

"We're good, Misses Vi. Malik's anger is warranted. Can you and Quentin give us a moment?" She wasn't asking them. The sternness of her voice commanded them to leave.

"Sure, but uh, one more question. Since it's obvious that you and I ain't going to hook up, do you happen to have any beautiful, smart, non-gold-digging friends such as yourself around?"

"Goodbye, Q," Malik said.

"I do, but we can talk later," she said to him before he left and then looked intently at Malik. "I really am sorry."

"You damned straight, you're sorry. Sorry and pathetic. I loved you, Eesh and this is how you do me? Just up and leave. No explanation. Just a little ass, impersonal note."

"Note? But I didn't – "

"All those nights I sat up, feeling like a bitch, crying for you. Wondering what I did so bad that you would leave me. Pssh, and then don't get me started on the money me and my mom spent on private investigators."

"Investigators? Your mom? But she- "

219

"Why me, man?"

She waited a few seconds before responding because he kept cutting her off before and she didn't want it to happen again. She inhaled deeply and exhaled slowly before speaking.

"Hurting you was the last thing I ever wanted to do. Words cannot express how sorry I am. It was hard for me to leave, but I did what I thought was best."

"Best for whom, Aisha? Me? You? Tell me. As a matter of fact, don't bother. I'm over this shit and over you. I have moved on. I'll be getting married in a few months anyway."

"I know. I read about it. Congratulations to you and your fiancé. I wish you well."

"So, are you seeing someone, too?"

"There is a man in my life. We have not been together long, but I can see myself spending a lifetime with him."

"Hmm, is that right? So, you got with ol' boy almost immediately, huh? Didn't waste no time. Were you with him before you left Atlanta?"

"Kinda. We had just met."

"Hmm, you talking about spending forever with him and shit, you must be in love for real."

"Yes, I am."

"Well let me not stand in your way. I left my beautiful fiancé alone across the street and must tend to her. Take care of yourself…Mimi." When he said her name, it dripped with malice. He held his head up and did not look back.

And for the second time in her life, Malik was gone.

Misses Vi rushed into her office when she saw Malik storm out the restaurant. Aisha sat in a chair; her shoulders shook with each sob.

"Let it out, baby. It's okay," the older woman said, rubbing Aisha's back.

The young woman lifted her head up and wiped her eyes. She sniffled a few times and then spoke.

"He was so angry, Misses Vi. I did not realize that my actions would cause him this much pain."

"I know you didn't, Sweetie. What did he say when you told him about what his mom did?"

"Nothing. I didn't tell him."

Ooh-kay. Well, at least tell me what he said about his son?"

"He doesn't know about that either."

"Oh no, baby girl. Zion needs to know his father. He deserves to know that he has a family out there who loves him."

"And he does know that, Misses Vi. My family has been here for him. Yes, Malik deserves to know but tonight was not the time to tell him. I'll give him some time to cool off and then tell him. But as far as his mother is concerned, she does not need to know my baby exists. She wanted me to kill him remember. It's because of her that I left in the first place."

Misses Vi sat next to her employee and hugged her.

"He's not the only one who is hurting right now. All those angry outbursts were nothing more than a cover to hide the fact that he is still very much in love with you. You can pretend that you are no longer in love with him all you want to, but we both know the truth. Tell that man about his son and please, tell him how you feel about him. If you let him go through with that wedding without saying anything, you will regret it. Mark my words.

Outside the restaurant, Malik and Quentin stood in silence. The breeze helped cool them both.

"Bro, you gotta know that I had no clue who she was."

"How could you, Q? I had never shown you any pictures of her and you hadn't shown me any either."

"She didn't even know who I was. I guess I should have known something was up when she told me that she stopped watching football. That was one of the reason's I liked her so much. Talking to her was easy and I didn't have to keep up appearances like I do with some chicks."

Malik nodded. "Yeah, she's always been genuine like that. That's why I love her."

"Love or loved?" Quentin raised his brow.

"Love. I never stopped. She's all I ever wanted."

"Well, then go back in there and get her. Shit, she didn't give me no play probably because she is still in love with your ass, too. Y'all are perfect for one another."

"Nah., She told me that is with someone else now and plus, I'm engaged remember?"

Quentin rolled his eyes. "I keep trying to forget that part. Man hey, you and I both know that that gold digger across the street don't give a damn about you. Fuck what your Mom thinks and love the woman you want. Not the one she loves."

"I hear what you're saying, but I'm gonna leave well enough alone. Selena has been a good woman to me, and I've treated her like shit. She's been existing in the shadow of another woman since we started dating. Because of Aisha, I never even tried to love her, but all that's about to change. Let's go. I've left my fiancé alone too long."

Q looked back at the restaurant and then to Malik, but reluctantly he followed his friend back to the party. As soon as they were inside, Malik walked off in search of Selena. Quentin went to the bar.

"Give me something strong. I don't care what it is," he told the bartender.

"Damn, it's like that?" She said, mixing up a drink and then handing it to him.

"You don't even know the half of it," he said before throwing the drink back.

"Slow down, bruh. You don't want to pass out at your own grand-opening, do you?"

Quentin sat his glass down and turned to see his good friend, Kyle standing next to him.

"KJ! Man, it sure is good to see you. I'm so glad that you and your daughter are okay."

The two men pounded their fists and gave one another a brotherly hug.

"Me too. It's a lot going on, but I wouldn't miss this for the world.

We go way back like Southernplayalisticadillacmuzik."

"A-T-L's finest."

"What's good with you?"

Kyle asked the bartender for a drink and sipped on it while Quentin filled him in on what was going on...with his cousin Malik.

"Damn. So, she's been here in Lagrange this entire time?"

Quentin nodded and sipped the drink the bartender had refreshed.

"Yep. I was gonna marry her too."

"Stop playing."

"Shit, I'm serious. Baby girl is bad."

"Yeah, she is. Humble about it, too."

Just then, a woman walked up behind Kyle. Quentin looked over his shoulder and saw a pair of the most captivating light brown eyes he had ever seen. This was a woman he wanted to know. He cleared his throat.

"Here you are. I was wondering where you had gotten off to." She spoke and placed her hand on Kyle's shoulder before Quentin said a word.

Disappointed, he took another drink and elbowed Kyle. "How long have you been dating this beauty?"

Kyle looked around. "Who? Her?" He pointed.

He and the woman laughed.

"You have it all wrong. I'm his sister, Kayla."

A smile spread across Quentin's face and he looked up. "There is a God. Kayla, are you single?"

"Very much so."

He picked her arm up and wrapped it around his. "So, what are you doing, let's say, for the rest of your life?" And the two of them walked off, leaving Kyle at the bar alone.

The band cued the music and Breeze stood in front of the microphone, preparing to serenade the party goers with his latest ballad, which was a cover of Jesse Powell's, "You."

Selena sat at a table, stirring the ice around in her drink. Malik stood, watching her for a moment. Her head leaned to the side and rested on the palm of her hand. He could see her chest rise and fall as she sighed deeply.

"May I have this dance?" He asked, holding his hand out to her.

She snapped her head up, surprised. "You want to slow dance? With me?" She looked around to make sure he was talking to the right woman.

"Yes. I want to slow dance with my fiancé. Will you do me the honor?"

"Yes, baby."

He held her in his arms as they floated around the dance floor.

"Next year let's call this day, our anniversary. The day I put, my heart in your hands and said that it was yours to keep," Malik sang along with Breeze.

"Okay then. I see you can hold a note. I've never heard you sing before."

"There are a lot of things you don't know, Selena, but you will. I'm in this with you. I can't wait for you to become my wife."

He lowered his mouth to hers and captured her lips between his teeth, sucking them gently before kissing her long and hard on the mouth.

Quentin and Kayla danced past them as they kissed.

Quentin heaved. "I think I just threw up in my mouth. I'm gonna be sick."

Kayla looked in the direction of his repulsion.

"Who are you talking about? Malik and Selena?"

"Yeah. I don't want to see him making a mistake, marrying her. There's something about her that's not right."

"You're right about that. I hope he finds out though before it's too late."

"Oh my gosh, babe. Tonight, was the best night ever," Selena said, falling backwards on the bed.

"You liked it, huh?"

She nodded.

"Well, get used to it. We are going to have many more like it and better. I'm going to spoil your ass."

Selena unzipped the back of her dress and let it pool at her feet.

"Babe, I'm not one to look a gift horse in its mouth, but what changed? I was starting to think you didn't want to marry me."

Malik loosened his tie and removed his cuff links.

"We need to talk."

"Oh, Lord," she said.

"Don't be like that. It's a good thing."

She sat at the foot of the bed in her bra and panties and waited for him to begin.

"When we first started dating, I only went out with you because I was trying to get over, Aisha."

"I kinda figured that."

"I was fucked up after she left me and didn't want to open up to you because I wasn't trying to get hurt again."

"But babe, I would never hurt you like that."

"I know that now, but then," he shook his head. "I was too vulnerable. Anyway, when I left you at the party, I went across the street to meet one of Q's friends."

He paused. She waited, expectantly for him to finish.

"His friend was Aisha."

"Excuse me?" She jumped to her feet. "Your ex is fucking your best friend?"

"Hell naw, he ain't fucking her."

Selena stopped. Her mouth moved to form an 'O'.

"Hold up. You sound a little pissed off. Are you mad that he's with her? It shouldn't matter. Especially since I am the woman you're marrying." She wiggled her ring finger in his face.

He smacked. "I'm not mad and they're not together. Q said she wouldn't give him no play."

"Really? That's surprising. Her kind usually tries to hitch her saddle to men of stature."

"Her kind? You don't shit about her and I'm not going to stand here and allow you to talk shit about her."

"Why are you defending her, Malik? This is the same woman who abandoned you. I'm the one who was there to help you pick up the pieces. If I didn't know any better, I would think you're still in love with her."

"I am," he yelled. The words flew out of his mouth so quickly he was unable to stop them.

His fiancé clutched her pearls and sat on the bed. "Wow. Just wow."

"Look, Lena. This is not how this was supposed to go. I don't want to argue. I only brought her up because I wanted to apologize to you."

"For what?"

"For giving you the short end of the stick. I realized that because I was so afraid of being hurt, that I didn't allow myself to try to love you."

"So, what are you saying?"

He inhaled and exhaled slowly. "I'm saying, I want us to start over. You deserve all of me and I want to give you that."

Happy, she threw her arms around his neck and showered kisses all over his face and neck. Her small hands parted his open dress shirt and she trailed kisses down his chest, making her way to his dick, that was hardening with each peck. Quick fingers unfastened his belt and slid the zipper down. His manhood sprang to life and she immediately wrapped her hot mouth around the head.

"Mmm," she moaned and twirled her tongue around the small opening in his penis. "Such a joyous occasion. I won."

He threw his head back and placed his hand on top of her head.

"What did you win, babe?" He thrust his hips upward off the bed.

"You." Suck.

"And not even that ghetto girl." Slurp.

"Or her bastard ass baby can steal you away now." Pop.

Malik jumped up so fast Selena fell backwards on the floor.

"What the fuck did you just say?" Zip. His dick had gone down, and he put it away.

"Huh?" She slapped her face at the Freudian slip. "Did I say that out loud?"

"Yeah. You did. What are you talking about, Selena? Who has a baby? Aisha?"

"I didn't mean her. Uh, there was something I heard on A-Tea-L Live about a groupie saying she was your baby's mama. Me and your mom were laughing about it."

"Nah. I ain't falling for that shit." He lifted her off the floor and her feet dangled in the air. "Your ass better get to talking or I swear you won't live to regret it."

"Stop, Malik. You're hurting my arms."

"That ain't all I'm gonna be hurting. Talk!" He shook her forcefully.

"Okay, okay." Tears began to pour. "Aisha does have a baby."

Like a balloon with a hole in it, he began to deflate and sat her down before sitting on the bed.

"Is it mine?"

She turned away from him.

"Answer me!"

"Yes. Yes, he's yours."

"He? How do you know so much about him?"

"Your mother. She told me all about it. She's been knowing where Aisha was and about the baby. It's the reason she left. Your mom told her to leave or else she was going to make something bad happen to Aisha's family."

"You fucking bitches. Get the fuck out of my house."

"No. We need to talk about this, Malik. I'm going to be your wife soon. We need to learn how to communicate now."

"Pssh, I know you don't think I'm still marrying you after all this? Your ass is dead to me. Kick rocks, Selena Get your shit and go before I have security come escort you out."

"Baby, please. Don't do this. I love you. If it's the baby, I will help you raise him and if you need to fuck her every now and then you can do that, too. Just don't leave me."

"Do you hear yourself? Love me? The only thing you love is my money and the status my name brings to you." He grabbed his suit jacket off the chair. "I meant what I said. Get your shit and get out. I'm leaving. If you're not gone by the time, I get back, you'll be sorry."

Malik walked out his bedroom, listening to Selena scream and hurl a slew of curse words at him. Once he got inside his car, he used his voice to dial his best friend.

"Yo, Q. You busy?"

"Nah. I just walked in the house. Man, your cousin Kayla is all that. I'm in love. For real this time."

Malik laughed. "That's good. Look, I know it's late, but I wanted to know if you would take a drive with me."

"Depends. Where we going?"

"Lagrange."

"Hell naw, I ain't driving almost two hours with your ass. You know how many cops are on the road this time of night?"

"Alright then. I thought we were boys. You're seriously not going to ride with me?"

"We are boys and no, I'm seriously not going to ride with you. But" he paused. "We can fly."

CHAPTER 20

After Burn

O FFICIALS RELEASED THE REPORT on the deadly fire that killed six people, including four children in a Buckhead townhome fire. The origin of the fire was determined accidental. A couple celebrating a wedding anniversary was having dinner by candlelight. A silver candle holder fell, breaking a wine glass. The wine acted as an accelerant and flames engulfed the unit, quickly spreading to surrounding townhomes. In a statement issued Wednesday, by the Atlanta Fire and Rescue Department, the loss from the fire at Windhaven Crossing was estimated at $2,585,000.

About thirty firefighters, using ten trucks, fought the blaze at its height, but were forced to retreat when two of the townhomes' roofs collapsed. The fire department stated that crews remained on scene for about twelve hours to make sure that the blaze was fully extinguished.

A spokesperson from the Red Cross is assisting the eight families whose units suffered secondary damage from the blaze. The children who perished in the fire were left alone by their mother's, who went out to a nightclub. Nine-month-old, Malia Hudson, the daughter of NBA All-Star KJ Hudson, suffered first-degree burns on her leg and smoke inhalation. The home was being rented by reality star Larissa MacIntosh who is the mother of R&B Superstar, Breeze Coleman's daughter.

An inmate switched the television set off when the news went to a commercial.

"Did you hear that bitch? They called me a star," Larissa said to her cellmate, Vonda.

"Ugh," Vonda growled, charging at Larissa. Using all her strength, she wrapped her small, chubby hands around her friends' neck and squeezed hard. She was angry at her friend for not telling anyone that she had no electricity. She was angry that Jarell and Brely were not even at home when Larissa dropped the kids off. But most importantly, she was mad at herself for not protecting her two angels, and now they were both dead.

"I hate you, hoe," she screamed with tears streaming down her face. "I should have listened to, Fatima. I should have listened to, Fatima."

"Guards, come quick. She's gonna kill her," one of the inmates yelled.

"Pop Cell 34," one of the officers commanded. It took three men to pull Vonda off Larissa. She coughed violently and gasped for air when she was finally free.

"I should have died in that fire with my babies, and you should have, too. You don't deserve to live." She spat on Larissa and the guards drug her away.

"That's pretty foul that you're the one who dropped the kids off and left them. Your girls trusted you with their kids and you let them down."

Larissa rolled her eyes. "And? They could have always found another babysitter. Hoes is always looking to me to handle shit for them. I'm sorry their kids died, but I lost things in the fire, too. Hell, my Birkin bags…my red bottoms…all that."

"Damn, Shawty, you're brutal. Comparing human life to some material shit shows just how fucked up you truly are," a thugged out lesbian said. "You better hope you get behind the wall. I know some people who'll be gunning for you. It'll be Hotel California for your ass."

Sitting down on the bunk, Larissa asked, "what does that mean? Hotel California."

"You can check in anytime you like, but you can never leave. In your case, it will be in a body bag."

She sat there for a moment and let that marinate. The woman was clearly issuing a threat to Larissa's life.

Damn, she thought. If I get some time because of those kids, I may not make it to see my next birthday, behind the walls.

"Oh, hell no," she said out loud. "It's time for a bitch like me to shake the spot."

Before she got up off the bunk, she wracked her brain trying to remember Phillip Drew's number. His was one that she had committed to memory, but with her increased drug usage, she had started to forget key things. She snapped her fingers when she remembered the number.

"Be still, bitch. I'm trying to sleep," Tika moaned. "Why are so antsy anyway?"

"Because I just remembered Phil's number. Before any of this shit happened, he and I were discussing a business opportunity. I'm going to tell him that I will accept his offer if he comes to get me out."

"Hoeing?" Tika sat up and rubbed her eyes. "Why you wanna do some shit like that?"

"'Cause, bitch. I would rather be set up in an upscale brothel than to do ten years in the pen. Wouldn't you? Hell, at least we'll be free. He said the house is a mansion and his partner only deals with high-end clientele. Plus, we will be able to shop, travel, and all that good shit that we do now. Except, we won't have the kids with us. You down?"

"Hell yeah. Ain't no judge on Earth gon' give me none of my kids back after this shit. Tell him if he will get me out, he got another girl, too."

"Bet. I'ma go call him right now."

There was a line of women waiting to use the phone. Larissa tapped her foot impatiently in the oversized, plastic, jail issued slides she had on. She looked down and frown. Everything that the jailers had issued to them had been used. Even the sports bra and panties. It wasn't no way that she was going to put her new ass in some old, nasty shit like that. They had her fucked up. Instead, she smuggled her own underwear in and washed them out on her hands every night.

The Fulton County jail was overcrowded and understaffed and that made for an extremely tense situation. Thankfully, the court system was moving a lot quicker than she expected and some of the women were going home. Most of them that left, either had their charges dropped altogether or they received light probation sentences. Although she really wished it were her leaving, she was happy that somebody got out of that hell hole.

Phillip answered the phone of the first ring.

"Please don't hang up," she prayed silently, while the automated voice announced that it was an inmate from a correctional facility.

"Hello." His deep voice sounded so sexy.

"Thank you so much for accepting my call."

"It's cool. How are you?"

"As well as can be expected," she said. "I don't have much time, but do you remember that job opportunity that we discussed before?"

"I do."

"Is the offer still on the table?"

"It is."

"Good. Then you have yourself two new employees."

"Two? You and who else?"

"Tika."

"Fuck, yes."

"There's a catch though."

"Isn't there always," he said, sighing in the phone.

"We need you to bail us out."

"Oh, is that all? I got you. You, I can get out in a few hours since your kids were not in the house, but Tika may have to stay one more night. Is that cool?"

"Yep. I'll let her know."

"You have one more minute," the automated voice said.

"Dammit. That was quick," she complained.

"Don't worry about it. Let me get everything started. I'll see you soon."

"Thank you, Phillip. I owe you."

"You'll pay me. Later."

"Your time has expired," the automated voice said then the call disconnected.

Light shown in Larissa's eyes as she walked toward Tika's bunk.

"It's on, best friend. He said he's gonna come get me tonight and then come get you tomorrow. It may take longer since your baby was in the house."

"I'm cool with that as long as I get out of this place. I swear I feel bugs crawling on me throughout the night."

"Ugh, me too."

The two ladies sat and talked about the things they would do once they were free. Before long, Larissa's name was called, and she was being processed for release.

In the parking lot, Kyle sat, contemplating if he really wanted to visit Tika. It had been almost three weeks since the fire and although Malia was home from the hospital, she had to use a nebulizer to help heal the damage her lungs sustained from the smoke inhalation. If it had not been for his family and Sunrise, he would have lost his mind.

His girlfriend helped him furnish a nursery for his daughter at the last minute. From start to finish, she oversaw the project and by the time his baby came home, the room was all set.

"What are you thinking about?" She asked him, caressing his hand.

"I don't know if I want to see her. Thinking about all that could have happened makes me angry all over again."

"Then stop thinking about it," she said. "You need to build a bridge and then get over it. Stop nursing and rehearsing bad things in your life. That's what the enemy wants you to do. While you're doing that, you are taking your eyes off the blessing that you and your daughter made it out alive when so many others didn't. Be grateful, babe. Go in there and see her. Let her know her baby is fine despite her lack of care or concern for her. Tell her you will pray for her and then come on out."

He picked up her hand and kissed the back of it.

"Yes, ma'am."

KJ made it through the checkpoint and was told to take a seat after he signed the visiting roster. Twenty minutes later, an alarm sounded and a few of the officers who were upfront, ran to the back. Despite the mayhem, it was finally his turn to visit. On his way to the back, he saw Larissa as she signed her release papers.

"They're letting you out of jail? There must be some mistake." He could not mask the look of disgust.

"They can't hold a good bitch down. I'm like cream baby. I always rise to the top."

"You're scum and you should be locked under the jail," Kyle replied before walking away from her. "I can't believe they let her out."

"She's just out on bail for now, but don't worry. People like her always get what's coming to them. Karma is real."

"Yes, it is."

He sat in a booth as instructed, while he waited on Tika to come out. The round metal seat was killer on his butt, and he kept adjusting himself trying to find a comfortable position.

There was a loud buzz sound and then he heard a heavy metal door slam. A few seconds later, Tika was in front of him. She pointed to the phone on the wall. He picked it up.

"Hey," she whispered.

"Hey. How are you?"

She shrugged her shoulders. "I've been better, but I'm here."

Kyle wiped his face with his hand. "What were you thinking, Tika? Our baby could have been killed with the others."

The dam broke and tears streamed down her face. "I wasn't thinking. I should have called you, but I was mad at you and being petty. I'm so sorry. How, how is Lee-Lee?"

"She's a tough cookie. The doctor said she will have to do breathing treatments for a little while, but she will be fine. Hopefully, this will not be a suppressed memory for her down the line. I'm not sure at what age that all starts. We've been keeping a close eye on her though." He looked around at the guards standing with their hands on their guns, the steel bars, and plexiglass and shook his head. "How is it in here?"

"The pits. We have been on 23-hour lockdown because the place is understaffed. They allow us an hour outside the cell to bathe. Thankfully, we have phones in the cell, but with six of us in there, it can get crazy. Two of my Bunkie's are gay and were in a relationship. One minute we hear them fucking and sucking on each other and the next minute they are trying to knock each other's teeth out. I don't think it can get any worse."

The buzzer sounded again, and another inmate walked in but stopped behind Tika.

"Yo, weren't you friends with the short chick that got taken to hole earlier?"

"Who, Vonda? Yeah, why?"

"That's what all the commotion was about. They just found her swinging in the cell by a sheet. She's dead."

And just like that, they did.

CHAPTER 21

Killing Her Softly

JUSTICE WAS A BALDHEAD, trout mouth bitch. Especially when it came to innocent, defenseless people like, Brely. Breeze could not believe that Larissa got out of jail. The court should have denied her bail.

"Who in their right mind, lets a woman out of jail who leaves eight children home alone, in the dark, with a seven-year-old babysitter?"

Caresse gently rubbed his back and shook her head. It was appalling how the legal system operated. They seemed to advocate for the guilty and penalized the innocent.

"It's sickening is what it is. Just because Brely, wasn't there, she was able to get out. The court placed the blame on the kid's mother's because they are the ones who left their children unattended, not Larissa. It is unfortunate that her friend killed herself."

"Yeah, that's messed up. Probably couldn't live with the guilt," he said.

"I'm sure she blamed herself. Those were her only babies. I could not imagine how I would be in her shoes."

"I don't even want to think about what could have happened if my daughter was there. Had KJ not come along when he did, we would be having a different conversation right now."

238

The implications of the "could haves" weighed heavily on him. Had Jarell not called him, he and Brely would have been in that house. They could have been burned. Or worse, they could have died.

"They just keep siding with her know matter what she does, babe. This shit ain't fair at all. Fuck! I was hoping that with the new child support bill, things were going to look up, but damn, ain't nothing changed."

"They are changing, baby. If they were not, the judge would not have given you temporary joint custody until this case is resolved. She is fair, honey. Give her a chance to review the case. I know that when we go back before her, the scales are going to tip in your favor."

He grabbed her around the waist and squeezed her.

"And this is why I love you. You always make me see things from a different perspective and you're right. It feels good to be able to get my baby and not have to sneak around with her and Jarell all the time."

"I must admit though, that little boy has been ride or die for you since all this mess began. It's a shame how they treat him," she added.

"Yeah, it is. But hey, it's almost over and when it is, both Brely and Jarell will be in a much better place. Let's go get her from the daycare early and me, you and Jarell can take her and go to dinner when he gets out of school."

"Sounds like a plan." Caresse pulled her cellphone out her pocket and called the daycare. "Hey, Londa. It's Caresse. We are on our way to get Bre. Can you all please have her ready?" There was a brief pause. "You what! What on Earth would possess you all to do that? Oh my gosh, you all will be hearing from our attorney."

Breeze's eyes bulged, questioning. "What's going on?"

"The daycare let Larissa take Brely."

"**D**ie, bitch, die!" Larissa yelled, covering Brely's face with a pillow. The little girl squirmed and fought as hard as she could. Her cries were muffled under the cotton.

"Ha, ha, ha," her evil mother laughed. "I don't know how you escaped that fire, but your ass should have burned alive."

"Wah," the little girl let out weakly. Her arms stilled, but her legs kept moving, albeit, not as fast as they once were.

"It's your motherfucking fault he ain't here. His heart was mine before you and now you and that stupid bar soap bitch are gonna pay."

Knock, knock, knock.

"Larissa, open this motherfucking door before I kick this bitch in."

Damn. It was her mother. She always managed to show up at the most inopportune times. Reluctantly, she lifted the pillow from her baby's face. Her lips were dark pink, but she was still breathing.

Gasping for air, Brely rolled slowly away from her mother and slid out the bed.

"Mommy hurt me," she said, grabbing her grandmother's leg.

"Gone with that shit, now," the woman said, kneeing the little girl, causing her to hit the wall.

She let out a loud scream.

Larissa walked over to her and slapped her hard across the face.

"Shut the fuck up, heifer." She turned to face her mother. "Now you see why I be fucking her up sometimes. Hell, this bitch is a royal pain in the ass."

Laquanda laughed. "She may be a pain in the ass but don't forget, she's still your got damned bread and butter. If she go, the money go. 'Member dat."

"You're right," she nodded. "Take your whining ass downstairs and watch TV. When Jarell comes home, he'll feed you."

Obediently, the little girl scurried like a mouse out the room and down the stairs to safety.

"Bitch where my fucking strap-on at? I got a client tonight who likes me to use it on him."

Larissa walked over to her drawer and handed the harness to her mom.

"Here."

"What the fuck is this? Where the damned dildo at?"

She shrugged. "I'on know. I let Tika use it, and this is all she gave back to me."

"Unh-uhh, hell nawl bitch. You gotsta break bread, hoe. This shit cost too much motherfucking money to let slide. I told your punk ass to buy your own."

"Damn, Mama. It ain't even that serious."

"If it ain't then pay me then."

"Ugg, you are so extra sometimes. How much did it cost?" Larissa pulled her wallet out of her handbag and began counting bills.

Her mother walked up to her and snatched five, one-hundred-dollar bills from her hand.

"This should do me just fine."

Angry, Larissa bucked at her mother, who side-stepped her so quickly, the younger woman stumbled into a chair.

241

"I wish you would try me, hoe. I'll beat you like a crackhead who stole something," Laquanda said. "Next time get your own shit. A bought lesson is a taught lesson. Stop acting like you don't know."

The door slammed when the older lady walked out the room.

"Bitch," she mumbled, rifling through her purse. She only had three-hundred bucks left. Disgusted, she threw her purse on the floor.

Jumping up, she went to the drawer where the dildo was supposed to be and pulled out a small glass mirror, a razor and small brown vile. Carefully, she dumped the white powder out and used the blade to make even, straight lines. She picked the mirror up and sniffed one line, then another. As she was about to inhale the last one, her door opened abruptly.

"You're on that powder again? Unh, unh, unh. That's a shame."

Her little brother stood in the threshold of the doorway, shaking his head. He looked at her with judgmental eyes.

"Fuck you, bastard. Don't your ass knock no more?"

"I would but what for? It ain't like it's a dude in here."

She sat the drugs down and walked toward him.

"What do you want?"

"Nothing, I just came to get Bre's jacket. I'm taking her to the park."

"She ain't going no fucking where. I got plans."

The little boy's eyes drooped. His niece had told him about the pillow on her face. He was trying to get her out the house and back to her father before his sister had a chance to do any more harm to her. She had never told him that he couldn't take the baby anywhere before. Whatever this new thing was that she was doing, he did not like.

"Man, come on. We won't be gone long."

"I said, no. If you want to play with kids so bad, go have your own or molest a few. I don't give a fuck. Just get the hell away from me."

Without closing the door, she walked back to the cocaine and snorted the last off the glass. Hungrily, she rubbed the remnants with her finger and wiped her gums with it.

"Ahh," she exhaled. The drug worked quickly, and she began to calm down. Swaying slightly from side-to-side, she began to sing.

"You took my love and I'm willing. But there's no limit to the love I'm giving. The love I'm giving."

Now this, he had seen before. Anytime his sister got high and began to feel sorry for herself, she always sang the old Michel'le tune, Something In My Heart."

He stood and listened to his sister's beautiful voice, float through the room. She hadn't always been on drugs or wild and loose. Once upon a time, about five years ago, she had dreams. Jarell could remember sitting in her room, listening to her talk about how one day, she was going to be a famous singer. She was on her way, too.

Even though he was only six or seven at the time, he remembered it clearly. Man of Steele Records had hosted a talent showcase at Greenbriar Mall and his sister entered it. There were lots of groups and rappers, even male solo artists, but she was the only female solo act. That made her stand out.

All the people were talented. Jarell remembered how nervous he was for her because no one had messed up. Not even a little.

"You gotta be better, Rissa if you want to win," he told her all those years ago.

"Don't worry about me, baby bro. This voice is going to sing us out the hood. Watch."

When it was her time to perform, she got on that stage and turned the people out. Singing "I Have Nothing," by the incomparable, Whitney Elizabeth Houston, Larissa had the audience captivated from the moment she opened her mouth. By the time the song ended, every mall employee had walked outside their stores just to see who it was singing. Even Keyon Steele, the company's owner, and his team, were blown away. So much so, that he signed her to a record deal on the spot.

Things were taking off, just like she had promised him. They had moved into the beautiful Buckhead home that they lived in now and even though it was still public, he attended a better school. She had just recorded her first single, when she was invited to do a duet with Breeze. That was a move that was supposed to catapult her career. She was about to go from backup singer to mega star. And because of her, they were all living the good life.

That is, until their older brother, Hakim, known on the streets as Hitta, caught a dope case. No matter how well Larissa's music did, he would not stay from out the trap house.

"I'm a motherfucking 'G' and we make our own money. The fuck I look like, living off my baby sister. I mean, I appreciate all the shit you do, but a nigga gotta get it how he lives," Jarell recalled him telling their sister.

That was the last time he saw his big brother. One of the houses he sold drugs at was busted and he was sentenced to thirty-years in prison. After that, their mother began to negatively influence Larissa and had even started her to using drugs. During one of their smoke sessions, the young woman had confided in her mother how much Breeze liked her, so Laquanda told her to use it to her advantage.

"What your ass needs to do is get pregnant. That nigga is worth millions. You can sit on your ass, eating bon bons and shit while the checks roll in."

Stupidly, that's what she did. His sister thought that by having a baby by Breeze, she would become a millionaire and a kept woman. But Breeze found out about the drug abuse and left her. Soon after, she lost her record deal and she had been angry and bitter ever since. Sadly, it was his niece who bore the blame for all her mother's failures. He turned on his heels and left her in the room alone, singing and crying tears of regret. Since she would not let him take Brely out, he had to stay home with her. Somehow, he would find a way to call Breeze and get them both to safety.

Later that night, Jarell was awakened by screaming and shouting.

"What the fuck happened to her?" He heard Breeze yell.

"Shit, I don't know. Why you think I called you?"

Jarell rubbed his eyes, thinking he was dreaming but he wasn't. Two Paramedics stood over Brely's little body, that lie on a gurney, giving her oxygen. Her body was listless as they wheeled her outside.

"Jarell grab your shoes and jacket and let's go."

"Hell naw, what are you doing, Breeze?"

"Ain't no way I'm leaving him here by himself at this hour. Your mother is not here."

"He eleven. His ass almost grown."

Breeze did not respond. He squinted his eyes and stared at her, stabbing her with his gaze. She looked away. Jarell, rarely listened to his sister, did not choose that moment to start. He got his stuff like Breeze said and went out to the SUV. Much to his surprise, Caresse was in the front seat, waiting on them.

"Awe man. Larissa is going to flip a lid," he said.

She hunched her shoulders. "It is what it is. But I couldn't let my man come here by himself."

For a moment, Breeze forgot that Caresse was in the truck. He was swiftly reminded when Larissa walked around to the passenger door and opened it, only to find his fiancé already buckled in.

"You can ride in the back with your brother," she said politely.

The tirade began.

"Ain't this 'bout a bitch! How in the fuck are you gonna come to my house with the next bitch?"

"You don't have any more times to call me out my name, ma'am. Because if you do, Breeze will be bailing one of us out of jail tonight for kicking the other one's ass, and it damned sure won't be you. Don't let this soft voice and pretty face fool you. I'm from the Bluffs baby, and we don't play that shit. So, get your ass in this truck, sit back, and shut the fuck up so we can get to this hospital. The only person who matters right now, is in that ambulance."

Both Larissa's and Breeze's eyes bulged. They looked at Caresse like she had grown two heads or something, but her tone let them know she meant business. Compliantly, Larissa got in the back seat and rolled her eyes at the back of her adversary's head the entire ride to the children's hospital.

Brely was immediately taken to a room where she was started on an I.V. While Breeze and Larissa went in to tend to their baby, Caresse stayed in the waiting room with Jarell.

"You should be in there, you know. You're more of a mother to Bre than my sister is."

"It's okay, baby. I love spending time with you."

A doctor, holding a chart came from the back, shaking her head.

"Justine? Is that you?" Caresse asked.

"Caresse? Oh my gosh girl, how are you?"

The two friends hugged and caught up on one another's current situations rapidly.

"You're engaged to Breeze? Damn. You did good girl."

"Thanks. He's a sweetie. Are you helping back there with his daughter?"

The doctor nodded her head.

"Yeah. I'm baffled at her symptoms."

Caresse placed her arm on her friends' shoulder and led her out of Jarell's earshot.

"Can you do me a favor? Run as many blood tests on that baby as you can. She comes to the hospital so much and we don't think it's because she is a sickly child. When she is with us, she is perfectly fine. I think her mother is doing something to her."

"Do you realize what you are saying? That mother in there does not seem like the type to harm a soul. I think you're wrong."

"But what if I'm right. Run the tests. Please. Hell, her daddy got money and he will pay whatever. Just do this for me. Please."

Her eyes pleaded with the doctor and she squeezed her hand, stressing the importance of her request.

"Okay, I got you."

The doctor returned to the room and looked at Brely's skin and nails. She noticed white lines across the little girls' nail beds but did not say anything about it. They were associated with the exposure to arsenic. Justine did not want to allow her friends concerns to cloud her judgement in any way, but she had to find out what was going on with the little girl.

"Miss MacIntosh, when you brought Brely to the hospital before, what were some of her symptoms?"

"Hell, if I know," she snapped.

Breeze rolled his eyes.

"Doctor, she has been in and out of the hospital with nausea, diarrhea, headaches, belly aches, you name it."

"Hmm, well I have ordered a battery of tests to be performed. Let me put on my thinking cap so I can accurately diagnose your little angel."

Maybe an hour had past, perhaps longer, before the doctor returned. By the time she did, Breeze was in the waiting room with his woman and Jarell. Larissa was getting on his nerves, so he left her.

The doctor returned and she was not alone. Two Atlanta police officers followed her into the waiting room.

"Caresse," she began, "please take this young man somewhere. I need to speak with Mister Coleman."

No one needed to tell either of them twice. They hightailed it out of there.

"What's up?" Breeze said.

"I hate to say this, but your daughter has been being poisoned. I found high levels of arsenic and diuretics in her system."

"Poisoned?" He looked at the cops. "I know you don't think I did it, do you?"

"Not at all. The same symptoms your daughter has in her nails are also present in her mother. Now that we know what chemicals are in her body, we know better how to treat her."

"Thank you," Breeze said.

From the moment they placed her in handcuffs, until she was placed in the back of the squad car, Larissa screamed. She kicked the back seat of the police cruiser hard, making the cop who was driving, happy that a fence separated them. Because of her antics, the ride over seemed much longer.

The jail was packed because it was 'sweeps' night. Dozens of women that were picked up on Fulton Industrial for prostitution milled around the holding cell. Most of them had already been there long enough to complete the booking process. A big, female guard took Larissa to get her fingerprints and picture taken, before throwing her in the overcrowded cell.

"Hoe, what is your bitch ass doing in here?" Laquanda asked.

"They accused me of trying to poison my baby. What are you doing here?"

Her mother shook her head.

"I kept telling your ass to leave that girl alone, but no, you gotta learn shit the hard fucking way. I'll be praying for you, Sis. You gone' need it. They popped me for prostitution, but I made bail."

As soon as she said that a guard came to the cell door.

"MacIntosh, Laquanda. Let's go."

The guard jiggled the keys in the heavy, metal door.

"Where Jarell's ass at?"

"Breeze took him," she said, nonchalantly.

"Good. He can keep him. I'm done being a parent. That shits for the birds. I quit."

"Are you going to get me out, Mama?" Larissa asked.

Laquanda doubled over at the waist and let out the loudest, longest laugh ever.

"Bitch bye, hoe hi, slut try – again. You know better than to ask me some shit like that. Deuces."

"That's alright. Fuck you, Laquanda. I have a way out."

There was not a line for the phone so when it was free, Larissa called Phillip. The automated voice announced her name and told the caller to press one if he was willing to accept the call. Much to her delight, he did.

"Phillip, baby. Oh my gosh, I need you. Can you believe that these people tried to say I poisoned my baby?"

"What do you want, Larissa?" There was no mistaking the agitation in his voice.

"Babe, please come get me. My bail is only seventy-five-thou. Ten percent of that ain't shit."

"So, yeah. About that. I'm not going to be able to do it. You're high risk and my partner doesn't want our clients to deal with jail birds. Plus, I have it on good authority that they are going to charge you with second-degree murder."

"Murder? I ain't done shit," she screamed into the receiver.

"Ma'am, it was you who dropped those children off at your home, alone in the dark. Not once did you tell your friends that they would be there by themselves. Had you told the truth, maybe Shannon's kids, Vonda, and her children would be alive today."

"Babe, I did tell them," she lied. "They are the ones who told me to do it."

Mch. He smacked on the other end. "No jury will by that."

"What about our agreement. You need me to run the operation like we discussed."

He laughed. "Actually, I don't need you. Tika has agreed to run things. I had forgotten how beautiful she is. Plus, she doesn't snort powder. Look, I have to go. I'll be praying you. And don't drop the soap. Do they tell chicks that? Oh well, you get the point. Goodbye."

The phone felt like lead in her hand. Her knees got weak, and she needed to sit down. Phillip was the only bridge that she had not burned. He was the only person who had money and all the qualifications to bail her out. Without him, she was screwed. She hated to think negatively, but Phillip was probably right, no jury was going to believe her. In her heart of hearts, she knew that if she made it to the prison yard, she would not make it out alive.

CHAPTER 22

Boys to Men

E COULDN'T STAY ANGRY with his mother forever, but he was not sure that now was the time for a reconciliation. Because of her, he had missed out on the birth of his sone and the first few months of his life. Moreover, because of her scheming and conniving, he and the true love of his life were almost over for good.

For years, his mother had made her dislike for Aisha known. However, he never knew her dislike was borderline hatred and he certainly never imagined that she could do something so grimy. All that just so he could marry a woman of her choosing. Someone who measured up to her unreasonable standards. And to think, if Selena had not accidentally spilled the beans, he would be married to one woman while secretly pining over the next.

"God was on my side when Selena told me the truth," Malik said.

"He's on your side with everything. We may not understand His plans all the time, but He does not make any mistakes. Perhaps it was meant for us to experience this if for no other reason than for you to see who your mother truly is. No matter how much I tried to talk to you about her treatment of me in the past, nothing seemed to get through to you

251

because you had never seen her behave in this manner before. What she did is reprehensible, but I think you should forgive her and allow her to meet our son."

"You are way nicer about this whole thing than I am. She tried to keep us apart. That shit is not cool."

"No, it's not. But I was going to tell you about Zion. I was just trying to muster up the courage. The letter that she gave me that she claimed was from you said some harsh things. I did not want to believe it was from you, but I didn't have anything to refute its validity."

"Ah, sooky sooky now. I see you over there sounding like an attorney."

She swat him on his arm playfully.

"Hush. I'm happy that I passed the LSAT, but I don't know if I'm more nervous or excited about entering law school in the fall."

"It's probably a mixture of both. I'm proud of you, babe. You never let anything stop you."

"Thank you. I couldn't. Honestly, I didn't know what was going to happen with us. Misses Vi told me to call you so many times, but I was scared. Not of what you were going to say or think, but about what could happen to my dad. My brother put my dad in harms way. The last thing I needed was a sickly mother and an incarcerated father. No, Sir."

"There's no way I would have sat by and watched your dad get railroaded."

She shook her head. "How were you to know that he was being set-up? Hell, he didn't even tell me that Cliff had been stealing. The whole thing was so jacked up."

He wrapped his arms around her and squeezed tightly. "Thank God, all of that is behind us now and we can move forward."

"You cannot move forward honey, with this anger in your heart. You must forgive your mother. You know she's going to be at KJ and Sunrise's wedding. Are you going to avoid her?"

"Yes. No. I don't know, Eesh. It's going to be hard for me to lay eyes on her. The night I confronted her about the blackmail, she denied it and straight up lied to my face. My Pops was blown away. I wish you could have seen the look on his face when I told him what happened. He was like a kid who had just found out his favorite super-hero was a fraud. What my mother did hurt so many people. She was out of line."

Aisha sat up in bed and turned to face him. "You don't get it do you?"

He looked confused by her statement, but she continued.

"Yes, your mother did some foul stuff, and she is wrong on so many levels but some of this is your fault, too. Had you protected me and stood up for me the way you were supposed to do as my man, she never could have taken things as far as she did. Long ago, you could have put her in her place, but you didn't. And when I asked you to do something about it, you blew me off. You tried to tell me to look over her and blow it off, yet things got worse. This is your fault too, buddy." She poked his chest with the last sentence.

He propped the pillows up, sat up, and leaned back. His head was down when he first began to speak, and he wrung his hands.

"So many times, I thought about ways that I could have changed things and prevented all this from happening and you're right." He lifted his head and turned to face her. "I did not stick up for you the way I should have, and I am so sorry, Aisha. Can you please forgive me?

She leaned in and kissed him on the lips. "I forgave you long ago. You are only human, and I am not going to hold your past against you. But the same way I have forgiven you is the same way you need to forgive your mom. When I had Zion, I understood why your mother did what she did. After they placed him in my arms for the first time, I knew that I would do anything and everything to protect him. In a way, that's all your mother was trying to do."

"Damn, you are so dope. I'm going to pray about it and turn it over to Jesus. He can work it out."

"Yes, He will. You cannot expect God to forgive you, and you are unwilling to forgive others."

"Caresse if you don't bring your ass on here, we are going to be late."

"I'm coming," she said.

Breeze tapped his foot impatiently, waiting at the bottom of the staircase for his wife. She was the matron of honor and he did not want her to be late. Usually, anytime they went anywhere, she was the first one ready, but not today.

His breath caught in his throat when she walked to the steps. Looking at her, she appeared to be an angel in the champagne-colored lace dress she wore.

"Mommy beautiful," Brely said.

"Yes, she is, baby girl. She's very beautiful."

Caresse blushed as she descended the stairs.

"Do I look fat in this dress? My hips have spread."

"You don't look fat. You're gorgeous. No one will even be able to tell that you are carrying my son because your tummy is so small."

She rubbed her belly. "Is it wrong of me to be this happy, with all that has happened in the past two weeks?"

Breeze stepped closer to her and put his arms around her waist.

"Not at all. Just because you are experiencing happiness does not mean you don't care about something."

She sighed deeply. "Brely, go get Uncle Jerry and tell him we are leaving."

"Okay," the little girl said.

Once she was out of the room, Caresse spoke freely.

"Burying Larissa last week was harder on me than I thought it would be. She didn't care for me much, but that was only because she was still in love with you. No matter what she did, dying was the last thing I wanted for her."

"I thought that she would have the chance to get herself together. You cannot do people wrong though and not think that it won't catch up to you."

"True that. Who knew that Vonda had family in that prison? They blamed Larissa for Vonda and her kid's deaths. Rightfully, she was responsible."

"Yeah, she was."

Against his better judgment, Breeze had spoken to Larissa while she was still in the county jail. She had told him that Tika made bail but refused to accept any of her calls. "So much for friendship," she had said.

Hell had Breeze been in Tika's shoes, he probably would not have had anything to do with the woman who was responsible for the deaths of so many either. His baby's mama had burned people she never thought she would need again. That was one of many mistakes she made.

She had told him that her attorney did not answer any more of her phone calls because she could not pay him. Later, he found out that was a lie. Nevertheless though, because of all she had done to people, she was left in jail. Alone. Shannon got out after her court date. She was placed on twenty-years' probation. Phillip Drew, who now represented Tika, got her off with a ten-year probation sentence. Since she had no money, things did not fair as well for Larissa. At court, her public defender tried to claim that she had Munchausen Syndrome by Proxy Disorder, but that was not the case at all.

Larissa was just plain evil, and the jury saw through her act. She was facing convictions on second-degree murder for the deaths of the children in the fire and child abuse, child neglect, and attempted murder charges for Brely. Three months later after weeks of testimony, she was convicted of all charges and sentenced to seventy-five-years in prison. Two weeks after she hit the prison yard, she was shanked on her way to the shower and died. Breeze and Caresse held a private memorial service for her. Laquanda did not show up.

"The best thing we can do is live our best lives. Let's try to move on from the past, okay."

"Yes, Sir. Now let's get to this wedding."

Jarell and Brely entered the foyer.

"Let's go, Bro," Jarell said. "I'm ready to eat some wedding cake."

"You're getting a kick out of us being brothers now, huh?" Breeze asked.

"Man, you've always been my brother. It didn't take your parent's adopting me to make that the truth."

Breeze hugged the young man.

"That's right. You are so wise, bro. When I grow up, I want to be just like you."

The ceremony was about to begin, and all Malik wanted to do was find his seat without being accosted by his greedy family. There was always at least one family member who had a great business idea or one who needed thousands of dollars to have some sort of surgery. He was sick of it. When his cousin Sherrod tried to hit him up for five grand, he sidestepped him but ended up running into his mother. At first, he simply stood there and stared. Then he opened his mouth.

"Hey, Mom. How are you?"

"I'm okay, Son. I've been better though."

"Look, Mom I'm- "

"Son, please forgive me."

They spoke at the same time.

"You go first," he said.

She took a deep breath and exhaled slowly.

"I don't know what possessed me to do what I did, but I am so sorry. I guess a part of me was jealous of Aisha and some of me was threatened by her."

"Jealous? Why?"

"Because she was taking you away from me and there was nothing, I could do to stop it. The only reason I pushed the union between you and Selena is because I would have been able to control her. Your girlfriend's strength was intimidating. Regardless of what insult I hurled her way she never stooped to my level."

Aisha walked up and held Malik's hand, lacing her fingers through his.

"You're wrong, Mom. Aisha is not my girlfriend. She is my wife."

Eloise touched her chest. "My apologies. Your father told me you were married. Congratulations, to you both."

"Thank you, Misses Jeffries."

"Aisha, dear. Can you ever forgive me? I am so sorry."

"Yes. I forgive you. We forgive you. And we want you to be a part of our lives and your grandson, Zion's life. But if you pull a stunt like that again, you can forget any of us exists."

"Trust me, I have learned my lesson."

"Good. Now let's go find your grandson. He's around here being a heartbreaker and he can't even walk yet."

His mother hugged him tightly and tears slowly streamed down her face. As he held her, he could feel the tension release from her body. Malik was not sure what the future held regarding him and his mother's relationship but for now, he was happy to be her little boy again.

KJ could not believe how blessed he was. He had just married his best friend. Sunrise was the most beautiful woman he knew inside and out.

"Misses Hudson, I promise I am going to make you the happiest woman on Earth," he said, twirling her around the dance floor.

"You already do, Mister Hudson," she said, leaning in to kiss him.

"Ooh!"

"Hey"

Cheers erupted around the dance floor.

"I think we are being watched," he teased.

"Hmm, seems like it. No worries. Later, the show I'm going to put on will be for your eyes only."

"Damn, my dick just got hard. Can we go now?"

"No, Silly. Your dad wants you and your bros to join him in the gentlemen's lounge and I'm going to join your mom and family. We'll meet up soon."

They kissed again then went to the lounges their bridal party set up for them.

Kyle Hudson, Senior raised his glass to his son in the gentleman's lounge.

"KJ, I want you to know that I am super proud of you and I hope God blesses your marriage as He did your mom's and mine."

The men raised their glasses and saluted.

"Thanks, Pops. I owe it all to you. Braden's Bill was life-changing legislature for me and so many men like me."

All the men present nodded and voiced their agreement.

"It's been a long time coming. But the bill is not just for men. There are many women who are paying child support to men who are just as much gold-diggers as the women you all have encountered."

"Really?" Breeze asked. "I've never heard of that."

"It's not broadcast as much. Same as male domestic violence victims. Some things are just not talked about openly."

"Mister Hudson," Quentin began. "Did you think that all the other states would come on board the way they have? The last I read, Cali, New York, Florida, and even Virginia have adopted the bill into their legislature. That's phenomenal."

"I'm glad that the bill is available now, but I am saddened that we needed it. Children are not leverage and they certainly are not meal tickets. All of this could have been prevented if you all would simply put on a Jimmy hat. Fifteen dollars in the beginning can save you fifteen million on the backend. You need to wrap it up. Every interaction. No matter how good that woman looks, do not play Russian Roulette with your lives. Y'all are blessed. The one thing I want you all to take away from this conversation is this: A baby is not the worst thing that you can get from having unprotected sex. Paying child support won't kill. But AIDS certainly will."

THE END